High Level

Colin Youngman

High Level

The Works of Colin Youngman:

High Level (Ryan Jarrod Book 4)

The Lighthouse Keeper (Ryan Jarrod Book 3)

The Girl On The Quay (Ryan Jarrod Book 2)

The Angel Falls (Ryan Jarrod Book 1)

**

The Doom Brae Witch

Alley Rat

DEAD Heat

Twists*

*Incorporates:
DEAD Lines
Brittle Justice
The Refugee
A Fall Before Pride
Vicious Circle

All the above are also available separately.

Colin Youngman

This is a work of fiction.

All characters and events are products of the author's imagination.

Whilst the majority of locations are real, some liberties have been taken with architectural design, precise geographic features, and timelines.

A SprintS Publication

Copyright 2021 © Colin Youngman

All rights reserved.

No part of this publication, paperback or e-book, may be reproduced, stored in a retrieval system, or transmitted, in any form or in any means – by written, electronic, mechanical, photocopying, recording or otherwise – without prior written permission of the author.

ISBN -13: 979-8-50316-970-6

High Level

DEDICATION

For the communities of Newcastle's East End

whose indomitable spirit, endless good humour, and resilience overcomes so much.

I have taken untold liberties with your good name within the contents of this book. Thank you for your forgiveness.

'In a huge city, it is a fairly common observation that the dwellers in a slum are almost a separate race of people with different values, aspirations, and ways of being.'

Wilfred Smith

'Through our sunless lanes creeps Poverty with her hungry eyes, and Sin with his sodden face follows close behind her. Misery wakes us in the morning and Shame sits with us at night.'

Oscar Wilde

High Level

CHAPTER ONE

SUNDAY

Her first glimpse of her new home came from the back of an Uber.

Maz Crawford stared up at the looming edifice of the Byker Wall, a mile and a half barrier of Erskine designed inner city sprawl, knowing it presented her with an opportunity to make amends, put the past behind her, and start afresh.

In 1960s Glasgow, it would have been called a tenement. When conceived in 1970s Newcastle, it was dubbed '*the Brasilia of the North.*' In 21st century Newcastle, it was universally known as '*The Wall.*'

The expansive mass of lurid coloured concrete and timber coiled like a serpent to the right of the A193 as the cab travelled parallel with Shields Road.

'Before its construction, Byker was just another east-end suburb of tightly-packed slum terraces,' the driver explained. The Uber app had told her his name was Pete and his voice came out muffled from behind the obligatory face-covering.

'They were razed to the ground as part of T. Dan Smith's 1980's vision to turn Newcastle into a city in the sky. Have you heard of him?'

'Who?' Maz asked, twisting her neck so her eyes could follow the curve of the wall.

'T. Dan Smith. He was leader of the council back in the day. Folk think he was a bit of a Commie. Actually, he was well-intentioned and much misunderstood. It's a pity it went tits up for him.' He glanced at his passenger via the rear-view mirror. 'Pardon me French, like.'

'It's okay. I've heard worse.'

'This place - the Wall - was about as good as it got for Smith.'

'What happened?' she asked, immediately regretting giving Pete an opportunity to continue his commentary.

'To Smith? He was jailed. Corruption charges. Part of the Poulson scandal. You know much about it?'

'Not that bothered, to be honest.'

'Okay. Excuse me saying, but it's part of the city's history. You might want to read up on it.'

'I prefer Tolkein.'

The cab doubled-back on itself and pulled into an inner courtyard decorated with graffiti and the hash markings of residents' parking bays. 'I'm a non-fiction man, me,' her chauffer continued. 'You pick up on all sorts of life tips, trust me.'

Maz flicked her blonde fringe from her eyes. 'I wouldn't have got in here with you if I didn't trust you.'

'Fair enough. Mind, this isn't the sort of place I'd want to live. Be careful, won't you?'

'I don't intend staying long. Just long enough.'

Maz directed the Uber to pull up alongside a white transit van parked in one of the numbered bays.

She waved at a figure standing alongside the van, but Howard Crawford didn't respond. He stood, hands on hips, gazing upwards. Inside the transit, his wife - Maz's mother - dabbed red eyes with a floral handkerchief.

Maz painted a smile on her face beneath the mask, touched her debit card against the cabbie's card reader, and climbed from the vehicle. The moment she set foot outside, the driver shot off, 'Before me wheels get nicked.'

High Level

'You don't have to do this, Marilyn. You know that, don't you?' Howard Crawford said, still staring up at the tiered façade of the Byker Wall.

'But I do, Dad. It's time I flew the nest.' She unhooked the mask from her ears.

Howard sighed. 'Two-thirds of chicks die before their first spring is over, you know.'

'Cheers for that. Thanks for the vote of confidence,' she snickered. 'I'm a big girl now. I'll be fine.'

'You're barely twenty-one years old. That's not big. Not in the grand scheme of things, it isn't. And, why now, in the middle of a pandemic? Are you really so desperate to get away from us?'

'Dad, it's not you. It's not Mum, either, before you ask. It's just the right time, that's all.'

'But why here, man? Your mum and I could help you find somewhere better than this place.'

She thought carefully before replying. 'It's something I have to do,' she said.

Her mother joined them. 'You don't have to do this, you know,' Eileen Crawford echoed.

'I've just been through this with Dad.'

'Then, why don't you listen to us?' She looked up at grey washing stretched across narrow balconies. Heavy bass music throbbed from an open window six stories up. A baby cried. Dogs barked. 'Do people really live like this?'

'Mum, it's not that bad. This is just the perimeter of the estate. It's built like this to shield the rest of it from traffic noise and winds blowing along the Tyne valley,' she said, repeating part of her cabbie's mantra. 'It's a bit like, I dunno,' she looked at her father, 'A bird's nest, I suppose. It shelters the hatchlings.'

Howard Crawford gave a mirthless snicker.

'I'm serious,' Maz continued. 'It's not all high-rise. In fact, this is the only bit that is. It's really quite green and pleasant once you get behind the wall.'

She wrapped an arm around her mother. 'The estate's won awards for its design. It's got loads of amenities. It's even got a gym for my workouts.' She flexed a bicep for effect.

Eileen took a deep breath and fought back her tears. 'So, does that mean you're in the other part of the estate?'

Maz looked skywards. 'No. That's mine, there.' She pointed to a tenth story window opaque with street grime. 'C'mon, let's get me stuff unloaded and up there.'

'I'm really not sure about this, Marilyn.'

'Well, I am. Are you going to help me or not?'

'Why don't I stay in the van? I'm not convinced your stuff will be safe out here.'

'You can if you want. But it'll take us longer if there's just Dad and me. Besides, me gear will be safe between trips with Willow in the van.' She smiled at the giant German Shepherd sitting alert in the driver's seat. 'Nobody will mess with him.'

Her mother cast a glance at two youths standing by the entrance, hands thrust in pockets, looking their way. 'I hope you're right.'

'Mother, man. Give it a rest. You'll feel different once you see inside.' Maz deposited a cardboard box in her mother's arms. 'C'mon. You can give me your verdict after you've seen it.'

Eileen Crawford had already reached her verdict. The Byker Wall was guilty as charged.

**

The lift shook and shuddered its way to the tenth floor before jerking to a halt. The elevator dropped six inches as its doors slid open.

'Jeez, it's like the Tower of Terror at Disneyland,' Howard Crawford said, only half-joking.

Maz was already inserting a key into the lock of the door nearest the lift.

'Here we are. Home sweet home.'

High Level

The door swung open to reveal a tiny living room. A TV unit, a tubular-legged steel table, and bottle green corduroy sofa left little room for manoeuvre.

A small kitchen area occupied the space to the left of the entrance. Against the right wall, a door opened into an evil-smelling shower-room. A second door led to a bedroom larger than the lounge area. A single wardrobe stood against one wall, a mattress on the floor.

'Where's the bed?' Maz's mother asked through lips curled in disdain.

'The mattress will do me for the first couple of nights. There's a Bed Shed on Shields Road. I'll get something from there next week.'

'Good luck getting it up here,' her father said, gently lowering two cardboard boxes to the floor. 'You stay here and empty these, Eileen. Marilyn and me will get the next load.'

Back in the lift, Howard Crawford asked, 'What do you really think?'

'Honestly? It's a bit shit, isn't it? It'll be better once I've put my stamp on it, though.'

Howard gripped a metal handrail as the elevator lowered itself in a series of random leaps. 'You could have stayed until something nicer turned up.'

Maz looked him in the eye. 'I couldn't. I need to do this.'

Howard began to protest but was cut off in his prime when the lift lurched to a stop. Maz hammered her finger against the exit button until the doors slid open with the reluctance of a stroppy child threatened with the naughty step.

At the van, Willow greeted them with erect ears, paws against the window, and a frenzied tail. Maz tossed him a handful of treats while they unloaded the next consignment. Howard said he'd take the boxes upstairs while Maz got the next lot ready. 'It'll be quicker that way,' he explained.

The two youths watched the activity from the courtyard. One laughed loudly at a ribald comment. Maz studied them before deciding they carried no threat. Not to a Second Dan like her.

Maz and Howard repeated the convoy two times without problem. The third time, the damn lift was stuck at the seventh floor and wouldn't budge. Howard took to the stairs while his daughter returned to the van for the final box.

She froze.

'Get away from that van!'

The youths stood either side of the transit, taking it in turns to rap against the window. Willow barked at them through the glass, frantically leaping from one side of the van to the other. The transit rocked like a rudderless skiff.

'I said, get away from the van.'

'Had yer piss, man. We're only admiring your dog,' the one closest to her said. Maz guessed he was no more than fifteen years old.

The second youth sauntered around the van. He was older than the first, and he tapped a bottle of cheap cider against bleached and torn jeans as he walked. 'Moving in, are you?'

She didn't answer.

He stepped closer. 'I'm Marv. Most people call me Rats. After the Rat Boy, y'knaa?'

Maz held her arms against her side. She flexed her fingers.

'I get to know most of the lasses round here.' He didn't need the leer for Maz to know what he meant. 'This is Scrapper.' He tilted his head towards the smaller youth, scrawnier than Rats. 'I call him Scrapper 'cos he feeds off me scraps. Me cast-offs, like. He spends half his life hanging around us like a right twat.'

He took a slug from the bottle and offered it to Maz. 'Wanna drink?'

Willow snarled a warning.

'Divvent say much, do you?' Rats said.

She said nothing.

High Level

'I like your hair.' He reached up and moved a blonde lock away from her eyes. 'Your eyes are nice, an' aal.'

His eyes shifted downwards. 'And I bet you've got a canny pair of tits on you.'

Scrapper laughed at his friend's comment. The laugh died in his throat when he saw Maz flick her right leg out and upwards, knee bent, toes pointing downwards, in a perfect Kin Geri.

Rats sunk to the ground clutching his groin. He gasped for air like a landed trout.

'What's going on here?' a voice echoed around the courtyard.

A man in a suit marched towards them. Scrapper darted for cover and Maz did a double-take before disappearing into the lift lobby, head down, leaving the newcomer to tend to the expanding gonads of Rats.

**

Eileen Crawford was out of there as soon as the last box was dumped on the floor. Howard wanted to stay a little longer. He sensed something was up, something he couldn't put his finger on, but Eileen held sway. They left Maz to finish unpacking.

It was hot work. The heating was stuck on maximum and hot air flushed into the room from a letter-box sized vent in the ceiling. Maz hunted high and low for the thermostat without success.

All of which meant she was lathered by the time she'd finished. Night had fallen and the flat was illuminated in stark white light from a single naked bulb hanging from a bare flex. She hadn't fixed the curtains yet, but no-one overlooked the tenth story window. She peeled off her damp T-shirt.

Sweat glistened and glimmered on her torso. Rivulets ran between the swell of her breasts. She reached behind her, unclasped her bra, and let it fall to the ancient sofa.

She didn't notice the letter box held open by stubby fingers, nor the wide eyes ogling her semi-nakedness through its maw.

'Welcome to the Byker Wall,' a voice whispered.

**

Ryan Jarrod closed the door behind him and stood with his back against rough brickwork. He couldn't remember where he was. A narrow terrace, for sure, but that's about all he could recall.

Relief flooded through him with the realisation he was pissed. It offered him a semblance of an excuse for his behaviour. What on earth had he been thinking?

He had no time to dwell on it because he had a decision to make: turn left, or right? He chose left. Either way would suffice as long it got him out of there before the platinum blonde he'd stupidly agreed to meet through a dating app re-emerged from her bathroom in 'Something more comfortable.'

At the corner of the terrace, Ryan stumbled out onto a main road. The street was well lit, wide, and lined by shops and takeaways. A bus lane hinted at it being a major transport route. He guessed it would normally be busy but, in the midst of a semi-lockdown, it was near deserted.

Ryan squinted up at a sign fixed to the wall above a chippie. *'Chillingham Road,'* it read. He remembered, now. He was in Heaton.

Ryan crossed the road and took refuge in the doorway of the locked and bolted Chillingham pub. He hunkered down like Marco Bielsa and kept watch for a bottle blonde stalker emerging from an alley. When she didn't appear, he decided it was safe to call a cab.

He withdrew his phone from a pocket. The display blinked at him. He'd missed a call from Acting Detective Sergeant Hannah Graves.

'Shit.'

High Level

Ryan spun the device in his fingers. That was the trouble with the world today: everybody was 'Acting.' DCI Stephen Danskin was Acting Superintendent, DI Parker Acting DCI, and Hannah Graves was Acting Detective Sergeant.

As for Ryan Jarrod, he acted as if life went on as normal. At least, he had until five minutes ago when he realised it was anything but.

'Get a grip on yourself, man.'

Ryan made to call the cab. The face of Acting DS Hannah Graves, framed by a halo of curls, glowed up at him from his screensaver image.

'Shit,' he said again.

CHAPTER TWO

MONDAY

His shirt tail, white with thin pink stripes, was untucked. The man wore trainers at odds with his tailored dress trousers. He lay face down and could have been sleeping were it not for the distorted angle of his neck.

The body was positioned smack bang in the centre of the lift shaft's cold floor. His left arm lay beneath him, the right splayed out as if he'd been dancing to Night Fever. Both feet had twisted one-hundred and eighty degrees and faced the wrong direction. There was no blood on the floor.

Detective Constable Nigel Trebilcock, or 'Treblecock' as he was known to all in the City and County police, looked down at the body and scribbled a sketch of the scene in his notepad. It was all they'd have until the Forensic photographer arrived.

'Think he fell?'

Trebilcock turned towards the source of the voice as Ryan Jarrod brushed past him to get a better sight of the body.

'Probably,' Trebilcock said, slightly annoyed.

'Just an accident, then?'

'Like I says: probably.'

'Good. What else do we know?'

Trebilcock's nose wrinkled. 'You bin' at the cider, boy?' the Cornishman asked.

'A bottle of cheap red last night, that's all.'

Trebilcock raised an eyebrow.

'Okay. A bit more than a bottle, actually.'

High Level

'That's a bad sign, that is; drinking by yo'self.' When he got no reply, he continued. 'I hope you didn't drive here.'

'Howay, man. What do you take me for? I'm not stupid. I got a cab.'

Trebilcock held up his hands. 'Okay. I'm sorry.'

'Aye, you should be. Right, we think it's an accident, then?'

'It's looking that way. Seems the residents have reported issues with the lift for a few days now. Look, if you'd turned up at Forth Street instead of coming straight here, you'd know all this already, so you would,' Trebilcock said, his Cornish burr echoing in the concrete chamber.

Ryan sighed. 'I know,' he agreed. 'But you know how things are. Best I keep out her way as much as possible.'

'She's worried about you, you know. We all are.'

'Hadawayandshite, man. There's nowt to worry about.' Ryan leant close to the body. The sour and sweet aroma of marijuana hung in the air, but it didn't come from the body. It emanated from a point above, one of the upper floors. Quite which one wasn't important. Not right now.

'She said she can never get hold of you.'

Ryan rubbed his forehead. 'There's no point even if she could, is there? I mean, I can't see her other than at work, anyway. My social bubble's me brother and dad, not Hannah. She made that perfectly clear.'

'Look, it's none of my business, but…'

'You're right, Treblecock. It IS none of your business.' Ryan closed his eyes. Softened his tone. 'I'm sorry. There was no need for that.'

'Apology accepted. But now you sees why we're worried about you.'

Ryan turned away from the body. 'It's the job. It gets to me, sometimes. I guess Frank was right after all, God rest his soul.'

'Frank? Who's Frank when he's at home?'

'My old mentor from me days as a Special. Frank Burrows. He said the job gets to everybody in the end.'

Trebilcock swallowed. He remembered Frank. One of his first assignments with the City and County force was to send Frank Burrows on a door-to-door in a Dunston tower block which was blown to smithereens with the old cop still inside.

'Could he have been pushed?' Ryan asked, turning back to the body.

'Possibly.' Nigel Trebilcock responded, relieved Ryan had changed the subject from Frank Burrows.

Ryan craned his neck to look up the lift shaft. He made the whistle of a dropping bomb. 'Splat. It would've been a hard fall. Health and Safety Executive been informed?'

Trebilcock nodded.

'What about the council? They'll be in deep shit over this.'

'Not council responsibility, so it seems.'

Ryan's brow furrowed. 'Thought this was council owned.'

'Not anymore. Byker Wall's been hived off to private landlords, same as most places nowadays.'

'Right. Well, either way, the owner's in for a hard time. Do we know who it is?'

'That we do.'

'Okay. Get one of the uniform lads onto it.'

'No point, Ryan. It won't help.'

'Mebbe not but they need to know.'

'I don't think they'll care, I's don't.'

'Why not?'

Trebilcock tilted his head towards the lift shaft. 'Because that's the owner, right there.'

**

Ryan squatted next to the body. He wanted to turn him over to inspect the victim but, with the forensic team on their way, it would wait. A cold blast of air, like a freezer door opening, hit the back of his neck.

'Okay, Treblecock, the cavalry's here. You're relieved,' a female voice said from the doorway behind them.

Ryan's eyelids slid shut. He remained where he was.

'Ryan?'

'What?' He heard her footsteps close in.

'What's wrong?'

'You mean, apart from the squashed fly at the bottom of the lift shaft here?'

'You're such hard work sometimes, you know,' Hannah Graves sighed.

Ryan stood but kept his back to her.

'I'm serious, Ry. What's wrong?'

He sucked in air between his teeth. 'You really need ask?'

Hannah glanced towards Trebilcock standing by the doorway. He shrugged and looked embarrassed.

'Let's just be professional about this, should we?' she said.

Ryan clenched both fists. Relaxed them and clenched again. 'Your idea this, was it?'

'Come again?'

'To turn up like this. To rub my nose in your so-called superiority.'

'Oh, grow up, man. Of course not. Lyall suggested it. Said he can't have any schisms in the team. Said we had to work together on this one.'

'Ah. Of course. Acting Detective Chief Inspector Lyall Parker,' he said, verbal speech marks around the word *Acting*. 'I don't suppose there was any outside influence from *Acting* Superintendent Danskin, eh? Your stepfather?'

Hannah signalled with her eyes for Trebilcock to leave. Once the door closed behind him, Hannah lowered her tone. 'Look. I know this is awkward, for both of us, but we have to get on with it.' She hesitated. 'I don't want to play on it, but I am your senior officer at the moment, and I need you to respect the rank, even if you don't respect me.'

He turned to face her. Tears sparkled in his eyes. 'Respect you? I don't respect you, Hannah,' he sobbed. 'I love you. God knows why after everything, but I still do.' He rubbed his eyes. 'There. I've said it. Now, can we just get on here, please?'

She blinked rapidly. 'We can, but we need to talk, as well. Next time I call you, pick up. It's the only way we'll get over this.'

He tutted. Shook his head. 'Hannah, you made it clear it was over the day you rejected me.'

'I didn't mean it like that, as well you know. Take my call – out of work – and we'll discuss it. Until then, we've work to do.'

'Whatever,' he said, indignation rich in his voice. 'So, do we have a name and address for our fella?'

'Name's Justin Warne. And he lives here.'

Ryan raised his eyes from the crumpled corpse and stared up into the blackness of the lift shaft. 'Which floor?'

'He doesn't live in the Wall itself. His address is Raby Crescent, just behind it.'

'Do we know what he was doing here, then?'

'Ryan: he owns the place. He can go where he wants. He might've been collecting rent. Checking what repairs needed doing...'

'Or jumping to his death.'

'Possibly. At the risk of sounding like DCI Danskin - or Acting Super Danskin, I should say - let's not see what we expect to see.'

Ryan sighed. 'I just want a nice, clean accident. Nowt more, nowt less. What do we know about him?'

'If you'd gone to Forth Street for the briefing, you'd have known.'

He tried hard to bite his tongue, but not hard enough. 'Just tell me, man, okay?'

'We don't know much about him yet. Sue and Todd are running background checks back at the station. We do have uniform presence at his house, though, so we'll shoot over there as soon as forensics arrive and see what we can find out for ourselves. The preliminary report I've seen sounds interesting.'

Ryan groaned. 'Don't tell me he's a weirdo. The last thing I need is a row of heads in a fridge or a wardrobe full of tutus and spandex hot pants.'

Hannah gave a genuine laugh. 'That's ma boy,' she said, her smile highlighting the dimple in her cheek.

'Aye, but I'm not your boy anymore, am I?'

Hannah saw the white forensics van pull up to the entrance. 'Let's go,' she said, diverting the conversation away from its destination.

They circumnavigated the wall and followed a sequence of narrow footpaths between grassed areas and shrubbery. The village behind the wall turned out to be more pleasant than either of them expected.

Raby Crescent and the adjoining Raby Street were narrow, graffiti-free, and lined with rows of privet. Behind the hedgerow stood low level apartments partly clad in bright yellow and blue timber. The front doors were painted either red, blue, or yellow.

'It reminds me of a holiday complex,' Hannah commented.

'Only if it's been designed by Ikea.'

'Yep. It is a bit like that, isn't it?' she laughed.

A uniformed copper barely old enough to have finished school stood on sentry duty outside Warne's property. Hannah flashed her badge in his direction.

'You'll need gloves and shoe coverings, ma'am.'

She fished into her pockets. 'They're always with me.'

'Of course, ma'am. Sorry, ma'am,' the constable said.

Hannah smiled. 'You haven't had much interaction with detectives have you?'

The young man straightened. 'No, ma'am.'

'We're just cops like you. I'm Hannah, or Acting DS Graves. Not ma'am.'

'Sorry, ma'am. Hannah. DS Graves, ma'am,' he mumbled.

'Has the apartment been tampered with since you got here? In any way at all?' Ryan asked.

'No, sir.'

'It's Ryan. Or DC Jarrod, if you prefer,' Hannah said as she scooped a showercap-like cover over her shoes.

'Yes ma'am.'

They both shook their heads as they stepped past the rookie into Justin Warne's abode.

**

Ryan and Hannah scanned the main room in silence.

Two bean bag chairs sat against a far wall. Directly opposite, a flat-screen TV hung low on a wall painted the colour of custard. In the centre of the room, a nest of two small glass-topped coffee tables stood on a beige rug. There were no photographs or other personal items on view.

'Minimalist,' Hannah said.

'To extremes,' Ryan agreed.

Ryan moved to the kitchen. A glass-fronted unit housed three glasses, three mugs, and an empty crystal decanter. Next to it, a second unit contained four plates and two bowls.

With a gloved finger, he slid open a drawer. It was bare. The one alongside it held knives, forks, and teaspoons - four of each – and a tin-opener-cum-corkscrew affair.

He opened the dishwasher. Empty.

Hannah left him to it and made for the only other room. She presumed it was a bedroom.

Ryan continued to rummage through the contents of the kitchen. He unearthed a jar of coffee, some Pot Noodles, cornflakes, seven tins of baked beans and a Fray Bentos pie. In the fridge, a food bag contained three or four slices of cooked ham, a pack of bacon, a carton of long-life milk, and a bottle of Peroni.

'Discover owt, Ry?' Hannah shouted.

High Level

'Apart from the fact Warne's not Jewish and has a serious baked bean habit, no; absolutely nothing. For a property owner, he doesn't have much property.' He thought for a moment. 'Unless he actually lives elsewhere.'

'Come and let me know what you make of this,' Hannah called.

'It's not the tutus and hot pants, is it?'

'No.'

'The heads, then?'

'Not them, either.'

Ryan gave up the guessing game and joined Hannah in the bedroom. A bedroom without a bed.

In its place, a giant wooden desk filled one wall. Three PCs and a laptop sat on its surface. A shelf beneath held two iPads and another laptop.

'Blimey. There's more kit here than Ravi and his geeks have in the station's tech room.' Ryan moved in for closer inspection while Hannah stepped to a built-in set of wardrobes.

'Very strange,' she said.

'Tutus and hot pants?'

'You're obsessed, man. Nope, not a tutu in sight. No hot pants, either. In fact, there's no clothes at all.'

Ryan spun towards her and saw the wardrobe contained two six-foot-tall bookcases. He held his head to one side so he could read the spines. Titles like '*No Money Down Property Investment,*' '*Your Property Jumpstart,*' and the snazzily-titled '*How to Dominate Property Development and Achieve Financial Freedom*' leapt out at him.

'Bet this Warne character was a fun bloke to spend a Friday night at the bar with. His mate's will be chuffed the pubs are shut.'

'It does confirm what we were told about him owning property, though. He's done some heavy research. All the books are about it.'

Ryan looked at the second bookcase. 'Not all, no.'

The shelves were filled with books on E-commerce and financial self-help. *'The Millionaires Fast Lane'* sounded appealing to Ryan, but it was one called *'The Laptop Millionaire'* which made him wonder.

He looked back into the main room, at the array of technology on the desk, and prepared to speak when Hannah's phone chirruped.

'That was Dr. Elliott. He says we can have the pleasure of inspecting the body with him now.'

'Wunderbar,' Ryan groaned.

CHAPTER THREE

Aaron Elliot sat cross legged on the lobby's concrete floor, facing the body.

The forensic examiner's long hair was bunched up beneath a scrub cap and he hummed a ditty to himself as he held an object between a pair of tweezers to the light for closer inspection.

A photographer at his side snapped away from a variety of heights and angles as Ryan and Hannah made their entrance. 'I'm done here, doc.,' the photographer said. 'Ready for him to be repositioned when you are.'

Elliot didn't look up from the corpse as he said, 'I'd recognise those footsteps anywhere. Young Sherlock's arrived, hasn't he? And just in time to give me a hand. Once you're suited up, of course.'

'Cheers, Aaron,' Ryan replied through a grimace.

'My pleasure.' The medic rose to his feet, knees popping like punctured bubble-wrap. 'These cold floors are a bugger. I'll have haemorrhoids before you know it, I don't doubt.'

Ryan shrugged into a paper suit he'd unsealed from a bag on the floor behind Elliot. He began pulling on the gloves and shoe covers he'd worn in Justin Warne's apartment.

'No, no, no. Fresh gloves and shoes, please. You should know by now we can't have you transmitting evidence from one scene to another.'

Ryan rolled his eyes but obliged. 'Do you want a hand turning him?'

'I will in a moment, but you might want a look at this first.' Elliot touched the back of the deceased's head and parted his hair. 'There's an abrasion here.'

'Howay, man. He's fallen God knows how far. Bound to be a mark or two.'

'You said it yourself, Sherlock: he's fallen God knows how far. If he'd got this in the fall, it would be a much more significant injury. No, this pre-existed the fall.'

'How much before?' Hannah asked.

'Impossible to tell from this inspection. Recent, for sure, but whether minutes, hours, or days, I don't know at this stage. I'll have a better idea once I have a little tour of him back in the lab.'

The photographer decided she'd take a close up of the wound and leaned in for the take. When she nodded, Elliot let the man's hair fall back into place.

'Okeydokey,' Elliot said. 'You know the routine. On three…one, two, three.'

Ryan and the medic flipped the corpse onto his back. As they did so, the angle of the man's neck became even more obscene. Hannah gagged.

'Step further back if it perturbs you, Watson.' Elliot always called Ryan and Hannah 'Sherlock and Watson.' They both found it - and him - eccentrically endearing.

'I'm fine,' she gulped, unable to drag her eyes from Warne's remains.

Justin Warne was younger than she'd anticipated, perhaps early thirties, quite attractive beneath the death mask. He had a square jaw and mop of dark brown hair. His eyes were open, staring up into the blackness from which he'd fallen. Beneath the milky fog of his passing, the irises were a pale blue colour. The sockets around them were circled by discoloured bruises which made him resemble a Panda.

Warne's forehead was marked, his lip swollen, and his cheek bore a deep indentation but, again, Ryan noted there was little or no blood.

He looked up the shaft and then down to the body, frowning. 'Why's there no blood?'

'If he landed on his cervix, or anywhere from the sixth thoracic vertebra up, which I suspect is the case, it doesn't necessarily follow that there would be blood. Not externally, anyway,' Dr Elliot explained.

'Aye, but he's got facial markings. Does that mean he's been roughed up beforehand? Maybe before he was thrown down the shaft?'

'Perhaps, perhaps not. He may have hit the walls on the way down. Could still have been an accident, but I'd remain on standby if I were in your shoes. I'll examine him properly once he's comfortably settled into my lab.'

Ryan thought for a moment. 'If you're right, and he landed on his back, how come he's face down now?'

Aaron Elliot held the tweezers at eye level and slowly, deliberately, opened his fingers. The tweezers tumbled downwards, hit the floor, bounced an inch or two, twisted, and landed other side down.

'Et voila.'

'Point taken.'

'Now, if you don't mind, we'll get some more pictures for my mantelpiece.'

Elliot moved aside and the photographer stepped forward as Ryan shook his head at the medical examiner's morbid humour.

Hannah had been making notes and snapped her book shut. 'Okay, Ryan. We've seen enough. I'll get uniform started on door-to-door, and to see if there's any witnesses on the upper floors. While they're doing that, we'll report back to Lyall and find out what Sue and Todd have found out about Mr Warne's background.'

Ryan puffed his cheeks as he blew out air. He'd felt comfortable interacting with Detective Sergeant Graves over the case. He dreaded the company of plain old Hannah Graves on a car journey back to Forth Street.

**

As it turned out, Ryan's fears were groundless.

Neither he nor Hannah uttered a word to each other on the journey because they were tuned in to updates on a protest near Newcastle's Moot Hall. Quite what the protest was about, neither knew nor cared. The important thing was it prevented them squabbling like a pair of politicians on Question Time.

They reported back to Acting DCI Parker who regarded them with the watchfulness of a Clownfish. 'Well?'

'It's still not clear whether it's an accident or not. Aaron Elliot didn't say as much, but I think he suspects Warne had been in a scrap,' Hannah said.

Lyall nodded. 'That's no' what I meant,' the Scotsman said. 'We'll get to that in a wee while. What I meant was, did you manage to work together wi'out coming to blows?' He saw them pout. 'Och, away wi' ye; you know you've been at each other like cat and dog for weeks now. I had to try something to get you together again.'

'We're not together, sir,' Ryan said.

'I dinnae mean in that sense. What you do or don't do off duty is your business – just remember it's against the Code of Ethics for officers o' different ranks to be in a relationship. You'd be skating on very thin ice, and I dinnae want either o' you to droon. What I do need, though, is to know I can rely on the pair of you to work together.'

'We can. We've just proved it.'

Satisfied, Lyall Parker hooked an arm around each of their shoulders. 'Good. Now, we all need to catch up wi' Todd and Sue. See if we can join the dots and work out whether we've a crime to investigate.'

Acting Super Stephen Danskin had rearranged the bullpen so it was Covid-secure, at least nominally. Only two desks on every bank of four were occupied. Sue Nairn sat diagonally opposite Todd Robson. Ryan disregarded protocol and looked over Todd's shoulder while Hannah perched on the spare desk next to Nairn.

High Level

'What you come up with?' Ryan asked.

'Ryan, other bank of desks, please. Back-to-back with Todd,' Lyall Parker instructed.

'Oh howay, man. It's fine us being next to each other in a car or interview room, but not in the bullpen. That's bollocks.' Ryan swapped desks regardless of his protest, but Todd rendered the change redundant when he spun his seat and faced Ryan.

'The bloke's name's Justin Bartholomew Warne. Thirty-three years of age. No record with us. He was a serial entrepreneur by the looks of it. He had fingers in more pies than Jamie Oliver.'

'Aye, Hannah and me have seen his house. Loads of finance books and get-rich-quick stuff.'

Sue Nairn picked up the baton. 'Mostly, he's into property development and real estate management, but he's involved in web-design and did a bit of freelance writing, too. He contributed to the Huff Post's lifestyle output, and ran a blog called More Money Matters.'

'Self-employed, then.'

Sue shrugged. 'A bit of both. He mainly did consultancy work, but he received a salary from High Level Properties. They're based in Cale Cross House.'

'Is that where he worked?'

'He rented office space from them, so I think it's safe to assume he did most his work from there, yeah.'

Ryan frowned. 'Seems a bit off, that does. I've never heard of an employee having to pay for his own office.'

'Like I said,' Todd interjected, 'He had other stuff gannin' on, an' aal. Warne also had a regular income from the Priory and Longsands Portfolio Group. They're based in Tynemouth, if you didn't guess from the name. I'm pretty sure High Level wouldn't want to pay for some other bugger's office space.'

'Makes sense,' Hannah nodded.

'Do we know if he did any work from home?' Ryan asked.

'Who knows?' Todd said. 'We can't ask the sod either, can we?'

'It's just he had a load of IT in his house. Hannah and me kind of assumed he used it as an office as well.'

'Which house?' Sue Nairn asked.

'What do you mean? The one in Byker, of course.'

Sue shook her head. 'Warne lived in a house overlooking Gateshead Fell cricket club. Nothing too grand, but canny. So, although he owned part of the Wall, he didn't live there. It's not unreasonable for him to have a property on the estate from which he could run that part of his empire, and I guess he'd stay there now and again, as well.'

'Have uniform checked out the place in the Fell?'

'Of course. Forensics, too. I'm awaiting their detailed report but the preliminary findings indicate it hasn't been lived in for a good few weeks. I'm not saying we won't find anything but, if we do, it'll be historic.'

Ryan considered Sue's contribution. 'I thought it odd he lived on the Wall if he's so successful, but if he owned a place in Low Fell as well, that'd explain it. Any clues as to why it hasn't been lived in?'

'Nope. He's a single man so I guess he had nothing particular to come home to. If he had lots of business interests, I can understand why he'd spend time on site, as it were, rather than rattling around in a large house.'

'He must be coining it in, two houses, and all.'

'Who said anything about two?' Sue added. 'He owns property in Gosforth and Stocksfield, too. Not to mention Portofino and Los Gigantes. He had a healthy rental income from them. More than he would the Low Fell one which I guess is why he leaves that one as a home base.'

Todd chortled. 'You'd get short odds on him doing a Dominic Cummings between all those places, I reckon.'

Lyall slurped coffee noisily. 'I think we've spent enough time on this for now. Until we hear back from Dr. Elliot or anything concrete crops up from the door-to-doors, let's shelve this. There's plenty more for you guys to get on with.'

'We should start getting some of the door-to-door reports through in the next hour or so,' Hannah pointed out. 'Should one of us monitor those?'

'Aye, that won't do any harm. Either you or Ryan can do it; I don't mind which. Decide between yourselves, unless you think it'll end up in a cage fight.'

'No, Lyall, we told you we're okay working together. I'll keep an eye on the reports. Hannah can get us a coffee.' Ryan winked at her, but no smile accompanied it.

'Get it yersel,' she countered. She saw Lyall Parker frown. 'Okay. Just this once, mind.'

Parker held a finger to his eye before pointing it towards Ryan and Hannah in turn. Hannah nodded and Ryan twisted his mouth, but both got the message, loud and clear. They were under scrutiny.

Ryan waited until Parker had disappeared into the office of Acting Super Stephen Danskin. Ryan had no doubt Lyall would be bringing Danskin up to speed on how he and Hannah were co-operating, more than on the case itself. Ryan sighed, tossed his notebook on his desk, and booted up a computer.

Soon, he was lost in the compilation of his initial report on the body previously known as Justin Bartholomew Warne. He tapped into a shared folder, copied the scanned image of Trebilcock's rough sketch of the scene, and pasted it at the head of the page. Later, he'd replace it with actual photographs once Forensics had logged their report.

In little over half an hour, he was left with nothing to do but wait. Wait until the Forensic report arrived, and the uniform guys filed the outcome of their enquiries. With a bit of luck, there'd be an eyewitness somewhere. Deep down, he knew it was a forlorn hope.

He'd experienced similar issues in closed communities before. Neighbourhoods like Elswick, Teams, and the

Meadowell Estate. Localities where residents closed ranks like the Praetorian Guard, protected their own, or were either too suspicious of the police or afraid of being labelled a grass to come forward. Ryan was sure the Byker Wall would be no different.

He released a sigh so loud Nigel Trebilcock looked up from behind a paper mountain of files.

'Bad news?'

'Is there ever any other kind? Nah, mate. Ignore me. I'm just pissed off with everything at the minute.'

'I had noticed.' Trebilcock smiled sympathetically. 'Why don't you have a break? I can man the fort for a while. I'll watch for the reports coming in. Let you know if anything turns up, so I will.'

'Cheers, Treblecock. I think I might take you up on that.'

'Good. Take yourself home, I say. Or even just goes for a walk around town, why don't you?'

Ryan stared out the bullpen window as he shrugged into his coat. He looked over the thick waters of the Tyne, as still and melancholy as the grey sky above it. A ribbon of traffic streamed across the Redheugh and Tyne Bridges while a Trans Pennine Express trundled over the upper tier of the High Level bridge.

'I'll settle for home. Can't trust mesel' not to chuck us off one of the bridges if I take a walk.'

'Come on, Ryan. Things aren't that bad.'

Ryan let out a moan. 'Aren't they?' he whispered.

CHAPTER FOUR

TUESDAY

Ryan lay as still as Justin Warne the previous day. He stared at the bedroom ceiling, cream with age, as daylight filtered through a gap between the curtains.

Specks of dust circulated in the sun's rays like fish food in an aquarium. Watching them had become part of his morning routine. He'd follow their aimless drift until memories of the dream faded into the recesses of his mind, even though he knew the dream would re-emerge like a stalker the following night, and the one after, and the next.

The thing that bothered him most was, it wasn't a dream. Not really. More a memory. A memory of the day the bottom fell out of his world.

**

He was on an island, at night. Waves crashed against rocks. When the clouds above parted, the moon was bright and full. It should have been idyllic. It was anything but.

Wind drove ice cold spray into his eyes. He was exhausted, mentally and physically. The old scars on his hands stung yet the pain from them was inconsequential compared to that of his arm. The bullet had only winged him, but the wound burnt like fire. The warm blood running down his arm and the cold which enveloped him were Yin and Yang.

He was on his knees. A figure stood over him. He looked up at her and opened his mouth to speak, only for the wind to force the words back down his throat.

He tried again.

'Hannah Graves: will you marry me?'

He held out his hands. Offered her the ring.

The clouds opened like eyelids. Hannah stood silhouetted by moonlight. Wind rippled her hair until her curls stood like serpents on Medusa's head.

'Oh, Ryan,' she said, 'I can't.'

**

Ryan thrust his hands in his pockets and wandered through the foyer of the Forth Street station. Folk bustled around him, lawyers, uniformed officers, members of the public: he didn't notice any of them.

'…I said, *'Good morning.'*

He looked up. 'Sorry. In a world of me own.'

'Aye, I could tell,' the Desk Sergeant said.

'Sorry.' Ryan stepped into the lift and pressed the button for the third floor. A woman walking towards him increased her pace so she could join him before the elevator moved off.

Ryan saw her and hurriedly jabbed the pushbutton marked << >>. The door shut in the woman's face.

'Well, thanks for that,' he heard her say, the voice rich in sarcasm.

He didn't care. Today, all he wanted was to be alone. That's all he ever truly was these days, anyway.

He collected a coffee on the way into the bullpen. He hoped its hit would help him re-join humanity. Until then, he'd keep his head down.

At a desk as far removed from anyone as possible, he booted up a computer and prepared to examine the results of the door-to-door enquiries. Four officers had been assigned to the exercise, each taking three floors. Although the Byker Wall contained six-hundred and twenty flats - which the developers laughably marketed as 'maisonettes' - the officers had been assigned to those closest to the shaft where Warne fell: fewer than sixty in total.

As Ryan anticipated, the officers failed to unearth much of value. Only fifteen reports were filed, and Nigel Trebilcock's initial scrutiny found only five merited an amber-flag indicator. None were worthy of a red.

Ryan opened the first report Trebilcock highlighted but he hadn't got past the first paragraph before Lyall Parker summoned him for a briefing.

He downed the dregs of his drink in the hope it would raise his sociability factor and ambled to where Lyall, Todd Robson and Sue Nairn stood, suitably distanced. Thankfully, Hannah Graves was nowhere in sight.

'Between me other cases, I've run a few more checks and they confirm what I said yesterday,' Todd recapped. 'Justin Bartholomew Warne is a nobody, as far as we're concerned.'

'No history at all?'

'Nope, sir. There's nowt on him. Zilch. Not a sausage. Bugger all. Any other way I can put it?'

'Not even a parking ticket?'

'Like I said: there's bugger all.'

'Could he be using a fake name?' Sue Nairn commented.

'Nah. He's just squeaky-clean, that's all.'

They took a moment to take it in before Lyall spoke to Ryan. 'You've been doing most the work on this one, Ryan. Found anything from the door knocks?'

'Howay, man. I've just logged in.' He remembered to be human. 'Sorry, sir. No, not yet. Treblecock's done some initial scrutiny. There's no red flags. He's identified five or six worth a second look and I'll follow them up when we're done here. I have to say I'm not holding out much hope, though.'

'Okay,' Lyall said. 'Let us know if anything shows. Otherwise, I suggest we park this until the post-mortem's done. Any news on it yet, Ry?'

'No, sir. It'll be a couple of days. Elliot's got it scheduled for tomorrow, so we'll probably get his report the day after unless he finds a silver bullet. I didn't think there was any need to bump it up the list or assign it to a duty FME.'

'Aye, right call, laddie.'

Out the corner of his eye, Ryan saw Hannah emerge from Stephen Danskin's office. He missed Lyall's words.

'Hmm?' Ryan said, absently.

'I said, it was the right call, leaving it in Elliot's hands. Let's see what tomorrow brings. We'll know soon enough whether we've an investigation or no'.'

'Oh, right,' Ryan said.

'We cannae spend all day hanging around. Back to work, the lot o' ye.'

Acting Superintendent Danskin stood at his door, staring in Ryan's direction. Anxiety washed over Ryan. No, not anxiety: paranoia. What had Danskin and Hannah been discussing?

He shook his head to rid himself of the thought. It was nonsense. Of course, it was.

'Jarrod. A word, please. In my office.'

Wasn't it?

**

'Take a seat.'

Ryan lowered himself into a chair opposite Stephen Danskin.

'So, how long you been with us now, Jarrod?'

Ryan narrowed his eyes. 'Look, you know fine well how long. You were the one who recruited me. Cut the crap and tell me what this is about.'

'It's cut the crap, *sir*,' Danskin replied, but he couldn't keep the affection for the young detective out of his voice.

'Sorry, sir.'

'Ah, hadawayandshite, man, Ryan. I'm only kidding. As long as you're respectful out there,' he waved towards the bullpen, 'We know each other well enough to be open in here.'

'Thanks, but I say again: what's going on?'

Danskin rubbed a hand against his shaven pate. Scratched the bristles on his jaw. He lifted a manilla folder from the desktop and revealed a sheet of paper beneath.

'This is confirmation from the Commissioner. We're getting a new Super from next month.'

'I'm sorry, sir. You've done a good job.'

'There's no need to be sorry, man. I only expected to be in the role a couple of weeks, not several months. I've had a canny run for my money and, if I'm honest, I miss proper coppering.'

Ryan smiled.

'What?' Danskin asked.

'That's one of your favourites, isn't it? *'Proper copper'*. That, and…'

'…*Don't see what you expect to see*. Aye, I know you all take the piss out of me about it, but it's true. Both of them.'

Ryan pinched his bottom lip. 'I still don't know what this has got to do with me.'

Danskin rubbed his palms together before interlocking his fingers and cracking his knuckles. 'Well, if I haven't long left before I go back out there, I thought I'd implement a few changes.'

'Such as?'

'Ryan, compared to the likes of Robson, you haven't been here long but, in your time, you've handled more major crimes than some see in a career. The Tyneside Tyrant, the vice ring, the …' he stopped short of adding The Lighthouse Keeper case to the list, 'Way you conducted yourself through all these cases is refreshing. Don't think it hasn't gone unnoticed.'

'I sense a *'but'* coming.'

'Not at all.'

'Then, what?'

Danskin opened the folder and slid a sheet of paper towards Ryan.

'There's a sergeant's exam in two weeks-time. I've recommended you for it.'

Ryan's eyes lit up. 'Seriously?' The smile faded. 'What about Hannah? She's acting DS. Shouldn't she be the one in for it?'

A light flickered in his brain. 'That's what you've just been telling her, isn't it? That you've recommended me for it, not her. Shit, I bet that didn't go down well.'

Danskin fixed him with a stare. 'What makes you think that?'

'Howay, man. You know what it's like between me and her at the minute. She's not going to take kindly to me leapfrogging her. Not that it bothers me, of course.'

Danskin smiled. 'Hannah's cool with it.'

'Really? Are you sure?'

'Yes, I'm sure. I'm sure because I've nominated her for it, as well.'

Ryan looked at the ceiling, not sure what to make of it all. 'That's all I need. Hannah and me in competition.'

'What if you're not in competition? What if I said there's two posts available?'

'I'd say you were spending money like it's going out of fashion, sir.'

'It's still my budget for the next three weeks. I can do with it as I think fit. Besides, it's not that costly.'

'How come?'

Danskin exhaled. 'Between you and me, and I mean strictly between you and me, Sue Nairn's leaving us soon. So, even if you both pass the exam and I keep the pair of you on here, it's only costing the difference between one DC and one DS salary. It's not going to break the bank.'

'So, only you and me know about this?'

'Aye. Well, and Hannah. And Sue, of course.'

Ryan nodded.

'Oh, and Lyall and the Commissioner,' Danskin added.

Ryan laughed. 'So, basically, everybody except Todd, Treblecock, Gavin O'Hara and Ravi Sangar?'

Danskin looked sheepish. 'O'Hara knows, an' aal.'

Ryan snorted a laugh. 'Okay. Well, I don't know what you expect me to say.'

'Nothing, Ryan. That's the whole point. You need to think about it because there'll be implications and ramifications. Not least in your relationship with the rest of the squad.'

Ryan slowly dipped his head.

'So, let me know by the end of the week,' Danskin concluded. 'Just make sure you think through the implications. All of them.'

He already was.

**

'Why can't you marry me?'

He remained on his knees, arms outstretched, his grandmother's antique engagement ring clutched in his hand, even though the jagged rocks beneath him cut into his knees like razors and his damaged arm weighed heavy.

'We've been through this, Ry. You know why.'

'No, we haven't. And no: I don't. Just seconds ago, you thought I was dead. You thought it was me who'd fallen from the lighthouse, not Ahmed Nuri. You told me you loved me.'

Tears streaked Hannah's cheeks. She wiped them away, sniffed back others, yet still more breached her defences.

'I do love you. But you've got baggage to get rid of. Remember the day we drove back from Corbridge? From interviewing the LeRoux's? We talked about it then.'

Ryan looked blank.

'We did, Ry. We both said we loved working together more than anything. We knew we couldn't work together and have a relationship if one of us were promoted. It's against regulations. And we both acknowledged our relationship wouldn't survive different shifts. We've seen what it does to others.'

Ryan shook his head furiously. 'But we're not of different rank. Not yet. We'll fight that fire when we come to it.'

Ryan saw Hannah look away from him. 'It's too late, Ry. Stephen's offered me a temporary promotion. And I've accepted. As of tomorrow, we are of different ranks. I'm your senior officer.'

Yes, Ryan Jarrod was thinking through the implications, alright.

CHAPTER FIVE

Peter Kirk texted his friend. 'You sick? Again? ☹'

It had been days since he'd last heard from him and, with the pink leaves of the Financial Times spread open in front of him, Peter could do with some advice. The markets had flatlined on the back of Brexit and COVID and he desperately needed to move some stocks. Where to, he didn't know. His friend would, if only he'd reply.

Peter called him for the third time, and for the third time the call went through to voicemail. He wasn't surprised. He rarely picked up, which is why Peter reverted to SMS.

He sipped his tea as he checked the markets. He wondered if shifting his investment into gold was the way to go, but he hadn't the courage of his convictions. Hence, the need for advice.

He had no-one else to turn to; no other friends, no family to speak of, and certainly no partner. A library of books, a day job in insurance which he currently worked from home, and weekends in his Uber. That was Peter Kirk's life in a nutshell.

He set the teacup down on a tray, grabbed his keys, and went for a drive.

**

Peter Kirk parked the car next to scaffolding. It would be safer there, with a squad of workmen walking the planks overhead while they tended to the apartment block roof.

He squeezed between the poles and cut across a semi-circle of worn grass. He stopped short the moment he rounded the corner into Raby Crescent.

Yellow tape emblazoned with the words DO NOT ENTER – POLICE provided a portcullis-like barrier to Justin Warne's apartment. A young cop stood by the door, stoically ignoring a volley of insults and abuse coming from a group of scruffy-arsed urchins.

Peter took a few steps towards the apartment, then stopped. The cop looked towards him. Mind made up, Peter strode forward.

'I'm sorry, sir. I have to ask you to move away,' the cop instructed.

'I'm his friend.'

'I'm afraid I can't let you in.'

One of the urchins picked up a handful of pebbles and threw them at Peter and the cop.

'Hoy, you lot. I've told you, clear off or I'll book you.'

Pete turned towards them but spoke to the cop. 'I think you're wasting your breath. That lot'll wear their ASBOs like a badge of honour.'

The cop laughed. 'I guess you're right.'

'Look, officer, what's up?'

'I'm not at liberty to say, sir. Could I ask your name?'

'Yes. It's Peter Kirk.' He gave the cop his address. 'Is Justin okay?'

'How long have you known Mr Warne?' The officer was taking notes, now.

'We went to Uni together. LSE, to be exact.' He saw the copper frown. 'London School of Economics,' he qualified.

'How long ago was that sir?'

'Twelve years. Fourteen, maybe. I quit after a term. We lost touch for years. Look, what's up? Is Justin in some kind of trouble?'

The cop ignored his question. 'When did you last see Mr Warne?'

'A few weeks ago.'

'Liar, liar, arse on fire,' a kid with a snotty nose sang. Peter shot the kid an even snottier look.

'Thank you, Mr Kirk. I really am sorry, but I do have to ask you to leave,' the policeman said.

'What? Just like that? With no explanation?'

'I'm afraid so.'

Peter opened his mouth to protest, realised there was no point, and turned back to his car. While he walked, he reached into a pocket for his phone, and tapped a finger against the name *Justin* on his contact list. The call went straight to voicemail.

'He's dead.'

Peter spun around in time to see a woman disappearing into an apartment.

'What?'

'He's dead,' her voice repeated from somewhere in the hallway.

Without a moment's hesitation, he followed her into the apartment. It stank of stale beer and Rothman's. Paper peeled from damp-infested walls and mould spots flecked the ceiling.

Close up, the woman was younger than Peter first thought. Late twenties, at most. Probably younger. She wore a baggy T-shirt off the shoulder. Tight denim shorts revealed a mid-thigh tattoo of an angel with horns.

She shifted a blue backpack from a futon and curled herself up on the seat, tucking her legs beneath her. The woman's feet were bare and Peter noticed the soles were grubby, her toenails jagged.

She tapped out a cigarette. 'Smoke?'

Peter shook his head.

'He broke his neck,' she said, matter-of-factly. 'I heard the cops say he fell doon a lift shaft.'

'God.'

'Nah,' she shook her head. 'There isn't one.'

Peter tried to take it in. 'Did you hear the police say anything else?'

She tipped her head back and blew smoke towards the ceiling. 'A lad and a lass were talking about it. Plain clothes. Said they were waiting for a medical bloke but they thought he might have been pushed.'

'Frigging hell.' He looked at the woman. 'Sorry.'

She laughed. 'For what? Swearing? There's a lot worse goes on round here, I tell you.'

He thought of Justin Warne at the foot of a lift shaft. She was right: there was a lot worse went on around there.

Something welled inside him. Something he hadn't felt for a long time. Emotion. A watery film distorted his vision. He blinked it away.

'So,' he said, suddenly uncomfortable, 'You knew Justin, as well.'

'Aye.'

'How?'

The woman leant forward. Hair the colour of pine streaked with indigo dye hung over her face as she flicked ash into a shot glass.

'We shared a drink or two together. Sometimes we'd share the occasional fuck. That's about it.'

Peter didn't know what to say, so he forced his open mouth shut and stayed silent. Silence brought back memories, and memories brought back emotion.

He felt tears dampen his cheeks. They took him by surprise. He wasn't even that close to Justin Warne. There again, he wasn't close to anybody.

He saw the woman stare at him and flushed with embarrassment once more. 'Sorry,' he said.

She smiled. 'You say that a lot.'

'Do I?'

'Yeah, you do.' She sucked on her cigarette. 'What's your name?'

'Peter.'

'Do you have a second name, Peter?' She reached for a can of Fosters close to her futon and snapped the tab.

'Kirk.' He rubbed the heel of his hands into his eyes.

The woman took a swig from her can. 'Well, Peter Kirk; never hide your emotions. When I'm upset, I do things to bury them. Have you tried doing that?'

Peter wondered if it was his imagination. She wasn't unattractive, in a hippy sort of way, but no; she wasn't suggesting what he thought, surely?

'I have to go,' he said.

'So soon? Ah well,' she shrugged. 'Win some; lose some.'

Bloody hell: she was!

'Thanks for telling me about Justin. I appreciate it.'

'No problem. And, anytime it gets too much for you, you know where I am.'

She held out her hand.

'I'm Sally, by the way. Sally Sykes.'

As Pete shook her hand, she leant forward.

'See you around, Peter Kirk,' she whispered into his ear.

**

At a desk on the perimeter of the bullpen, Ryan put his hands on the keyboard and pulled up the reports Nigel Trebilcock had highlighted for him.

He finished reading the report he'd opened earlier. It contained nothing significant.

The second report was from a guy who lived on the sixth floor. Geoffrey Allan reported hearing loud voices outside his flat. He said it sounded like a heated argument. He couldn't say how many voices he'd heard, what the argument was about, or recall any names being mentioned. Mr Allan said, 'This sort of thing happens all the time around here.'

Ryan shook his head. If that's what Trebilcock thought worthy of highlighting, it didn't augur well for the other reports.

An Olwyn Farmer on the eighth floor described hearing breaking glass outside her apartment. Someone swore and kicked her door. She'd been wary of opening it so it was fifteen minutes later when she peeked out. A bottle of Smirnoff lay smashed in the corridor. *Big deal*, thought Ryan. *Some drunk's dropped his medicine and kicked out in frustration.*

When the fourth statement turned out equally bland, Ryan wondered how much time and energy the force had expanded on sod all. He rotated his neck until it cracked, adjusted his posture, and opened the final statement.

Rosina Durrant lived on the second floor. Her flat overlooked the courtyard. She'd seen an altercation involving three men and a woman escalate into a minor scuffle. She didn't recognise the woman and couldn't be sure of the men.

Ryan doubted it was the truth. She either knew them but didn't want to get involved, or was too frightened to name names. He made a physical note of Rosina's number and a mental note to come back to her if, and when, Aaron Elliot concluded they had a murder investigation on their hands. Until then, he had no authority to quiz Rosina Durrant again.

Ryan glanced around the bullpen. With nothing better to do, he logged into the National Police Promotion Framework intranet website, called up the Step Two Examination Candidate Information Booklet and, after tilting his screen out of view of prying eyes, he scanned the sample questions.

They were all multiple-choice questions around two-hundred and fifty words long, each describing a scenario an officer was likely to encounter on duty, and offering four outcomes. Ryan picked a question at random.

'SIMPSON *has found out that his wife is having an affair with* WEBB. SIMPSON *abducts* WEBB *and drives him around Anytown. He has an imitation gun in the glove compartment.*

High Level

SIMPSON tells WEBB he has a firearm and will shoot WEBB if he does not promise to stop seeing his wife. WEBB is unconcerned by the threats, so SIMPSON drives his car in a dangerous manner intending to endanger both their lives. Does SIMPSON commit the offence of possessing a firearm with intent to endanger life, contrary to Section 16 of the Firearms Act 1968?

(A) No, because the firearm is an imitation and it is not the means by which WEBB's life is endangered.

(B) No, because WEBB does not believe that his life is endangered by the firearm.

(C)...

Ryan's eyes glazed over. He hated exams, found them boring, and thought multiple-choice questions a false measure. They allowed for too much guesswork rather than 'proper coppering,' as Danskin would call it.

Or was he just fed up with the life, the Universe, and everything?

He logged out of his computer, pulled on his jacket, and headed home.

**

Maz Crawford struggled into the lift lobby with her Morrison's shopping overflowing from within an XL Sports Direct Bag for Life.

She set the bag on the floor and shook out her arms to relax her muscles. Maz knew she had the length of the Wall to walk to reach her flat once she reached the tenth-floor corridor.

Her nostrils flared. The lobby this side of the Wall smelled like a Bigg Market urinal. She curled her lips in distaste as she waited for the lift. The sooner the police opened her end of the building again, the better.

The grey metal doors in front of her were etched in lurid coloured graffiti, most of it pornographic, all of it grammatically challenged. She thanked God she wouldn't have to stay here long.

'They think they're funny.'

Maz jumped at the sound of the voice close by her. 'I'm sorry?'

'The knacker Dans who do this,' the woman said, tilting her head towards the doors, 'Think they're funny. They're not. They wouldn't get away with it in old Byker. They'd get a reet clip around the lug, they would.'

Maz offered the woman a smile and returned her gaze towards the metal doors.

'New here, are you?' the woman continued.

'Yeah.' Maz jabbed at the lift button again.

'Thought I hadn't seen you before. Why in buggery do you want to live here?'

'It's okay,' she lied.

'Hadawayandshite. It's bloody awful, man. Old Byker might have been a bit run down but we looked after our own in them days.'

'It's okay,' Maz said again, hammering at the lift button.

'Terrible business the other day, wasn't it?'

'Hmmm?'

'The man who got killed. It's a terrible business. It was only a matter of time before summat like that happened, though. Nowt surprises me these days.'

The ping of the elevator's arrival lightened Maz's spirits. She stepped in and pressed number 10. 'What floor?' she asked.

Her companion looked at the panel, saw the green light alongside the number 10, and said, 'Same as you, pet.'

Maz's eyelids slid closed.

'All I'm saying is, keep your wits about you, lass. There's lots of wrong uns here. Don't let yersel' be taken in.'

The doors opened with a squeal. Maz struggled out with her heavy bag. The woman followed.

'I'll see you again, nee doubt,' the woman said.

'Yes, I'm sure.' Maz forced a smile and trudged along the corridor.

The woman didn't follow, but Maz felt the hackles rise on her neck. She knew the woman's eyes remained trained on her back.

Silently, the woman stepped back into the lift and hit the button for the second floor.

CHAPTER SIX

WEDNESDAY

Ryan stared blankly out the kitchen window like an automaton. Work beckoned but, as was increasingly the case, he had no appetite for it.

He took a pack of raw dog food from the freezer, tipped the solid mass into a large Tupperware box, and popped the sealed container into a carrier bag next to a Smart Price pasty and bag of Quavers.

The old Fiat which Hannah had always looked on with disdain navigated its way from The Drive, along Front Street, up Rectory Lane and onto Larkspur Road via Holme Avenue. Before he knew it, he'd pulled up on Newfields Walk.

'Bloody hell, man. Just come straight in and give me a heart attack, why don't you?' Norman Jarrod said as Ryan entered the house.

'I've brought old Spud some food. I know you'll feed him that Heroes shite if I don't give you the good stuff.' The pug skipped and danced around Ryan's feet as he put the Tupperware on the bench to defrost. 'It'll be ready for his tea.'

Norman Jarrod appraised his elder son. 'You lost weight?'
Ryan shrugged.
'You're not yourself, are you?'
Ryan sighed. 'I'm okay. Life's a bit shit, that's all.'
'Want to talk?'

'Bloody hell. Who are you? What you done to me dad?'

'Funny. No, seriously, if you want owt, just say.'

'Thanks, Dad. I appreciate it. Nah, it's just this COVID thing. Not being able to see me mates. It's hard enough as it is with this job, but I'd just like to be able to have a pint in the Horse now and again, you know? Or even the Crown.'

'Bloody hell. You must be desperate.' Norman Jarrod switched off the TV. 'So, it's nowt to do with Hannah, is it?'

Ryan gripped the bench. 'It's just everything, man. I worry about Gran. Not being able to visit her. If I'm struggling, what must it be like for her?'

'Son, she's got the carers around her in the home. Her friends are there. She's surrounded by people.'

'I guess, but it doesn't stop me worrying.' He hesitated. Swallowed hard. 'Will she even remember me by the time I'm allowed to visit her again?'

His father looked at him but had no words of reassurance. Except, 'She doesn't really know any of us anymore. Not really.'

Ryan shook his head. 'You're not helping, Dad.'

'And you're changing the subject. Are you pining over Hannah?'

'That might be part of it, but it's just everything. The job, missing me mates, not being able to gan to the match…'

'Howay, man; that's a blessing, surely?'

'Fair point,' he laughed. 'No, I'll be okay, Dad. Honest. Thanks, anyway. Listen, I'd best be off. If James ever gets out his pit, tell him I've been, yeah?'

'Aye, I will.'

Ryan picked up the bag containing his packed lunch. 'See you.'

'Love you, son.'

Ryan put down the bag containing his packed lunch. 'Are YOU okay, Dad?'

'Ah, get yersel' off to work, man. I'm just a silly old duffer who's gone soft in his old age. Now, bugger off and leave me in peace with Susanna Reid.'

'Not Piers Morgan?'

'I'm not that soft. Get out of here and dole out a few parking tickets or whatever it is you detectives do.'

With a laugh, Ryan got out of there.

**

'You're late,' Hannah Graves admonished.

'Don't get high and mighty with me, Hannah. Not today. In fact, not ever: okay?'

'I'm only saying.' She held her hands aloft. 'Don't be so defensive. We're on the same side, you know.'

Before Ryan could reply, Lyall Parker scurried towards them.

'You're late, Ryan,' he said, checking his watch.

'Sorry, sir.' Ryan saw the dimple bloom in Hannah's cheek. Despite himself, he found it cute as a kitten.

Lyall gave him a dismissive wave. 'You've missed nothing. Until now, that is.'

'What's occurring?' Hannah asked.

'Elliot's report on Justin Warne's just arrived.' He'd printed off the report and handed them a copy each. 'Let's have a wee chat in ma room.'

Ryan and Hannah read through the forensic report as they wheeled their chairs towards the Acting DCI's desk.

The cause of death was asphyxiation due to a broken neck which cut off airflow to the lungs. Elliot surmised Warne may have lain at the foot of the lift shaft for anything up to thirty minutes before succumbing to suffocation.

The fact the impact itself didn't kill Warne led Elliot to conclude he had fallen no more than three floors.

Elliot made reference to a fractured left ankle, and several breaks to tibia, fibula, and ankle of Warne's right leg. These were impact injuries sustained by the fall.

High Level

The report noted the contusions and abrasions Ryan had seen on Warnes head and face during the initial on-site inspection. Elliot was unable to determine with certainty how the wounds were obtained but they were consistent with injuries caused by collision with the walls of the shaft during Warne's descent.

Inspection of Warne's upper torso revealed several other semi-formed bruises. Aaron Elliot concluded they were highly unlikely to have been received during the fall, nor were they significant enough to be the result of hitting a solid surface after a three-story drop.

Not only that, but the bruises were also the wrong shape. Specifically, two below the left rib cage were the size of a small foot.

Lyall waited until they'd finished reading the report. When they raised their eyes to meet his, he spoke.

'It looks like you two have a case to investigate. Justin Warne had been in a fight in the moments leading up to his fall.'

**

Rosina Durrant was in her late sixties and had steel grey hair which matched the colour of her eyes. Beneath a pink cardigan, she wore an ill-fitting bra which gave her an odd, lop-sided appearance. She also wore too much perfume.

'Mrs Durrant? I'm Acting Detective Sergeant Hannah Graves and this is my colleague, DC Ryan Jarrod. I wonder if we could have a word?'

Rosina stared at Hannah, then at her badge, then along the corridor, before ushering them in.

'This'll be about the other day, is it?'

'It is, yes,' Hannah replied. 'I gather you witnessed a disturbance outside.'

Ryan stood by the window, looking out over the courtyard. From his vantage point, he could see two-thirds of the car park, the entrance road, and had a clear view of the entry to the Byker Wall.

Rosina Durrant watched him as she answered, 'I talked to the other policeman about this already.'

'We know, ma'am. We're just trying to work out what happened, that's all.'

Rosina perched on the edge of a seat, hands clenched together in her lap.

'Could you tell us exactly what you saw?'

Rosina shrugged. 'Not much. I saw four people in the courtyard, a woman and three men. The woman was arguing…'

'You could hear them?' Ryan asked.

'No. No, I couldn't. But you can tell when somebody's arguing, can't you? They throw their arms about. They point. They stand differently, don't they?'

'So, these four people were *standing differently*,' were they?' Ryan said.

'The woman was, yes. She seemed to be having a right go at one of the men.'

'If I showed you a photograph, would you be able to tell me if it was the man?'

Rosina Durrant looked down. Toyed with an imaginary thread on her polyester trousers. 'No. I wouldn't. None of them.'

'Were they fighting? Physically, I mean.'

The woman hesitated. 'Well, I didn't see it, if they were. I went to do something – can't remember what – and when I looked back, one of the men was kneeling on the ground. He was holding his…, you know – his bits.'

'But you didn't actually see anything?'

'No, officers, I didn't.'

Ryan stood alongside Hannah. 'And, you didn't recognise the men?'

Again, Rosina Durrant averted her eyes. 'No.'

'But you saw enough of the woman to know you hadn't seen her before. That's a bit odd, isn't it?'

Rosina continued to stare downwards. 'My old eyes aren't what they were.'

Ryan began to speak but Hannah hushed him. 'It's likely we'll need to talk to you again, Mrs Durrant,' she said. 'Meanwhile, I'll give you my contact details. If you remember anything else, please let us know.'

They both knew she wouldn't.

They were wrong.

'I don't know who she is, but I know where she lives,' Rosina Durrant said. 'I've seen her since. We don't much care for strangers around here, so I followed her. Just so I knew where to find her if…well, if anything happened.'

She made eye contact with Hannah.

'You'll find her on the tenth floor. Now, let yourselves out, and make sure no bugger sees you leave.'

**

'What did you make of her?' Hannah asked as they stepped from the lift at the tenth floor.

'Not sure. She knows the blokes, I'm sure of that much, but I can't decide whether she's scared of them or scared of us.'

They walked along the corridor past a row of doors which could have been clones of each other. 'Yeah, I agree. Let's see what we find out here before deciding whether to pay her another visit.'

The corridor arced gently until they could see the elevator door at the far end.

'The woman Mrs Durrant reported lives right by the elevator. She'll already have been interviewed by Uniform. We'll check out the original report when we get back to Forth Street,' Hannah said.

'Aye, that's a good point. Treblecock didn't flag her up so she mustn't have said owt to the door-to-doors, which poses a question in itself.'

They reached the flat Rosina had indicated.

'What the hell?'

Splashed across the front door in red paint were the ill-formed words 'YOULL PAY.'

**

Ryan and Hannah stood while Maz Crawford sat on the battered bottle-green sofa.

'You admit to having a run in with three men on Sunday evening?'

Maz Crawford met Hannah's eye without flinching. 'No. I had a disagreement with a kid. Two kids. They were tormenting my dog.'

'You do realise we have CCTV we can check?'

Maz snorted a laugh. 'I wish. There's no way the folk around here would put up with that. I bet all the cameras are smashed. But, if they're not, go ahead and check. Be my guest.'

Hannah nodded to Ryan. 'Do you know this man?' He produced a picture of Justin Warne.

Maz gave the photograph due consideration. 'Nope.'

'Are you sure?'

Maz looked directly at Ryan. 'I'm sure. Besides, the kid I had a run-in with was much younger than this. He called himself Rats. You'll know him if you see him. He'll be the one walking with a limp.'

She gave Ryan a curious look. Her lips curved upwards.

'Have I said something to amuse you, Miss Crawford?'

'What did you say your names were again?' she asked Hannah.

'DS Graves and DC Jarrod.'

Maz squinted at Ryan.

'Are you related to Jam Jar?'

Ryan's mouth dropped open. 'Aye. James is me brother.'

'Thought you must be. It's an unusual name.'

'Do you know him, like? Sorry, obviously you do if you know his nickname.'

'He was a year below me at school.'

'Are you from Whickham, an' aal?'
'Marley Hill originally.'
'Small world.'
'Isn't it just? Tell me, does Jam Jar still have Jedward hair?'
Ryan laughed. 'Aye. He's toned it down a bit now. More Tin Tin these days.'
Maz flicked a strand of blonde hair away from her eyes. 'I used to fancy him in an odd sort of way.'
'Wor James? Never.'
She laughed. 'Yeah. You remind me of him. You've got the same eyes.'
Hannah coughed. 'A word. Outside. Now.'
Ryan followed her out into the corridor. 'What?'
'What the hell do you think you're playing at? She's a bloody witness. A suspect, possibly, and you're flirting with her.'
'Don't be daft, man.'
'Well, if you're not flirting with her, she is with you.'
'Don't tell me your jealous.'
Hannah barked a laugh. 'Jealous? No way. But I am professional. And I expect you to be, too. Now, let's get back in there and find out what this is all about.' She pointed to the words on the door.
'You win,' he said. 'Sir.'
Hannah gave him the finger as they re-entered the flat.
'Miss Crawford, could you tell me about the graffiti on your door?'
'It just appeared. Monday night. No idea what it means.'
'You don't seem too concerned.'
'Probably, because I'm not.'
Hannah looked at her long and hard. 'The day after you have a heated argument with a man, the day after a man is found dead at the bottom of a lift shaft next to your front door, you find said door daubed with threats - and you're not concerned?'

'Not really, no. There's graffiti all over the place. Whoever did it probably doesn't even know I live here. It's probably aimed at the previous resident.'

'When did you move in?' Ryan asked.

Maz softened her voice. 'Sunday. I only moved in on Sunday so, you see, I can't possibly know anybody here, can I?'

Hannah and Ryan exchanged glances. 'You only moved in on Sunday?'

'That's what I just said, yes.'

'Can anyone vouch for you?'

'I'm sure there'll be records. And I got a cab here. Look, it'll be on me app. You can check with the driver, if you like.' She held her phone up so Hannah could read it.

Hannah and Ryan jotted down the driver's details. 'We will do, I promise. Okay, Miss Crawford; that's all for now. Thanks for your time.'

Maz directed her reply to Ryan. 'My pleasure. Any time. Oh, give James my love, won't you?'

She saw Ryan and Hannah out, returned to the sofa, and gnawed on a fingernail.

CHAPTER SEVEN

They squinted into the sun as they surveyed the exterior of Justin Warne's Byker apartment. A neighbour with badly dyed hair watched them until Hannah gave her the eye. The woman stared back, sneered, but retreated into her apartment.

'What did you make of the warning on Crawford's door?' Hannah asked.

Ryan thought for a moment. 'Whoever did it was uneducated. No punctuation.'

'Have you seen the state of the graffiti around here? That rules out precisely no-one.'

'True, but if it had been an associate of Warne's, I think they'd know an apostrophe when they saw one.'

'Unless they wanted to make it look like a local.'

'So why pick on Maz?'

'I dunno, Ry. Perhaps she's right. Perhaps it was aimed at a previous occupant. Or, perhaps someone knows she did kill Warne and was telling her she'd pay for it.'

Ryan waved to the young uniform cop standing guard outside Warne's house. 'Let's see what we find in here, should we? If we find naked posters of Marilyn Crawford hidden in a secret panel behind a wall, we'll bring her in.'

'You're fantasising now, Ry, aren't you?'

'Nah. Not my type.'

'Ha! Could've fooled me.'

'She isn't. I mean, she hasn't got a dimple, has she?' With that, he clambered through the tape into Justin Warne's apartment.

Ryan and Hannah found it the way they expected: untouched and unchanged since the day Warne's body was discovered.

They loaded his IT equipment into large sacks marked *Evidence*. 'Ravi will be like a pig in shit weaving his technological voodoo over these hard drives once we get them back to Forth Street.'

Hannah laughed. 'Aye, but he'll come up with the goods. We'll have a list of his contacts in no time.'

'I'll let him know we're on our way.' He dipped into a pocket for his phone and froze.

'What's the matter?'

'Warne's contacts. He must have had loads.'

'And?'

Ryan rubbed the side of his face. 'There wasn't a mobile phone on the body when he died.'

Hannah waited for him to make his point.

'We haven't found one in here, either. Where's his phone, Hannah? Who's got it?'

They hunted the apartment again. It didn't take long. There weren't many places where it could be hidden, other than in the bookcase. They checked, but Ryan and Hannah both knew it was too Agatha Christie for it to be concealed there.

'Shit.'

Hannah looked at him. 'What now?'

'We should have photographed the desk when we got here the first time. When I think about it, I'm sure there was a blank space as if something had been removed.'

'You think somebody took the phone?'

'Aye, possibly. Possibly something else, an' aal. The space was too big for just a mobile. You know, I think someone might have removed a laptop from here.'

He looked back at the desk.

'If Ravi Sangar can't find owt on the kit we've parcelled, I reckon we'll know for sure that there IS a missing laptop. And I bet it's the key.'

**

The rap on the door startled Rosina Durrant. If that was the cops back again, she prayed no-one had seen them.

It wasn't the cops.

'Fifty quid, missus,' Rats snarled.

'I haven't got it. I haven't got me pension yet.'

Rats barged past her. He picked up a figurine and weighed it in his hands.

'Please, don't hit me. I'll get you the money. I just need time. Tomorrow. Yes, tomorrow. I'll have it then.'

Rats put his face into Rosina's. Garlic and stale alcohol invaded her nostrils. She tried to show neither fear nor disgust.

'Today,' he sneered. 'You'll get it today.'

He raised the figurine above his head. Brought it towards the woman. Rosina Durant cowered from him.

The ornament slipped from his fingers and shattered on the floor.

'Ooops,' Rats said. 'Never mind. It'll be yer telly next time.'

'You can't keep doing this, week after week.'

'Yes, I can. Who's going to stop me?'

'Somebody will report you.'

'Are ye stupid, or what? No fucker would dare. Besides, who are they going to report me to?'

Rosina Durrant's eyes widened. 'You! You did it, didn't you? You killed him.'

'That's for me to know and you to find out.' He exposed yellow rotting teeth. 'Fifty quid. Cheap at half the price. Y'knaa what, it IS half the price. Next week, it'll be a hundred.'

'I can't afford it. I can't.'

'You can. You'll make sure you can 'cos you know there's neebody to stop me now.'

'Please. Leave me alone. Leave all of us alone.'

'Fifty quid by six o'clock or yer telly's gannin oot the window. Next week, it'll be you that goes out.'

Tears streamed down Rosina Durrant's cheeks. She knew he meant it.

'Stop yer bubbling, woman. Think yersel lucky yer such an ugly sod or I'd have me payment some other way.'

Rosina Durrant's eyes yawned.

'With a bag ower yer heed, I still might. I'll make it a plastic bag. That'll be even better, watching yer eyes bulge and yer face turn purple.'

He turned his back on her.

'Fifty quid by six or I might just give that a go.'

The door slammed shut behind him. Rosina slumped to her floor sobbing like a two-year old.

She almost wished it had been the police at her door.

**

The police themselves were busy.

Ravi Sangar was in the tech room tinkering with Justin Warne's hard drive as if he were a model railway enthusiast fine-tuning his replica Mallard. Hannah Graves updated Lyall Parker, Nigel Trebilcock chased up Forensics for the fingerprint results from Warne's apartment, Ryan cross-checked statements, and Todd Robson picked his nose.

'Is there nowt I can do, man?' he pleaded. 'I feel as useless as a eunuch in a brothel here.'

'Robson,' Stephen Danskin's voice boomed across the bullpen, 'We're not in the seventies now. Less of that.'

'For fuck's sake, how does he always know when I say summat I shouldn't?'

'Probably because you've a voice like a leafblower and you're as subtle as dysentry,' Danskin shouted.

The bullpen exploded with laughter.

'Aye, I am a bit, like,' Robson chuckled.

High Level

'Tell you what,' Ryan said, 'Check the Uber records for Sunday night. See if you can confirm this bloke dropped a Marilyn Crawford off at the Byker Wall sometime Sunday afternoon.' He handed his notepad to Todd. 'She might be known as Maz, and the driver's name is Pete, according to the App and Crawford. If he can verify her story, we might be able to rule her out.'

While Todd set to work, Ryan called up Marilyn Crawford's discussion with the officer conducting door-to-door.

The report was bland. She hadn't mentioned any altercation, hadn't reported anyone trolling her dog, failed to mention she'd only just moved in. In fact, all the report said was, *'The occupant, Marilyn Crawford, saw or heard nothing on the day of the incident.'*

Ryan steepled his fingers and rocked back and forth in his chair. 'Now, why would you say that, Maz?' Ryan asked himself aloud.

Out of curiosity, he checked the report of Maz's next door neighbour. It read, *'The occupants, Wendy and Thomas Bull, saw or heard nothing on the day of the incident.'*

It wasn't unheard of for a bored officer to file bodged 'copy and paste' reports at the end of a long, fruitless day. Ryan wondered if that was what this PC had done. He called up another three reports filed by PC Gary Paddock.

The first read, *'The occupant, Edwina Noteman, was out most of the day, delivering shopping to her disabled sister. Story checks out.'*

The next report, from the floor below, followed the 'saw or heard nothing' mantra, while the final report came from the flat directly above Maz Crawford.

'The occupant, Derek Hazell, heard sounds below and went to check out the source. He says the noise was of someone moving in. No other suspicions reported.'

Ryan couldn't decide whether he was relieved Maz Crawford's story held firm, or irritated that the system – and Nigel Trebilcock - hadn't made the connection earlier.

'Well, knock us sideways with Barry Manilow's sneck,' Todd Robson said. He glanced towards the Acting Super's office like a meerkat. 'Looks like that one's acceptable to Herr Gruppenfuhrer.'

'Story checks out, Todd?'

'Aye. It does. You'll never guess what, though.'

'Am I going to like this?'

'I don't know, to be honest.'

'Howay, man. Spit it out.'

'I've cross-referenced the name through the statements. The Uber gadgee's called Peter Kirk, and we've a report of him snooping around Justin Warne's gaff, that's what.'

**

Hannah insisted they took her Renault. Ryan didn't know why it needed the two of them to speak to Peter Kirk, but he went along with her. He hadn't much choice. She was his senior officer, as she frequently but good-naturedly reminded him.

They parked outside a modest new build in a rapidly expanding development north of the West Allotment suburb, spreading almost to Backworth and Shiremoor.

The GPS found Peter Kirk's street easily enough, but Cloverfield wound a circuitous route of ever decreasing circles and they backtracked several times before finding the right house.

'Looks like he's in,' Hannah said, pointing to the car on the drive.

'How do we play it?'

'I think we stick to questions about Maz Crawford, at least to begin with. Watch for twitchiness. Once he's backed up her story, I'll let you hit him with the Justin Warne questions.'

High Level

'Sounds like a plan.'

They left the Renault and made their way up Peter Kirk's garden path. The man who answered the door was a wiry, nondescript individual. He was neither plug ugly nor knock 'em dead hunky and could have been any age between thirty and forty-five.

Peter Kirk was someone who'd blend into the scenery.

'Not interested,' he said. 'I've got my own religion. You shouldn't be doing this in the current climate, anyway. Not exactly essential business, is it, Jehovah's-bloody-Witnesses? We're in the middle of a Global pandemic if you hadn't known.'

He closed the door on them.

Ryan raised his eyebrows at Hannah as he knocked on the door again. When there was no answer, he slipped his face covering beneath his chin and opened the letterbox.

'Mr Kirk. We're not Jehovah's Witnesses, Latter Day Saints, or double-glazing salesmen. It's not Avon calling, either. We're from City and County Police. We'd like to ask you a few questions if we may.'

Through the letterbox, he saw the slippered feet of Peter Kirk head towards the door.

'I'm sorry,' Kirk said. 'I don't get you guys knocking on my door every day.' A thin film of sweat slicked his forehead. 'Come in. Please.'

He escorted them into a coffin shaped living room, tastefully decorated and furnished in a way which maximised space.

Hannah asked Peter Kirk if he wanted them to remove their face coverings so he could identify them from their ID. Once he'd agreed and the formalities were over, Hannah moved to the purpose of their visit.

'We'd like your help in confirming the statement of someone, Mr Kirk. We'd be grateful if you could tell us whether you had a fare on Sunday afternoon. More precisely, a fare to the Byker Wall.'

'I did, as it happens; yes.'

'You're certain?' Hannah asked. 'Don't need to check your records?'

Peter Kirk snickered. 'We Uber drivers aren't exactly busy these days. Not many folk out and about with everything being shut, and all. Yes, I took a woman to the Wall. Short lass. Quite pretty. She was moving in.'

Hannah flicked a glance at Ryan. He nodded. Everything Peter Kirk said backed up Maz Crawford's story.

Hannah showed him two photographs: one of Maz Crawford, the other some random blonde-haired woman of about Maz's age she'd picked from an archived file.

'That's the one,' Kirk said, tapping Maz's image. 'Definitely.'

Hannah smiled. 'Thank you.'

Peter Kirk stood. 'No problem, Detectives.'

Hannah and Ryan remained seated.

'Is there something else?'

'Did you go back to the Wall at any time that day?' Ryan said.

Kirk sat back down. 'No, no. I try to avoid it if I can. It's a bit rough, to say the least.'

Ryan watched for a reaction as he said, 'Aye. A bloke was killed there on Sunday. Fell down a lift shaft.'

Peter Kirk maintained eye contact for too long. He forgot to blink. When he did, his eyelids fluttered rapidly.

'We think he was pushed.'

Kirk swallowed.

'Mr Kirk, have you been back to Byker since you dropped off Miss Crawford?'

'Yes.' The word was quiet, almost inaudible.

'I didn't quite catch that, Mr Kirk,' Ryan lied.

'Yes, I have. But you obviously know that already, don't you?'

Hannah spoke. 'Yes, we do.'

'What were you doing there?'

'You'll know that, as well. I went to see Justin.'

'Ah, yes. Justin Warne. The same Justin Warne who broke his neck by falling down a lift shaft the evening you were placed at the scene.'

'It wasn't me.' Even Peter Kirk thought it sounded pathetic.

Ryan looked beyond Kirk, who turned and followed the line of sight.

'Is that your computer on the table?'

'Of course.'

'Then, you don't mind if I take it in to be checked out.'

Kirk stood. 'Yes, I most certainly do. I need it for work, and it contains personal details of my clients. I'm in Insurance.'

Ryan laughed. 'Good, because I think you might need some insurance of your own. You're in a spot of bother, Mr Kirk.'

'Look, why would I hurt Justin? He was a friend.'

'WAS a friend?'

'Oh, come on: I used the past tense because he's passed away, not because he's no longer a friend. You're trying to catch me out.'

Ryan locked eyes. 'Did you go to see him for a specific reason?'

Kirk looked at the floor. 'I was after some financial advice.'

Hannah stepped in. 'Do you have money troubles, Mr Kirk?'

'No! Well, no more than anyone else does, these days. Justin often gave me advice.'

'Was it good advice?' Ryan's turn again. 'Or did his advice cause you to lose money?'

'No! Justin was sound. He knew his stuff.'

'So, did you take his computer from Byker so you could continue to benefit from his advice after you'd killed him?'

Peter Kirk dropped into a chair like a sack of coal. 'It's my laptop, and I didn't kill him.'

He looked at Ryan, then at Hannah, then back to Ryan. Something flickered in his eyes.

'Wait a minute. I know you, don't I?'

'Why? Have you been in trouble with us before?' Ryan countered.

'No, not like that. Wait a minute,' he clicked his fingers, 'Of course I know you! I couldn't possibly have been at the Wall on Sunday when Justin died. I couldn't because I was working.'

'Officially? You have the records to prove it?' Ryan asked.

Peter Kirk laughed. 'I have, but I don't need them. I don't need them because you know I was working. I picked you up. I picked you up on the corner of Chillingham Road. On Sunday night: the night you've just accused me of killing my friend. THAT, Detective, is where I know you from.'

Ryan's eyes flicked towards Hannah. He felt the heat rise to his cheeks, fought against it, and began to lose the battle. 'I think you're mistaken,' Ryan said.

'I think I'm not. I took you from Chillingham Road and dropped you off in Whickham.'

Ryan felt Hannah's eyes burn into the side of his neck, but not as much as the blush burnt his cheeks.

He'd lost more than a battle. He might just have lost everything.

CHAPTER EIGHT

'Ryan, what the fuck was all that about in there?'

Ryan stared straight through the windscreen as he clipped the seat belt into its holder. 'I don't know. I'm not sure what to make of him. He could be telling the truth, but we'll only know if Danskin authorises a warrant for us to impound the laptop. I'd say he was genuine, which isn't what I expected, although I think he does know more than he's letting on.'

'Stop waffling, Ry. That's not what I mean, and you know it. I meant what was that about you and Chillingham Road?'

Ryan shrugged and jutted out his lower lip.

'Ry?'

'Maybe he was trying to distract us. Throw us off the scent.' He knew his cheeks were flame red.

'Howay, man. I've done this long enough to know when someone's lying and, right now, I trust Peter Kirk with the truth more than I trust you.'

Ryan rubbed his forehead. 'Y'know what? I think we should get ourselves over to Warne's office. See if we can find owt in his desk. Talk to his associates in, what was it called, High Level Properties?'

'Stuff Justin Warne for a minute,' Hannah yelled. 'What aren't you telling me?'

Ryan exhaled so long he became light-headed. 'Okay.'

Hannah waited. And waited.

'Well?' she asked finally.

'I was in Heaton on Sunday. I did hire an Uber. It might have been Peter Kirk driving.'

She narrowed her eyes. 'What were you doing in Heaton, of all places?'

'It's got nowt to do with you, Hannah. Nothing at all. So, are we going to High Level or not?'

Hannah started the Renault, engaged gear, and pulled away with the velocity of a bullet from a rifle. 'I don't know you anymore, Ryan Jarrod. And, you know what? I'm not sure I want to, either.'

They wove out of Cloverfield and queued in traffic at the Holystone roundabout in icy silence.

'One last thing, Ryan. We remain professional at work. Out of work, we have nowt to do with each other.'

'Fine,' Ryan sulked.

The hollowness he'd felt in his stomach for weeks was filled by a lead weight.

**

At sixty-one metres tall, the eighteen story Cale Cross House, home to High Level Properties, was for many years the tallest commercial premises in Newcastle City Centre.

With supreme irony, it stood like a sentry on duty at the north western tip of the Tyne Bridge, not the older High Level Bridge, and afforded panoramic views of the River Tyne and all its crossings.

Hannah strode through the entrance into a plush-carpeted reception area with Ryan trailing behind like a chastened puppy. Hannah flashed her ID at a security officer who ushered them through a turnstile to a desk where a receptionist sat behind a polished redwood desk. The nameplate on its surface introduced her as *Lynne Casey*.

Lynne Casey was middle-aged and wore a pale blue blouse above navy blue slacks, the corporate colours of High Level Properties. She looked over her glasses as she asked, 'May I help you?'

'Yes,' Hannah said. 'We'd like to speak to someone who can tell us about an associate of yours, a Justin Warne.'

The woman rolled her eyes. 'What's he done now?'

'Could we speak to someone in authority?'

High Level

Lynne Casey pursed her lips. 'Mr Warne is no longer connected to our company.' She looked around her, conspiratorially. 'His contract was terminated.'

'Who do we need to speak to, Ms Casey?'

'You'd be best off talking to Beth Richards, but she's on holiday. I'll see if anyone can help you.'

She swung her back to them as she dialled an extension. After a few moments, she announced, 'Twelfth floor. Ursula Maddox will meet you. Lift's through the first set of doors.'

Ursula Maddox did indeed greet them outside the lift, and she shepherded Ryan and Hannah into a glass-walled office facing upriver, towards the High Level Bridge. While Hannah made the introductions, Ryan watched an Intercity 125 roll across the upper tier of the structure on its route out of Newcastle Central Station towards London King's Cross.

'I understand you have, or had, a Justin Warne work here?' Ryan heard Hannah ask.

'Had, Detective Sergeant. He was an independent consultant. Our relationship with him is at an end.'

'Why was that?'

Ursula Maddox looked between Hannah and Ryan. 'You should talk with Beth Richards. She worked closest with Mr Warne. I really don't have the authority to release confidential information. In our business, lawsuits are thrown around like confetti. I don't want Mr Warne suing me.'

'That's not possible,' Hannah said. 'Justin Warne is dead.'

Ursula's hand went to her mouth.

'We have reason to believe he was killed, and we're here to determine why.'

Ursula sipped water from a glass. 'His work for us was good, perhaps a bit tardy with his paperwork, but he brought in plenty of business. I'm sure you know Mr Warne worked for other companies, too, and Mrs Richards had suspicions he may have been using information obtained from us to further his other business interests.'

'That'll be Priory and Longsands, is it?' Ryan asked.

'Others, too, but as I far as I know it was mainly P&L, yes.'

'So, that's why Mr Warne was terminated?' Ryan used the word ambiguously, watching for a reaction.

He didn't get one.

'Partly, but mainly because we had a complaint. About his ethics.'

'Who filed the complaint?'

Ursula looked away. 'I can't tell you.'

Hannah smiled. 'Can't, or won't?'

Warne's erstwhile colleague grimaced. 'I might get into trouble for this,' she said, but she pulled out a file, nonetheless. Ursula licked her fingertips and leafed through it.

'It came from a Lola Di Marco. She owns an Agency called North Umbria Estates. That's three words; not two.'

She snapped the file closed.

'Now, I really must get on with my work. Good day, Detectives.'

**

Peter Kirk sat in his car attempting to gather thoughts which whirled through his brain like leaves in a tornado. The only thing he knew for certain was that he was in deep shit.

He'd seen too many TV shows where police fabricated, or planted, evidence so there was no way Kirk was letting them take his IT kit without a warrant. God knows what they'd do to it.

What he couldn't prevent them doing was leaving something incriminating in Justin's Raby Crescent residence. The only thing for it was to find the killer before the police did the dirty on him, poor, innocent Peter Kirk.

Which is how Kirk came to be parked at the rear of the iconic Wills Building off the Coast Road, east of Newcastle.

He bounded up the stairs and pressed the buzzer at the door to the building.

High Level

'Yeah?'

'It's Peter Kirk. Do you remember me?'

There followed a lengthy silence. 'No. Am I supposed to?'

'Not a good start,' Kirk thought. 'We were at LSE together. Well, briefly. I was friends with Justin Warne.'

'Oh-kay. And?'

'We met again a couple of years back. You were with Justin at Raby Crescent. I had a cup of tea and spilled it all over the new dress you had on.'

'Oh God, yes. I remember. It was from Monsoon. Cost a fortune.' After a pause, she said, 'What do you want?'

'I need to talk with you.'

'About?'

'Justin.'

'Look, I don't want to know. He's trouble.'

'Please. Five minutes, that's all.'

Peter heard a resigned sigh. The magnetic lock clicked, and he pulled open the heavy door.

Inside, the building was cavernous. A former tobacco factory, it had been transformed into top-end apartments and flats. The lobby looked like the atria of a swanky office building, tiled floors, palm trees, lots of glass, mirrors, and light.

Peter walked to the glass-fronted lift, thought of Justin Warne, and took the stairs instead. The second-floor corridor transformed the appearance of the building from office to that of a hotel.

The door to number seven opened at the same time as he raised his hand to knock.

A dark-haired woman in skinny jeans and baggy sweater pointed to a small screen inside the door. 'Saw you coming. You've five minutes. Stay at the door. I don't want a fine for breaking lockdown.'

Hayley Mack had been Justin Warne's girlfriend at the LSE. They'd hooked up during fresher's week, were together during the length of their time in London, after which she'd followed him to Newcastle. She stayed even after they'd split six months later. Hayley and Justin kept in touch, met occasionally, but never shared a bond and fell out more often than they made up.

Hayley walked from him and stood at the floor-to-ceiling window overlooking Wallsend golf course. Sun streamed in, tinting her black hair with the orange reds of henna.

Without turning to face him, she said, 'You've lost a minute already. If you want to talk, talk. If you don't want to talk, go.'

'Justin's dead,' he said, immediately wishing he hadn't been so brusque.

She brushed a few strands of hair from her eyes. 'Okay.'

'Is that it? *'Okay'*? He was your boyfriend. Don't you care?'

'*Was* my boyfriend. Past tense. It was years ago.'

'But you had feelings for him.'

'Feelings change.'

'Aren't you even a little sad?

'Why should I be? Our lives followed different paths. That's the way he wanted it.'

'That's cold, Hayley. He still talked about you, now and again. That's how I know where you live.'

She sniffed a laugh. 'He talked about me, yeah? Big deal. I talk about Boris Johnson. Doesn't mean I have feelings for him.'

'Look,' Peter said, 'I get that, but I really need your help. I think the police suspect I had something to do with it. I need you to tell me everything you know about him. Did he have enemies? I need something that will get the cops off my back.'

'I can't help you, Peter. Justin harped on at me about the way I lived my life, how I handled my money, how I SPENT my money. God, we weren't together - but he wanted to control me. When it became obvious I wasn't prepared to be controlled by him or anyone else, he said I'd regret not being

High Level

friends with him. I laughed, told him we hadn't been friends for years, and I cut him out of my life. That was two years ago. I haven't been in touch since.'

She held Peter's eyes with hers. 'I couldn't tell you anything about him even if I wanted to. Your five minutes are up. Close the door yourself.'

**

Lola Di Marco's North Umbria Estates operated from a property just off a roundabout in Tynemouth which separated Beach Road from Grand Parade. As Hannah's Renault pulled into the entrance, Ryan broke the silence hanging heavy between them.

'Whoa. Did you see that? Do you reckon it's a coincidence?'

'It might have escaped your attention, but I happen to be driving. I was watching the road. Did I see what?'

'The sign on the entrance. Seems like North Umbria aren't the only ones to have a base here. The sign said they share the building with none other than Priory and Longsands Portfolio Group, would you believe?'

'Does seem to stretch coincidence a bit far,' Hannah conceded. 'They are separate companies, aren't they?'

Ryan looked up at the white-walled building. 'Let's find out, shall we?'

The building was a converted hotel, and the renovators had spared no expense updating it. North Umbria catered for the upper end of the market, and the office reflected it.

Glass walls separated the lobby from an oval, open-plan office which wrapped itself around the reception area. People could be seen talking with headsets on, others sat hunched over their IT, still more stood by metric boards discussing performance figures.

'Busy,' Ryan said. 'Didn't think there'd be much movement in the property market these days.'

'Aye, I thought more would be working from home, I have to say.'

The receptionist was a thin young woman with a Black Cat tattooed on her wrist.

'Mackem,' Ryan whispered.

'Or she might like cats. Or she might be a witch. Either way, we're not here to see her, are we?'

The young woman smiled broadly as they approached. 'How may I help you?' she said from behind a perspex hygiene screen.

'We'd like to see Lola Di Marco.'

'And you are?'

'Detectives from City and County Police.'

The receptionist raised her eyebrows and tapped a couple of buttons on her phone. She whispered into it, then said, 'Ms Di Marco will be with you in a moment' as she put down the phone.

Ms Di Marco was as good as her word.

She was a well-proportioned woman dressed in a black pencil skirt and bright orange silk blouse. 'I'm Lola Di Marco,' she said, looking from Ryan to Hannah before settling her gaze on an appraisal of Ryan's shoes.

The look on her face told them she was neither intimidated nor impressed by Ryan and Hannah. Or Ryan's shoes.

'Mrs Di Marco…' Ryan began.

'It's Ms,' Lola interrupted.

Ryan glanced at Hannah who shrugged and hid a smile at his uncomfortableness.

'Ms Di Marco, we're here about your complaint against Justin Warne.'

Lola looked Ryan up and down once more. 'Why does it take two detectives to investigate an ethics complaint?'

'We're just trying to understand why you filed the complaint and…'

'She sent you to intimidate me, didn't she?'

Ryan looked nonplussed. 'What?'

'You can tell her I'm not dropping my complaint. In fact, tell her I'll file one against her as well.'

'No, ma'am, I think you've misunder…'

'I want my solicitor present if you insist on interrogating me further, or I'll report you for harassment.'

'What?' Ryan spluttered again.

'When my solicitor gets here, we'll reconvene. Until then, I'm not talking to you. You can't intimidate me.'

Lola spun around, grabbed a glass door almost invisible against the wall, and stalked into her office. The door slammed shut with a thud which caused the window to shimmer like a lake.

This time, it was Ryan's turn to ask Hannah, 'What the fuck was all that about?'

CHAPTER NINE

THURSDAY

At the appointed hour of ten a.m, Hannah parked her car in a bay alongside a cherry red Porsche at the rear of Lola Di Marco's company HQ.

'I'd recognise that car anywhere,' Lyall Parker said. 'It's William Vermont's. At least we know Mrs Di Marco cannae refuse to talk to us now her brief's here.'

'For God's sake divvent call her Mrs. She'll have your nuts for breakfast,' Ryan warned. 'It's Ms Di Marco.'

The low-level building was barely discernible even at close quarters, so thick was the fret drifting in on the North Sea tide. Lyall wiped at the rear window for a better view before realising the fog was outside, not inside.

'Let's get this show on the road. From what you told me o' this Di Marco woman, I think it's best I lead on it. While we're here, we'll kill two birds with one stone and have a wee chat with Priory and Longsands, too.'

The entrance to Priory and Longsands lay at the far end of the building, closest to Tynemouth Aquarium, though the dense cloud made it invisible.

Lyall looked in its general direction as he continued. 'Ma hunch is, we'll get more from Di Marco but in case we need the extra clout a DS carries, Hannah – you take P&L. Ryan, you're with me.'

As Hannah disappeared into the mist, Lyall turned to Ryan. 'Don't think I hadnae noticed the atmosphere in the car. It was chillier than it is out here. You need to try harder, you two.'

'It's not me, man; it's...'

The Acting DCI held up a palm. 'I dinnae want to hear it. I'm just saying I'm watching you. We all are – Danskin, included.'

Ryan huffed and puffed as if he were about to blow the house down, but he kept his counsel and followed Lyall into North Umbria Estates.

The receptionist with the cat tattoo escorted them into a conference room obscured by closed blinds. Inside, Lola Di Marco and William Vermont, dressed in a suit which Ryan guessed cost more than his own monthly salary, sat at the far end of a long rectangular table more befitting an Elizabethan banqueting hall.

Ryan and Lyall took the only other seats in the room, at the other end of the table. They removed their face coverings and Lyall introduced himself as Detective Chief Inspector, rather than 'Acting.' He knew it wouldn't fool Vermont but hoped it might gain traction with Di Marco.

It didn't.

'I'm an extremely busy woman. Let's leave the formalities and get on with it.'

'Suits us all fine, then,' Lyall smiled, watching the woman at the far end of the table. Her tanned skin, raven hair, and eyes so dark they were almost black, betrayed her Adriatic heritage as much as her name.

'We're here about Justin Warne.'

'Did she send you?'

Lyall frowned. 'Who?'

She gave a dismissive wave. 'What about Justin Warne?'

'He's dead.'

She blinked several times.

'We have reason to think he was murdered.'

She exchanged glances with William Vermont. 'And you think I had something to do with it?'

Lyall Parker studied her. 'Why would we think that?'

'Because you know I filed a complaint against him.'

'Aye, you did, Ms Di Marco. I understand he was a friend. So, why file a complaint against him?'

'He used to be a friend. Friends and business aren't a compatible marriage, Detective Chief Inspector.'

Lyall cracked his knuckles. 'We're trying to find out why Mr Warne died. Tell us what caused you to make a complaint.'

Lola Di Marco didn't speak. William Vermont slowly nodded, but still Lola sat quietly. Finally, she relented.

'He acted as a broker between a client and me. Just as I thought the deal was all sealed and delivered, the client refused to sign and said he wanted to cancel. He refused to give an explanation; just point blank insisted he didn't wish to proceed.'

'And you believe Mr Warne had something to do with your client's decision to pull out?'

'I don't *think* that. I KNOW he did.'

'Go on.'

'I heard rumours that the seller of the property had agreed a deal with somebody else. It all moved so swiftly it had to be negotiated while I had it listed. That's underhand, Detective Chief Inspector. In layman's terms, it's corporate gazumping and caused my client to withdraw his offer.'

Lola's lips curled, and she tapped the conference room table as she battled against her emotions. Once she regained her composure, she inhaled through closed lips. 'The sneaky bastard Warne double-crossed me and stole my commission. He brokered the transaction with a third party.'

'It was a big deal?'

'Oh boy, yeah. It was big, right enough.' She rocked in her chair. 'The biggest.'

'Care to share?'

Lola Di Marco's knuckles drummed against the tabletop. 'Moot Hall.'

'It's listed, isn't it? Got a preservation order on it. What would he want with that?'

'The exterior has the preservation order on it. And the inner grand staircase. The rest of it doesn't. Not any longer.'

'How come?'

She stared the length of the table. 'Because, shall we say, I facilitated it.'

'Bribed, you mean?'

Vermont spoke up. 'Acting Detective Chief Inspector. My client is helping your enquiry here. I suggest you listen to her without interference, or I shall instruct Ms Di Marco to withdraw her co-operation.'

Lyall and Ryan remained silent. Eventually, Lola spoke again.

'The important thing is, Moot Hall now has outline planning permission for conversion to apartments. With its location and its history, they will be amongst the most expensive apartments in the city. Gentlemen, it cost me a fortune – and not a small one, either – to have the plans passed. And Justin Warne lost me the deal.'

She raised her eyes to meet Lyall Parker's. 'THAT's why I lodged my complaint. But that's all I did. Am I sorry he's dead? Not at all. No-one deserved it more. Did I kill him? No, I didn't.'

Lyall considered her words. 'If the deal was that big, that costly, how could a wee small player like Warne afford it?'

Lola Di Marco laughed, though it came out as a bark. 'You don't understand this business at all, do you? As I said, Warne was just a frontman. A go-between if you will. Warne didn't actually buy the property, he facilitated it. He gets a fee – a very generous one, I have no doubt – with not a penny in outlay or risk.'

'Who bought it?'

'Doesn't take a genius to work it out. That's why I thought she'd sent you to bully me into dropping my complaint.'

Lyall leaned forward. 'Who's *she*?'

'Beth Richards, of course. I'm betting High Level Properties are the buyer.'

**

On the drive back to Forth Street, they discussed what they had, or hadn't, discovered.

'The case is disappearing up its own backside,' Ryan began. 'Justin Warne was kicked out of High Level Properties because of a complaint raised by Lola Di Marco. Di Marco accuses him of working with High Level to sabotage a deal, yet Ursula Maddox told Hannah and me that they thought he was using inside information to sell THEM down the river. They can't both be right.'

Lyall thought for a moment. 'Unless there's a third party he's using against both of them. Och, Hannah, what did you get from Priory and Longsands? It would be great if you told us Warne had stitched them both up in favour of P & L.'

Hannah stayed silent as she observed traffic at the Swan House roundabout and swung left towards Melbourne Street and down to the Quayside.

'Nah. Sorry. Bit of a red herring, that one. Seems Warne did do some work for them, but it was more linked to their business investment portfolio, not property. He wasn't a big player with Priory and Longsands.'

'Where does that leave us?' Lyall muttered.

'I think it leaves us with Ravi Sangar and Justin Warne's IT,' Ryan said as the Renault passed along The Close beneath the shadow of Moot Hall and the High Level bridge.

'Y'knaa what it is… just when you think you've got an easy case, it all goes to buggery.'

**

It wasn't exactly buggery, but thirty quid and a blow job was enough to send Rats whistling his way along the length of the eighth floor corridor of the Byker Wall.

High Level

'*Sometimes,*' he thought, '*It's better when they don't have the money.*' Unless, of course, it was that old hag, Durrant, on the second floor.

'How, Scrapper,' he shouted into his phone, 'Get yersel up to the eighth floor. The tart with the limp's ready for you.'

He laughed as his protégé said something. 'Aye, I'm done with her. Mind, yer might want her to brush her teeth first, like.'

He held open the door to the stairwell. 'I'm on me way up to the ninth now. I'll see you doonstairs soon. I expect you to have a fair whack for us, mind. Divvent let us doon.'

Rats took the stairs two at a time and emerged into a dank corridor. Three apartments along, he kicked against a door the colour of wet clay.

'Come oot, come oot, wherever you are.'

A woman in her late thirties answered.

'I've come for me money, love. It'd be pretty shit if somebody broke this nice door of yours. I'll make sure they don't. Fifty quid should see to it, as usual.'

Ailsa Black's hand trembled as she unfurled her fingers to reveal a ten- pound note. She sniffed twice.

'A tenner? Are you takin' the piss?'

Rats brought a Stanley knife from his pocket. Dragged it across the door's surface.

'Ah, look what it's done, man. Sorry aboot that. I'm sure nowt else will happen if you go and get the rest. There's a good 'un.'

Ailsa sniffed again, her eyes glassy and vacant. 'I've got nee more.'

'Well, I'm sorry to hear that, missus.'

Rats lay the Stanley blade against the woman's cheek. Moved his hand a fraction. A crimson teardrop of blood seeped from the incision.

Rats brushed past her into the apartment. The woman snorted noisily. One nostril flared wide.

Rats studied her.

'I've got an idea,' he said. 'Why don't you just give us whatever it is your using? On account, like?'

Ailsa glanced behind her towards the bathroom.

'In there, is it? Champion.'

'Divvent take it all. Please. Leave me some. I need it.' She hugged herself with skeletal arms.

'Nah. I'm doing you a favour, man. This fucking stuff's nee good for you. You'll thank us for it one day.'

He slipped the polythene bag inside his jacket. 'See you next week. Same time, same place.'

He squeezed the woman's atrophied breast as he left.

Until next week.

**

Half an hour later, he was counting their spoils beneath a wizened bush and sniffing Ailsa Black's coke through a twenty.

'It's bloody great without that poncey Warne bloke on the lookout,' he laughed. 'Three hundred and fifty quid, just like that.' He snapped his fingers. 'Here's fifty for you, Scrapper.'

'Is that aal?'

Rats flicked out a leg as they sat. It caught Scrapper in the throat.

'Fuck off you scrawny twat. Be thankful for it. You got yer leg ower an' aal, divvent forget.'

'Not this time. She wasn't having it.'

'What? Seriously? Bloody hell. I've never known her to be fussy before.'

Scrapper struggled to his feet and rubbed his throat. 'To be honest, I didn't even try.'

'What the fuck? Are you on the turn, or summat?'

The younger boy moved a safe distance from Rats before saying, 'It's aal wrong, this. I mean, with this Warne bloke dead, the coppers are going to be back. They'll find oot what we're doing.'

High Level

'Ah, man. Divvent tell us your scared of that lot? Listen, man, nee bugger on the estate's going to say owt. They're even more scared of the cops than they are of us.'

Scrapper shook his head. 'Maybe. But what if the cops do find out? We're screwed. I'm not gannin to nee detention centre for neebody.'

Rats stared at his friend. 'Well, if that's the way you feel.'

Scrapper nodded. 'Aye, it is. You're on your own, mate. Sorry, like, but I cannot risk it.'

To his surprise, Rats just shrugged. 'Suit yersel. Nee hard feelings, eh?'

He held his hand out for Scrapper to shake. When the younger lad reached for it, Rats whipped his other hand around and slashed out with the Stanley knife.

Scrapper's eyes widened as he attempted to close the gaping wound on his right wrist with his left hand.

'Fuck off, Scrapper. Hope you bleed to death, you miserable twat.'

CHAPTER TEN

Ravi Sangar led the City and County Police computer forensic team from its base in a small tech room adjacent to the third-floor bullpen.

Ravi had stripped and reassembled Justin Warne's IT kit after first scanning evidentiary copies of the hard drives in case someone – probably Todd Robson – cocked-up big-style.

Ravi unlocked all four computers and replaced their passwords with simple alternatives for Lyall Parker's team to access. He'd networked the kit and placed it on desks evenly distributed within the room; not quite two metres apart but respectably distant.

Lyall himself sat in front of one piece of kit, Ryan another, and Todd Robson the third. Ravi accessed the PC he'd allocated as the master.

'Right, lads,' he said, 'You're good to go.'

Lyall told them they had an hour to ferret around and find what they could before they'd get together to discuss.

Ryan typed in the password he'd been given – TOON2 – and was greeted with a wallpaper image of a young woman in shorts and bikini top sitting aboard a yacht. She had one arm wrapped around the back of her head holding her hair while the other waved at the camera. Her head was tilted at an angle as if she were about to toss it back and laugh.

The fact other folk could be seen milling around on shore, out of focus, told Ryan it was neither a stock image nor a professional shot. The photograph, he concluded, was personal to Justin Warne. It meant something to him.

Ryan jotted down a couple of questions in a notebook. *'Who is she?'* and *'Where is this?'*

High Level

They spent the next hour in quiet solitude. Lyall Parker focussed on Warne's browser history, social media and blogs, Ryan on the man's contacts and e-mails, while Todd broke the silence with the occasional 'Buggeration' and 'Ah shit: where's that gone?' as he lost himself in the maze of files, folders, and datasheets on the piece of kit in front of him.

An hour later, Nigel Trebilcock marched in carrying a tray laden with coffee cups and pre-packed sandwiches.

'Just the horse's knob,' Todd said as he grabbed a BLT. 'Hungry work this, like.'

'Let's start with you, Todd. What did you find for us?' Lyall Parker asked.

Todd wiped a sliver of lettuce from his lips and spoke through a mouthful of food. 'Nowt jumped out and hit us. It was all bollocks to me. Spreadsheets, mostly. They showed some of his transactions but I suspect not all of them. In fact, I know it's not all of 'em. There's no mention of Moot Hall, for one. A lot of the other stuff seemed to be draft documents for his Money Matters Most blog thing.'

'I've got his finished blogs on here,' Lyall reminded them. 'We'll cross-match 'em to see if they marry up to his drafts.'

'What will that tell us?' Ryan enquired.

Lyall shrugged. 'Och, who knows? Perhaps that someone might have tampered with them. Edited them. It might prove useful once we know what we're looking for, but probably not before.'

He took a bite of sandwich. Cheese savoury filling dribbled onto the keyboard. 'Ry? Anything from you?'

'The most interesting thing for me was the bloke's screen wallpaper. We might learn more about him if we can trace the lass on it. Mind, she might be a holiday romance cos there weren't any other pics of her, but I feel in my gut they were close. Something about the look in her eyes. It might help if we know where it's taken, an' aal.'

Ravi called up the image on all their screens. 'Is she one of his Facebook friends? Instagram?'

Lyall shook his head. 'Och, she's a bonny lass. I'd have recognised her if she'd been amongst them.'

Ryan and Todd quickly scrolled through Warne's friends and agreed none resembled the girl on the picture. Ravi, meanwhile, copied and pasted the image into Google Search.

'I can help you with your last question, Ryan,' Ravi said. 'The picture was taken on Lake Windermere.'

'How you work that one out?'

'Simple. I reverse Googled it.'

'Is that even a thing?'

Ravi laughed. 'Of course. Doesn't always work but, look – it's picked up the background scenery and confirmed it.' He shared his screen with the others.

'Wheeyabugger. It's never been that sunny whenever I've been there.'

'Do we know when it was taken?' Lyall asked.

'No. The metadata tags have been erased. I don't think it'll be anytime in the last twelve months, though. It's too busy. A lot of folk have broke lockdown if it is.'

Lyall sipped his coffee and pulled a sour face at its coldness. 'We've no' got much to show for an hour's work.'

'True,' Ravi said, 'But I've been at it longer than you lot and I noticed a couple of things. Firstly, all the kit is surprisingly clean. And I don't mean physically clean. All the cookies have been removed, there's no errant files, no junk at all, really. Even his e-mails aren't stuffed with spam ads for Viagra or Russian brides.'

'You been hacking my e-mails again, Ravi?' Todd questioned.

They snickered.

'Anyway,' Ravi continued, 'The whole kit 'n' kaboodle is squeaky clean. Like it had just been tidied up.'

'After he'd been killed? Someone's wiped trace evidence, you mean?'

'It's possible, although Warne could have done it himself if there was anything in his files that tied him into any dodgy deals.'

Lyall pulled a face realising it didn't prove anything, one-way-or-another. 'You said there were two things.'

'Aye. It might be summat or nowt but see what you make of this.'

Ravi Sangar called up one of Warne's blog posts and, again, shared his screen with the others. At the foot of the article, readers posted their comments, whilst others left a 'thumbs up' like or 'thumbs down' disagree.

The screen settled at a specific comment from a subscriber with the username *'Beer.'*

It said, *'Warne: you are high-level filth.'*

Thirty-six people had rewarded the comment with a thumbs up.

**

'Forensics have got back to us with the fingerprints from Justin Warne's apartment,' Hannah said as Ryan passed her on the way to his desk.

'About bloody time. Anything to learn from them?'

She coiled her hair around a finger. 'Five sets altogether. Warne's, predominantly, and two we've no record of.'

'The other two?'

'Ah, the other two. Interesting. One set belongs to Beth Richards.'

'From High Level Properties?'

'The very same.'

Ryan thought for a moment. 'That means she's got a record with us, yeah? What for?'

Hannah sighed. 'Don't get your hopes up. It's nowt, really. Beth Richards was one of five served with a penalty notice for Disorder after a minor skirmish outside the Tup Tup Palace nightclub eighteen months ago. Another couple of months and her prints would have been wiped so it's a lucky break but I'm not sure of its significance to us. She's no other record.'

'Aye, we know they worked together so it's not too much of a shock she's been to his place but, given what Lola Di Marco said, we definitely need a chat when Richards gets back from holiday.'

'I agree.'

'The other prints?'

Hannah looked at her screen. 'A neighbour. Sally Sykes. She's previous for a string of drunk and disorderlies and a couple of minor drug offences.'

Ryan's brow furrowed. 'Was she spoken to as part of the door-to-doors?'

'Aye. She denied seeing or hearing anything related to Warne's death. She also didn't mention we'd find her prints all over Warne's place.'

'Sounds like Maz Crawford all over again. Still, I think I should pay her a visit.'

**

This was the riskiest thing he'd ever done.

Peter Kirk stood in shadow cast by the Byker Wall's scaffolding and pondered his next move while nerves gurgled in his stomach like a bilious hippopotamus.

If the police saw him, it'd add to their suspicions. On the other hand, if there was anything in the apartment to indicate who Justin's killer was, he'd prove his own innocence.

Mind made up, he took a deep breath and marched onto Raby Crescent. The police tape still lay across the front door, but the police guard had gone; the door locked.

Peter guessed this meant that the police had taken everything they needed. If so, he'd find nothing.

Still, what harm could it do?

He stole around the back of the apartment. The small garden was littered with junk spilling from a ripped binbag. An old car battery had been thrown over Warne's fence, dog mess covered the tiny square of lawn, and a battered rucksack lay discarded atop a rockery. Peter shifted the backpack with his foot, lifted a heavy stone, and threw it against the window.

He ducked behind a wall and waited.

No-one came to investigate. Wanton vandalism was commonplace around the estate. Nobody batted an eye.

Peter clambered through the broken window into his old friend's home.

He stood for a moment weighing up the implications of what he had done. 'You've already broken and entered,' he whispered encouragement to himself, 'It doesn't matter what more you do now.'

He walked to the lounge. Apart from the bookcase, the place was barren. The police had taken all Justin's iPads, laptops, and desktop computers. He moved to the bookcase. Took out a book he recognised, T. Dan Smith's biography. He smiled at its familiarity.

'What are you doing here?'

Peter jumped, his heart thundering against his chest wall. He turned to face the voice.

'Jesus Christ,' he gasped, 'You! How did you get in?'

'I think that's what you should be telling me.'

'I came to see if I could find who did it. I think the cops might try to frame me.'

Sally Sykes twirled a key between her fingers as she leaned against the doorjamb. She ran a hand through her dyed hair. 'Why would they do that?'

The question hadn't occurred to him. 'They do it all the time on TV.'

She tisked. 'Well, did you find who did it, Peter Kirk?' Her voice teased him.

'No. The cops took everything he had, by the look of it.'

'What did you expect?'

He gave a rueful smile. 'That the cops would take most of his stuff.'

'So, what you really mean is, you came to see me.'

'What?'

'You heard me. You want to see me. No, scrub that: you WANT me, full-stop.'

'I've got to go,' he said.

'I'll tell the cops you've been here.'

'You won't.'

'I might, if you don't come next door with me.'

He watched her stand against the doorframe like a pouty child.

'You won't,' he repeated and rushed past her, breaking the police tape like a hundred-metre sprinter over the finish line.

Sally Sykes shook her head.

'What's a girl got to do to get a decent fella round here?' she said to herself.

**

A mud-splattered low-loader, its rear empty apart from brown pools of sludge, was parked next to Peter Kirk's car when he reached the scaffolding. *WOOD BUILDING CONTRACTORS*, Peter deciphered the livery on the cab door said beneath the grime. A logo depicting the pyramids of Giza sat next to the lettering. Peter assumed the truck belonged to the company carrying out the renovation work.

He nodded an acknowledgement to a bloke leaning against the truck and unlocked his own car with the fob button.

The other guy levered himself off the truck and stood in front of Peter's car.

'Scuse me,' Kirk said, 'This is my car.'

'And that wasn't your apartment,' the man said. He was taller than Peter had first thought. Broader, too, with a labourer's muscles pulling his shirt sleeves taut.

'What are you talking about?'

High Level

The man pointed towards Raby Crescent. 'I saw you break the window. You broke into the house. What did you take?'

'Nothing. I swear.' The man leant towards him. Peter recognised a veiled threat when he saw one. 'My friend lived there,' he explained.

'Lived, you say. Not lives. Which means you don't have any right being there. So, I ask again: what did you take?'

'Nothing. I just want to know what happened to him. You can search me if you want.' Peter held his arms out wide.

'How about I knock your lights out instead, clever-dick?'

Peter swallowed. 'Okay. Sorry. I didn't take anything. There was nowt to take even if I'd wanted to. Police cleaned it out.'

The man from Wood's stared at him. 'What's your name?'

'John,' Peter lied.

'Okay, John. I believe you.'

Peter expelled air.

'Or I'd like to. But, you see, the Uber sticker in your windscreen says your name's Peter Kirk. So, if you're lying about that, what else might you be lying about?'

Peter inspected the kerb in front of his feet. He came clean about his name and, for good measure, threw in his address as well.

'Good. You're a fast learner. I like that. Now, piss off Peter Kirk. And remember, I know your car registration, your name, and your address.'

Peter climbed into the car. From its safety, he said 'You have the advantage over me.' He attempted a smile which ended up more like a gurn minus the horse collar. 'You know I'm Peter Kirk – I didn't catch your name.'

'Mine? Oh, don't go worrying yourself about me. I'm a nobody, me. Unless you decide to do more snooping, of course. Then, you might just find I'm the death of you.'

CHAPTER ELEVEN

In the station and around others, he just about held his shit together. Away from the focussed environment of Forth Street and his colleagues, demons emerged from the shadows of Ryan Jarrod's thoughts.

Ryan sat in the driving seat of his Fiat, hands locked behind his head. He allowed his eyelids to slide shut. He inhaled through his nose to the count of three, held it for three seconds, and exhaled slowly through his mouth.

Tomorrow, he had to let Danskin know whether he wanted to sit the sergeant's exam. He knew the answer to that one.

The more pressing question was, what would he do about Hannah Graves afterwards? Was it too late to rekindle the flames of their relationship? Is that what she wanted? More to the point, did HE want it?

Ryan repeated the breathing exercise, but still his mind raced.

Memories of the day Hannah had been taken hostage, and the pain he'd felt believing he'd lost her to a people-trafficking gangmaster, overcame him. He remembered thinking his world had collapsed. The feeling of utter emptiness he'd experienced was worse, even, than the death of his mother and the cognitive decline of his grandmother.

When he remembered the heart-swelling joy he'd felt when he discovered her alive, he knew he'd answered his own question. Yes, he wanted Hannah Graves.

Until a horned, scaly creature snuck out from his dorsal cortex and whispered its negative thoughts.

High Level

It asked him to remember the day Hannah had told him she'd lost their baby; the baby she hadn't thought to mention she was carrying.

The creature didn't stop there. It conjured up images of him kneeling in front of Hannah, blood running down his arm, ignoring the agony of the bullet wound, to propose to the one he loved.

Only for her to turn down the proposal. Coldly. Clinically.

The demon asked him to gauge his reaction to her trauma against hers to his. Compare and contrast.

'Ah, fuck, man!'

He rubbed his face with both hands before slamming the door of the Fiat shut as he climbed out.

**

Music played softly inside the house, so soft he heard the footsteps pad towards the door.

'Shit,' a woman's voice said from the other side. 'Just a minute. Door's locked. I need to find me keys.'

With no sign of the woman's return, Ryan knocked again. 'I'm DC Ryan Jarrod of City and County police. I need to talk with you.'

'Bollocks,' he heard the voice say. This time the inflection was anxious, not frustration. 'Hang on. I'm on my way.'

The music stopped as the footsteps returned. A moment later Ryan heard the rattle of keys and watched as the door edged open.

'Yeah?' the woman said.

Ryan lowered his face covering and showed her his ID. 'May I come inside?'

The door swung wide. Sally Sykes's fair, indigo-streaked hair was tied in a straggly bun. She twisted her mouth and blew a loose strand from her eyes. She wore jeans, ripped with age rather than design, and a cut-off T-Shirt imprinted with the Bridge Over Troubled Water album cover.

Despite his dark mood, Ryan tried to his best to present an affable image. 'Aren't you a bit young for Simon and Garfunkel?' he smiled.

'Aren't you a bit young for a Detective?'

Ryan coughed. 'Sally Sykes?'

'Aye.'

'Can I come in and talk?'

'I'd rather you didn't.'

Ryan grabbed her by the elbow. 'Fine. We'll do this at Forth Street.'

'Okay, okay. We can talk inside. Don't lose your cum over it; it's just a bit of a state in here, that's all. Oh, and the neighbours aren't too fond of your kind.'

Sally Sykes's apartment smelled like the old S&N Brewery on Pitt Street. An empty gin bottle and half a dozen lager cans littered the floor.

'Can we open a window, Miss Sykes? I could get drunk on the air in here.'

'Maybe it'll make you nicer,' she said as she tucked her legs beneath her. 'Look, can we get this over with? What's this about?'

'It's about your neighbour, Justin Warne.'

She curled her mouth. 'Again? I already told you lot that I didn't see or hear owt.'

'The houses are pretty close together on this estate. I imagine you'd hear a fight.'

'People argue all the time around here. There's not much else for them to do. I wouldn't take much notice even if I did hear a row.'

'I didn't say a row. I said a fight.'

Sally lit a cigarette, inhaled, and blew a perfect smoke circle in Ryan's direction. 'I heard nowt.'

Ryan tried a different approach. 'How well did you know Justin?'

She shrugged. 'We were friends, I suppose.'

'Good friends?'

Sally smirked. 'Why don't you come out and say it? *Did we fuck?* is what you're asking, isn't it? Well, yes. We did fuck, now and again.'

'And did this fucking take place here or in Mr Warne's house?'

Sally used a hand to unfold a leg from beneath her. 'I like it when you talk dirty,' she smiled. 'Both. Here and there.'

Her lips formed an 'O' as she blew more smoke towards Ryan. As the ring drifted out, her lips remained open.

Ryan looked away. 'Miss Sykes, did you and Mr Warne ever fall out?'

'No, we weren't that close.'

Ryan's eyebrows arched. 'You were never jealous?'

Sally tossed her head back and laughed. 'No.'

'What? Even when he had another girlfriend?'

'You've got this wrong, kidda. We were never serious. We fucked, that's all. Don't tell me you don't fuck, Detective.' She spoke the profanity slowly, her tongue clicking against the roof of her mouth to emphasise the 'k'.

Ryan ignored her. 'Did Mr Warne have a serious girlfriend?'

'Nah. There was one lass popped in now and again, but she hasn't been for ages.'

'Do you know why they stopped being friendly? Do you have a name?' he placed his pen against his notebook.

'I remember her name because of what she did. It kind of sticks in the memory, even for these parts.'

'The name, please.'

'Hayley Mack.'

She smiled for the first time. More a childish smirk than a smile.

'I remember her because she used dog turd to write *'Die, you shit'* across his window.'

**

Peter Kirk's nerves still jangled from the run in with the man driving the Wood Building Contractors truck. The whole incident had been so surreal for a moment he thought he'd imagined it.

What connection would a guy working on the Byker Wall refurbishment scheme have with Justin Warne? They weren't working on the part of the wall Justin owned. It didn't make any sense – unless he had something to do with Justin's death. Again: why would he?

Peter hadn't dared return home in case he found the man parked outside his house, waiting for him. Instead, he'd logged in with Uber and drove around town hoping the App would ping him a fare.

It was a fare which never came.

Eventually, after an hour of aimless miles, he pulled into a cobbled courtyard and tucked into an early-evening Subway meal.

In front of him, the brick façade of the Bridge Hotel stood lonely and forlorn; doors locked, beer taps dry. Through the rear-view mirror, the rugged stone walls of the Castle Keep – the Norman fortress from which the city took its name – loomed menacingly. This was no Baronial hall. The Keep was a grim symbol of royal power; a place where armies once gathered, and criminals were imprisoned.

And executed.

Peter thought of Justin and the man in the van. He shuddered violently. Felt a cold sweat dampen his back and forehead. The confines of the car closed in on him. Gastric matter burnt his throat. He needed air.

Peter Kirk flung open the door and deposited his liquidised tea onto the cobbles of Castle Garth.

Groggily, he set foot on the uneven surface and rested a hand on the car roof to steady himself. After a few moments, he moved off towards the High Level Bridge where he knew he'd feel a revitalizing breeze from its heights.

High Level

He folded his arms over the barrier of the rusting bridge and gulped in air. Slowly, his breathing settled. He raised his head and took in the quintessential views over Newcastle and Gateshead.

Far below, pedestrians on the Quayside marched back and forth like soldier ants, vehicles rattled over the Swing Bridge - the smallest of the seven bridges - and, tucked behind the Bridge Hotel, the Doric pillars of Moot Hall enticed the inquisitive away from the city walls.

Feeling himself relax, Peter retraced his steps to the parking bays lining Castle Garth.

Where he froze to the spot.

Next to his car stood a familiar low-loader coated in familiar muck and an all-too-familiar driver. The man spotted him.

'Hey, Kirk!'

Peter turned and raced back to the bridge. He thundered along its narrow footpath. Its tight-knit, cathedral-like metal arches hemmed him in. He risked a glance back. As he did so, his shoulder crunched into a support beam, winding him.

But it had been worth it. He'd discovered he wasn't being followed. Peter slowed to a walk. Glanced over his shoulder a few times. Eventually, he remembered to breathe.

The bridge was deathly quiet. The railway line on the upper tier remained clear, there were no other pedestrians on his level, and the roadway alongside the footpath was deserted. Restricted to one-way traffic and open to bus and taxi only, it bore no comparison to the crowded Tyne and Redheugh bridges either side of it.

Peter Kirk walked the bridge in isolation, through alternate patches of shade and sun which illuminated him like a moth by flickering candlelight. He scurried past the areas of darkness and looked back along the bridge during the sunlit sections. No-one pursued him.

When he reached the Gateshead side of the bridge, he veered left and perched himself on a wall outside a second-hand car dealership built into a railway arch. His seat bordered a busy crossroads where traffic from the Tyne Bridge bisected the apex of the High Level. Any assault on him would have countless witnesses. Peter felt safe, in relative terms, for now - but he needed his car. And his car lay at the other end of the bridge. Next to the man from Wood's.

The sun dropped like a stone. Soon, darkness would settle over the city. Peter pictured the rat run of the High Level footpath. Imagined the menace lurking in its shadows. It was now or never.

A couple pushing a child in a buggy walked by. They turned right towards the bridge. Peter fell into step behind them. He kept far enough away so as not to creep them out – but close enough to prevent the man from the building contractor's launching an assault.

Peter's heart raced. Adrenalin coursed through his veins. Tension clamped his jaws tight, made his hearing more acute, and his breathing shallow.

The couple were almost at the end of the bridge now. A pink blanket slipped from the buggy. The man stopped pushing, the woman fussed and tended to the child, wrapping the blanket around the infant.

If Peter stopped behind them, he'd arouse their suspicions. He had no wish to frighten them. He had to keep going. He held his breath as he passed them, slowing slightly so he remained in their sight.

He took comfort in the weight of traffic heading towards him before the vehicles swung sharply right, following the one-way system up towards the Central Station. Their presence afforded ample cover.

To his right lay only the gloom of Castle Garth and the empty shell of The Bridge Hotel. This is where the attack would come. He steeled himself for it. Prepared a scream in his throat.

High Level

Peter stared into the darkness as he left the confines of the bridge. There, alone and abandoned, stood his car. No truck. No muscle-bound labourer. Only Peter Kirk's car.

Peter laughed. A loud, insane giggle of relief. He hurried towards his vehicle, unlocked the door as he approached - and then he saw it: the note tucked beneath a wiper blade.

With trembling fingers, Peter unfolded the paper. The words, scribbled in pencil, read:

'Why waste energy following you? I know where you live. I'll be seeing you, Peter Kirk. Soon.'

CHAPTER TWELVE

FRIDAY

'So, I assume I can put you down for the sergeant's exam, Jarrod? Looking forward to it, I bet.'

Ryan surprised himself with a sigh. 'Yes, sir.'

Stephen Danskin set down his pen. 'Then I think you should tell your face, son. You don't look too happy about it if you ask me.'

'I think I'm going through one of the phases you warned me about. You know, the *'am I right for this job?'* phase. That's all.'

Danskin narrowed an eye. ''Course you're right for it. You're one of the best. Keep telling yourself that and remember what you told me the first time we met. *'This is what I've always wanted to do,'* you said.'

Ryan gave an ironic snigger. 'Aye, and old Frank Burrows kept telling me the job gets to everybody in the end. I think Frank was more right than me.'

'Hadaway, man. You love it really. Don't you?'

Ryan shrugged. 'Yeah. I suppose so.'

'Look,' Danskin said, 'You've got to be certain about this. You've got a career ahead of you – but only if that's what you really want.'

'It's hard, you know. I didn't expect the job to make me feel so isolated.'

The Acting Superintendent wafted a hand. 'That's not the job, man. That's Covid. Everybody feels isolated. The

High Level

vaccinations will soon be rolled out to those that matter. You'll be back in the pub before you know it.'

'But not with Hannah,' Ryan whispered. He felt the Acting Super's eyes on him. 'Sorry, sir. Did I say that out loud?'

'Aye. And I'm pleased you did. We're getting to the bottom of it now. It's none of my business, but...'

'With respect, sir, you're right. It is none of your business.'

'When it affects your work, it is my business – regardless of whether Hannah's my stepdaughter, my Aunt Fan, or any other officer. Listen, Jarrod, I knew this would be hard for you. For both of you. But, the job's hard. So, call this the first part of your sergeant's exam. Deal with it, yeah?'

Ryan thought for a moment. Stared into space. 'Okay. But, have a word with Lyall. Tell him I can work with Hannah, but we don't need be joined at the hip. Tell him we don't have to buddy up on everything we do. It's not the States. We don't have partners. He doesn't seem to get it.'

'It's his investigation, Jarrod. He'll do it his way. I won't tell him how to run the case.' His look softened. 'But I'll ask him. I'm sure he'll give it consideration.'

Danskin's fingers skipped over his keyboard. 'There. That's you entered into the exam. Now, bugger off and do some proper coppering. Lyall's waiting for you by the crime board.'

**

Ryan joined Lyall Parker, Ravi Sangar and Hannah for the briefing.

After giving his update, Ryan's thoughts drifted. He studied the photographs on the board. At its top, two images of Justin Warne's body framed a map of the Byker Wall estate, yellow pins indicating the spot he was discovered and the location of his apartment.

Displayed directly beneath these were the faces of Lola Di Marco of North Umbria Estates, Beth Richards of High Level Properties, and Peter Kirk of nobody in particular.

Finally, bottom centre, the flushed face of a glassy-eyed Sally Sykes mugshot stared out across the bullpen.

As Lyall wrapped up the briefing, Ryan picked up a marker pen. 'Before we go, can I throw something into the mix here?' he asked. 'I think there's a couple of things we're missing.'

'Such as?' Lyall encouraged.

'Well, I agree we've got the main players on the board. Most of them, anyway. But as well as the persons of interest, I suggest we keep in focus the threats made against Warne.'

'Come again?'

'You noticed it first, Ravi.' Ryan walked to the board. To the left of Sally Sykes photograph, he drew a large question mark. Beneath it, he wrote *'Warne: you are high-level filth.'* Then, *Beer* and another question mark.

'Good point,' Lyall conceded. 'We need to find this Beer bloke. Any ideas how we do it?'

'Hang on a bit. We might already know,' Ryan continued.

He turned to the board, obscuring it from their view as he wrote. When he stepped aside, they saw the words:

'Die, you shit.'
HAYLEY MACK.

**

Ryan pressed the call button.

'Yep?' a tinny voice came through a speaker next to the door.

'City and County Police.'

Pause.

'What do you want?'

'I'd like to talk to you, if I may.'

'About?'

'Justin Warne.'

Several seconds later, the lock buzzed and Ryan entered the Wills Building. On the second floor, the door to Hayley Mack's apartment stood open.

High Level

A woman dressed in black jeggings and a Guinness T-shirt stood several steps inside. She sipped from a bottle of Fenteman's cloudy lemonade as her eyes surveyed Ryan.

'Hayley Mack?' he said, holding out his ID. 'I'm Detective Constable Ryan Jarrod. May I come in?'

The woman turned her back on him and he followed into the apartment.

When they were seated, Ryan on a sofa which almost swallowed him in its cloud-like softness and Hayley Mack on a wicker chair suspended from a ceiling beam, Ryan said, 'I'd like to ask you some questions about Justin Warne.'

'So you said. I know he's dead, if that's what you've come to tell me.' She swallowed some lemonade.

'How do you know?'

'A friend told me.'

'Which friend?'

She hesitated for a fraction of a second. 'She's called Lesley. More his friend than mine but we know each other from Uni, years ago.'

It was a lie, Ryan knew for sure, but he let it pass for now.

'What did this Lesley tell you?'

'Just that he'd died. Then I told her to leave.'

'What? Just like that?'

'Yes. Like I say, she was more his friend than mine.'

'I know you were in a relationship with Mr Warne. Did you break up with him because of Lesley?'

'Good God, no. I broke up with him, not the other way around. We'd run our course. We never fell out, as such.'

'How did you feel when you heard Mr Warne was dead?'

Hayley Mack shrugged. 'I wasn't bothered, really. It was years ago.'

'I see.' Ryan looked directly at her, 'And yet you were bothered enough about him to write threats across his window.'

Hayley lifted the bottle to her lips, realised it was empty, and set it on the floor. The chair swung slightly as she lowered the bottle. She gripped the ropes. Ryan noticed her knuckles were bone white.

'You've done your homework,' she said.

'That's what I get paid for. The threat was pretty strong, wasn't it?'

She pointed to the Guinness harp logo on her T-shirt. 'I might have had a few too many of these at the time.'

'You like a beer?' he asked, putting all the emphasis on the final word.

'Occasionally. Why?'

'Tell me: do you ever comment on media posts?'

The woman pulled a puzzled expression. 'No. Why?'

Ryan studied her for a moment before saying, 'Have you ever posted anything along the lines of '*You are high-level filth?*'

'What?'

'Miss Mack, did you consider Mr Warne to be high-level filth?'

'No. No way did I call him that.'

'Where were you on Sunday evening?'

'Why?'

'Because that's when Mr Warne died. He was murdered.'

She didn't bat an eye.

'You don't seem surprised.'

'I'm not. I wouldn't have a detective sat here interrogating me if it was natural causes, would I?'

She had a point. 'So, where were you?'

'Here.'

'All night?'

'All night.'

'Can anyone vouch for that?'

She looked around the apartment. 'I can't see anyone else here, can you? I live alone, Detective.'

'Do you sleep alone?'

'I beg your pardon?'

'It would be helpful if someone could corroborate your story, that's all.'

She shrugged.

'Do you know anyone who might want Mr Warne dead?'

She shook her head. 'Don't know him well enough, these days.'

'What's Lesley's second name?'

'Don't know. It was Smith back in the day. Could be anything now.'

'Lesley Smith. Really?'

'Yes, Detective. Really.'

Ryan fixed her with his most frigid stare. 'Are you lying?'

'No.' Her chair swung as she kicked her legs like a child in a playground.

'I hope not. For your sake, I really do.' He struggled to extricate himself from the sofa. 'That's all for now, Miss Mack. I'll see myself out. Call the station if you think of someone who might want him dead. I'll be talking to you again at some point. Don't go anywhere, will you?'

As soon as Ryan exited Hayley Mack's apartment, she retrieved her mobile from the windowsill.

'I thought you should know the police have just left. I think they might suspect me.'

She looked out over the deserted expanse of Wallsend golf course.

'Don't worry,' she said. 'I kept you out of it.'

**

Hannah Graves tapped a fingernail against her teeth. 'Have you got a minute, Lyall?'

'Och, I've always got time for you. What can I do for you?'

'I'm just looking at the board here. The stuff Ryan added. There's something missing, but I don't know if it's relevant.'

'I'll never know if you dinnae tell me.'

'Well, there's another message linked to the case. Possibly, anyway. This one wasn't aimed at Warne. The first person we spoke to about the case was a Marilyn Crawford.

Someone scrawled 'You'll pay' on her door. Now, we all but ruled her out but summat tells me it might be connected.'

Lyall Parker supported his chin with a hand. 'Won't do any harm to look at her again,' he said. 'I'll send Ryan out for a wee chat wi' her.'

Hannah gave it some thought. Remembered the cosy nature of Maz's previous chat with Ryan.

'No. I'll do it,' she said.

**

'Oh. It's you. Come in.'

'Thank you, Maz,' Hannah said. 'I'm just checking how you are. You know, with the warning painted on your door, an' all.'

She walked into the tiny flat. Tiny but, actually, quite welcoming now Maz had spent some time on it.

'You've got a good eye,' Hannah smiled. 'I approve.'

'Thank you. It's not much but it's mine. That's important, while I'm here.'

'Are you thinking of moving on already? Has something else happened?'

Maz shook her head. 'Oh no. Nothing like that. I never intended being here long. I just had to start somewhere, that's all. I'm not going, like, tomorrow or anything.'

Hannah looked through grime coating the outside of the window. She couldn't decide where dirt finished, and grey sky began. 'So, about the *'You'll pay'* thing. Have you any idea why someone might target you?'

'No. None. Like I said, it's probably not aimed at me at all. There's been no follow up so I'm not exactly quaking in my size fours.'

Hannah laughed. Without Ryan at her side, she was beginning to warm to Maz Crawford. 'Have you seen any more of the blokes who you said were after your dog?'

'I didn't SAY they were after my dog. They WERE after him.'

High Level

Hannah sensed a defensive tone. 'Where is your dog, anyway?'

'Willow's a German Shepherd. Wouldn't be fair keeping him here, would it? No, I left him with my folks. Best place for him.'

Seems plausible, Hannah thought. 'True, but...'

A knock at the door interrupted her.

'Excuse me. I'll get rid of them.'

Hannah took the opportunity to go to the bathroom while Maz went to *'get rid of them.'*

'Aal reet, pet?' the caller leered.

'You!'

'Aye, last time I looked, I was me,' Rats smirked, leaning against the brick corridor wall.

'You've got a short memory. Don't you remember what I did to you last time?'

'Oh aye. That's why I've come prepared.' He brought the Stanley knife out of his pocket.

Maz's eyes homed in on it. She swallowed. 'What do you want?'

He dipped his head towards the door. 'I see you've cleaned it up.'

'That was you?'

Rats shrugged. 'Might have been. Might not. The most important thing is, do you want it to happen again? I bet you divvent, seeing as you cleaned it up nice and tidy, like. Fifty quid and I'll make sure it never happens again.'

Maz spat out a laugh. 'You're kidding, right? You think I'm scared of a runt like you?'

'Mebbe you should be.' His finger flicked the blade in and out.

Maz stood defiant. 'No chance.'

Rats looked past Maz into the flat. 'Your sofa's a bit grotty. It'll be a lot worse with the stuffing ripped oot, though.'

He stepped towards Maz, knife in one hand, the other hand subliminally protecting his Crown Jewels. He brushed past her into the flat just as the toilet flushed and Hannah emerged from the bathroom.

'What the hell?' she said.

Rats looked her up and down. 'You didn't tell us you had company, missus. Never mind. I've had two lasses before,' he laughed. 'More the merrier.'

'What's going on?' Hannah stepped towards him.

He raised the blade to her face.

Hannah froze.

'Feisty bitch, aren't you? I wouldn't mess with Rats if I were you.'

Maz inched up behind him. Hannah's glance betrayed her.

'Nee good trying to catch us out,' Rats said. 'I know you're behind us. Get ower there with your mate.'

Hannah's eyes signalled to Maz. *Do as he says*, her look said. Maz nodded.

'Your pal's canny looking, like. What's her name?'

'I can speak for myself. I'm Hannah.'

'As in Montana,' he laughed.

'No, actually. As in Graves. Detective Sergeant Hannah Graves.'

'Fuck!'

Rats spun on his heels and raced to the door. He used its frame to swing himself left, back along the corridor. The blade slipped from his hand. 'Fuck.'

Hannah sprinted after him. 'Stop!' she shouted. Then, over her shoulder, 'Don't touch the knife, Maz.'

The echo of footsteps resonated along the corridor. Rats flung open the door to the staircase. Hannah followed, closing in on him.

The boy spiralled down the staircase, taking three at a time. No sooner did Hannah get a glimpse of him than he disappeared around the next bend.

She followed the sound of his raspy breath and the heavy footfall. Then, suddenly, all was quiet.

High Level

Hannah stopped. Listened intently. There was nothing to hear but the yelp of a dog far below.

Hannah lay her head against cold brickwork, panting from the exertion.

'Shit.'

She kicked the wall.

'Shit, shit, shit.'

Rats had vanished into thin air.

CHAPTER THIRTEEN

SATURDAY

A scratching at the door woke him. Ryan pushed himself up from the sofa and winced in pain. He rubbed a hand around the back of his neck, but his head refused to straighten and hung limply to one side.

'Ry, are you up?' a voice said from outside the door.

'Aye, man. Give us a minute.' He stood, discovered he had jelly legs, and promptly sat back down again. 'Jesus.'

'Howay, man. I'm freezing me bollocks off out here.'

Ryan tried rotating his neck but, with the stubbornness of a mule, it refused to comply. 'I'm coming.'

The second the door inched open, Spud burst through closely followed by James Jarrod.

'Bloody hell, get the heating on, will you?' James said. He studied his elder brother. 'What's up with you?'

'What do you mean?'

'You're standing there like Quasimodo, that's what I mean.' James stooped, raised a shoulder until it reached his ear, and tilted his head. 'The bells,' he slurred, 'The bells.'

Ryan rubbed his neck again. 'Bad night, that's all.'

'Aye, I can tell. To top it all, you've got comb-over hair, as well.'

'I've just got up, man. What do you expect?' Spud set both front paws against Ryan's shins and looked up expectantly, tail a blur. 'All right, Spuddy-boy. I'll get you summat in a minute.'

High Level

'I haven't seen or heard much from you all week so thought you might want to take Spud for his walk this morning,' James said.

'You mean you can't be arsed.'

'Well, there is that.'

Ryan smiled, softened his voice. 'Yeah, give us ten minutes. It'll be good to be somewhere other than here or the station.' He bent down, ruffled the fleshy folds around the pug's throat, and found he couldn't straighten.

'You okay? You're less mobile than Dad and he hasn't left the couch for the last month.'

Ryan chuckled. 'That's my trouble. Fell asleep on the sofa myself last night. Woke up on it, as well.'

'You mean the sainted Hannah's choice of sofa's not so comfortable after all?'

'Look, let's agree on one thing. I'll walk Spud with you if you'll not talk about her. Deal or no deal?'

'Deal.'

Ryan hobbled to the hallway like an octogenarian and began his search for a matching pair of trainers.

**

By the time they reached Millfield Road, the brothers' conversation had dwindled to weather references, Gogglebox-like comments on TV programmes most of which Ryan hadn't seen, and bets on which of the village pubs would open first. Ryan put his money on Wetherspoon's whilst James went for an outsider: The Woodman's Arms. Both agreed The Crown would be last.

They cut into Chase Park via an entrance close to the Neuro Centre Care Home and Ryan unleashed Spud who made a beeline for the Skate Park where he unashamedly did his business slap-bang in the centre.

Ryan groaned with effort as he bent to pick up the mess, though his moan may have been more to do with James's question.

'Howay, then. What's up with you and Hannah?'

'We had a deal, remember?'

'Aye, but that was just my cunning plan to get you out.'

'Bastard,' Ryan half-smiled.

'Perhaps, but I'm a concerned bastard, if it helps.'

'Actually, it does. Thanks, James.'

'So, what's the crack, then?'

Ryan sighed. 'I think it's over. I'm not sure it's right for either of us. I just need to get me head around it, that's all.'

'Right.'

'What's that supposed to mean?'

James Jarrod pulled at his quiff like Stan Laurel. 'I like her, that's all. It's a shame.'

'That's one way of putting it. I dunno, we still care about each other, but I'm not sure it'll ever work. Not now, anyways.' Ryan whistled Spud back as they neared the park exit.

'Can't be easy at work, though,' the younger Jarrod said.

Ryan considered the comment. 'It's weird. Sometimes, it's okay. Other times, it's a nightmare. I asked Danskin if he could keep us apart, just for a while, like, but nowts changed so far. Anyway,' he said, changing the subject, 'How's your love life?'

James waited for a gap in traffic before they crossed the foot of Rectory Lane. 'Earth calling Ryan. We're in the middle of a pandemic. Not exactly the ideal time to start a relationship.'

Ryan felt something curdle in his stomach. It was the unpalatable memory of an ill-judged blind date in Heaton with a girl whose name he'd already forgotten.

'Actually, I think I might be able to help you once lockdown's over,' Ryan said.

'Yesss!' James punched the air. 'You've got Pixie Lott's phone number, haven't you?'

Ryan laughed. 'No, but I do know somebody's got the hots for you.'

'Oh aye? What's the punchline?'

'No. Seriously. It's a case I'm working on. A lass we talked to recognised my name. She asked if I was related to Jam Jar.'

James stopped, brow furrowed. 'Who?'

'Somebody you went to school with. I think she said she was a year above you. Might have been two. Anyway, she definitely knows you; you and your hair. She told me she used to fancy you.'

Ryan's phone vibrated in his pocket. He pulled it out and looked at the message. 'Ah, man. Sorry, kidda. I've gotta go. It's work. Something's come up.'

James took Spud's leader from Ryan. 'Okay, but you can't leave me hanging. Who was it?'

Ryan had burst into as much a sprint as his aches allowed. As he headed back towards the park, he shouted over his shoulder.

'Her name's Maz. Marilyn Crawford.'

**

By the time Ryan arrived in the bullpen, Lyall Parker, Todd Robson, and Stephen Danskin were already gathered around the crime board. He was surprised to see Hannah upfront, a second board standing blank alongside her.

'Thanks for joining us, Jarrod,' Danskin said. 'DS Graves has some interesting developments to bring us on the Justin Warne case. She's been with forensics most of the night and can now bring us up to date. Hannah – the floor's yours.'

'Thank you, sir. As you know, to date our focus has been on tracing those who had business interests with Warne.' She pointed to the pictures of Lola Di Marco and Beth Richards. 'Also, some of his friends and acquaintances,' she indicated the bottom row of the board, Peter Kirk, Sally Sykes and a fresh image of Hayley Mack.

'Now,' she continued, 'We also have the messages, thinly veiled threats, made against Warne. We've assumed all along that they're linked to the killing. What if they're not?

Let's assume for a moment we're wrong; that we've fallen into the trap of seeing what we expect to see.'

'Bloody hell,' Todd grumbled, 'We've another one saying that now.'

'Robson,' Danskin warned, 'Let DS Graves finish.'

'What if all of this,' she waved a hand over the board, 'Is all coincidental? What if the murder has nothing whatsoever to do with Justin Warne's business interests?'

'I'd say we were up the creek without a paddle,' Lyall Parker said. 'I'd say we'd lost a week of the investigation.'

'And, I'd say you're wrong,' Ryan interjected. 'There's too much pointing towards it. The dodgy business deals. The complaints against Warne. It's got to be one of those on the board. If not the SEOs, Di Marco and Richards, it'll be Hayley Mack, I'd lay odds on it. What else could be behind it?'

Hannah gave a triumphant smile. 'Yesterday, I went back to the Byker Wall.' She turned to the blank board and blue-tacked a photograph on it. 'I spoke to this woman. Marilyn Crawford. She's also received a threat.'

Through a yawn, Ryan said, 'But Hannah, man, we don't even know the threat was against her.'

'We didn't, but we do now. While I was speaking to her, she had a visitor. Someone was trying to extort money from her. Threatened to damage her property.'

'And?'

'And, it seems Maz Crawford wasn't the only one. Getting information from the neighbours was like blood from a stone. They close ranks and protect their own, but a couple of them told me there was some reet dodgy stuff going on.'

'*Reet dodgy stuff,*' Ryan mocked. 'Can you be a bit more exact than that?'

Hannah looked at him coldly. 'Yes, as a matter of fact. There's a protection racket rife on the estate. A couple of thugs are threatening residents. Demanding money in exchange for *'looking after'*, Hannah made air quotes, 'The property.'

Lyall Parker whistled. 'I'm ahead o' you here. You think they killed the owner of the properties so they had no resistance?'

'Precisely, Lyall.'

'They'd have a free hit once Warne was out the way. Good work, Hannah. Brilliant work, in fact.'

'You said you were there when Maz was threatened,' Ryan said. 'Does that mean we have him in custody?'

Hannah looked sheepish. 'No. He got away.'

Ryan didn't want to smirk. He really didn't. But smirk he did. And he hated himself for it.

'I do know who he is, though. He's one of the two youths Marilyn Crawford had a confrontation with on her first day at the Wall.' She produced an evidence bag from behind the board. 'And his prints are all over this Stanley knife which he used to threaten Marilyn Crawford.'

'We have an ID?' Danskin said.

'Yes. He goes by the name of Rats. Real name, Marvin Scully.' She attached a mugshot of a sour-faced, sneering youth. Printed across the bottom of the image was a tell-tale sequence of numbers.

'He's got form, then?' Todd asked.

'Oh aye. Assault. GBH and ABH. Carrying a bladed weapon. Aggravated burglary. Yep, he's got form, all right.'

'He looks a bit young to be running this himself. Is he a stool pigeon? Somebody else pulling his strings?'

'Impossible to say for sure, but the little I've been told doesn't suggest that's the case. As for being too young, he's nineteen. That's around the same age Bonnie and Clyde were, and Scully has a bigger back catalogue than they had.'

'Let's bring him in.'

'I wish we could, Todd. He's gone completely off-grid since he threatened Maz. Uniform are carrying out door-to-door checks throughout the estate, Ravi's undertaking digital traces on him, and we've patrol cars roaming the East End. No luck so far.'

They let out a collective sigh. 'We'll find him, ugly wee bastard that he is,' Lyall said.

'Yes,' Danskin agreed, 'But we can't afford to put all our eggs in one basket. Not again. Lyall – you and Graves focus on this Scully character. Rope Treblecock in if you need extra hands. I'll work with Jarrod and Robson on the original line of enquiry. Ravi and DS Nairn will assist both teams. I want us to keep two balls in play for now.'

Danskin clapped his hands. 'Howay, then. Let's crack on. And, just to echo what Lyall said: that's real proper coppering, DS Graves. Well done.'

The team went their separate ways. As Hannah passed Ryan, he caught her wrist. 'Look, I'm sorry. About before. I was way out of order. Not what I said, but the way I said it.'

'Actually, you were out of order with both.'

Ryan breathed out. 'Aye. I was. Well done, Hannah. The girl done good. I mean it.'

She beamed at the compliment. 'I know you do, Ryan. And it means a lot.' Hannah slid her hand downwards and interlocked her fingers with his. 'More than you could know.'

She released her grip, ruffled his hair, and walked off towards Lyall Parker.

Ryan shook his head. *'Understanding women,'* he thought, *'Is like trying to describe what colour the number five smells like.'*

CHAPTER FOURTEEN

Peter Kirk noticed the teacup tremble in his hand as he set it down.

Yesterday, he'd been preoccupied by thoughts of the thug from Wood's. Given the fact he'd woken up, he assumed he hadn't been butchered in his sleep on either of the last two nights so, today, his worry bubble was the call from Hayley Mack.

'*I kept you out of it,*' she'd assured him yet the very fact the police had spoken to her at all meant they might be onto him. He needed to know more, but three times he'd tried to call her and three times she hadn't picked up.

Kirk's imagination ran riot. She must be in custody, he thought. She'll be singing like a bird, as they said in the movies. Doing everything she could to prove her innocence. Including dropping the name of Peter Kirk to the cops.

Peter gnawed on his lower lip. He felt his bowels contract with fear. There was only one thing for it – he had to prove it was all in his imagination. He had to see her once more, then he'd know everything was okay.

He grabbed his car keys from the hook by the back door and hauled a plastic bag full of kitchen detritus outside with him. As he turned from locking the door, the punch floored him.

'I told you I'd see you soon.'

Peter lay in the shadow of the man towering over him. He raised his hands to protect his face.

'What were you doing by Moot Hall?'

'Moot Hall? I wasn't...'

The man's steel-toed work boot dug into Peter's side.

Kirk spluttered as he tried to regain his breath.

'Did that hurt? The next one will be worse, I promise.'

Peter squirmed away, coughing. 'Okay, okay. Give me a second to breathe first, though.'

He used the moment to think of a way out. There wasn't one. The only escape lay at the other end of the side alley, and it was so narrow the construction worker's bulk filled it.

The man stood over him, arms by his side, fists clenched, legs apart. 'I'm waiting,' he growled.

'I'm...I'm just gathering my breath,' Peter gasped. He raised himself onto one knee. Coughed again for effect. And launched himself between the man's legs like an Olympic sprinter out the blocks.

Except, it was a false start. Peter's feet became tangled together and he stumbled face-first onto the path.

He felt the man's weight land on top of him, a knee crunching his spine. The man grasped the back of Kirk's shirt collar, raising his head from the flagstone.

The man pushed down, hard.

Peter Kirk saw the flagstone race towards his face before his world spiralled.

**

Moot Hall, home of Newcastle's Crown Court until 1998, was little more than a stone's-throw from the Forth Street station, but it was a steep uphill walk.

Stephen Danskin doubled over, hands on his waist. 'Sooner I'm off the desk job and back on real work, the better,' he gasped. 'I'm so out of condition it's untrue.'

'It's your age,' Ryan smiled.

'Cheeky bugger.' Danskin straightened himself. 'Right. What are we looking at here?'

They stood at the hall's gated entrance, eyeing the Grade 1 listed building. At its base, six full-width steps led up to a symmetrical main frontage of Greek Revival style. A portico supported by Doric columns shielded the central double-doors, at each side of which elaborate brackets housed tapered lamps.

'I thought it might help if we saw what the fuss was all about,' Ryan said. 'Get a feel for the place, like.'

'Aye. I reckon you'll be like me. Passed it hundreds of times but never really seen it.' Danskin scanned the length of the building. 'I tell you what, it's a canny impressive structure.'

Its three storeys were arranged beneath a hipped roof which included elements of glazing, bounded by a parapet.

'I agree, sir. I can see why Lola Di Marco would be pissed off at losing out on it. Look at the views, man.'

Moot Hall sat between the Tyne Bridge and its elder sister, the High Level.

History lay, literally, at the old courtroom's doorstep while beneath it, the splendour of the modern-day quayside with its bars, hotels, and restaurants on one bank and the Baltic Art Gallery and Sage Concert Venue on the Gateshead side, stretched out into the distance.

'Any idea how much one apartment here would fetch?' Danskin mused. 'I reckon you'd be looking at quarter of a million, minimum. And there's space for, what, two dozen apartments inside?'

'Probably. There's private parking in the courtyard. Security gates. I think you might be underestimating the value, sir.'

Danskin let out a whistle. 'How'd they keep this under the radar?'

A thought struck Ryan. 'What if they didn't?'

'What do you mean?'

'I mean just that. What if someone leaked news of the plans for it? Sir, the day Justin Warne's body was discovered, there was a protest going on here. Hannah and I listened to the reports of it on our way back from the Wall. It kind of distracted us from each other.'

'Aye. It was uniform who dealt with it. Not CID work.'

'Precisely, sir. In other words, we didn't get told what the protest was about. I bet it concerned the development, in which case someone let the cat out the bag.'

'Which gives someone yet another motive for seeking vengeance against Justin Warne.' Danskin mulled the thought over. 'Problem is, that widens the net still further.'

Stephen Danskin stared up at the old courtroom before giving his verdict.

'Bollocks and bugger.'

**

'What have you got?' Hannah asked, looking over Lyall Parker's shoulder.

He'd pulled up Marvin Scully's history on a PC and was scrolling through the data.

'You pretty much nailed it earlier, Hannah. He's a string of offences to his name, starting when he was only eleven years old.'

'Christ, what were his parents doing?' Her comment was more social observation than question, but Lyall answered all-the-same.

'His father was doing time, that's what he was doing. Still is. He's in Frankland.'

HM Prison Frankland, in the village of Brasside three miles from Durham city, is a Maximum-Security prison housing Category A inmates. Dubbed Monster Mansion, it has counted some of Britain's most notorious criminals amongst its inmates. Peter Sutcliffe, Charles Bronson, Ian Huntley and Harold Shipman have all found themselves within its confines at one time or another.

'Not a petty criminal, then,' Hannah said with understatement.

'Och, no. Lee Scully's about as un-petty as they come. Multiple rapes. Arson with intent to endanger life, and a list of domestic violence offences longer than a roll o' Andrex.'

'Domestic violence? Against our lad's mother?'

'Among others, aye.'

Hannah let out a sigh. 'Jesus.'

They spent a moment in contemplation until Hannah said, 'We need to speak to her.'

'She's no use to us. She's under witness protection in Hampshire. Has been since she helped put Scully away.'

'But we've an address for Rats, or Marvin, or whatever you want to call him. It was the first place uniform went looking for him. Who's he been living with, if not his mother?'

Lyall popped a piece of gum into his mouth. Tossed the wrapper into a bin. 'We dinnae have an address for him.'

'But…'

'We have a last-known address, Hannah, not an address. He's been living anywhere he can and with anybody who'll have him. No fixed abode, you'd call it.'

Hannah groaned. 'Which means he could be literally anywhere. Just. Bloody. Great.'

She sat upright.

'Wait a minute. What about his mother? Might he be heading for Hampshire?'

'Doubt it. He doesn't know where she is.'

A pained expression crossed her face. 'Even her own son doesn't know where she is. That must be so hard for her.'

'Not really. It's what she wanted.'

'Why? I don't understand how a woman could do something like that.'

Lyall Parker looked her in the eyes.

'That's because you haven't had an eleven-year-old son coming after you with a bladed weapon.'

**

Rats lay still as night in the drainage channel beneath Byker Bridge. The Ouseburn was never the most fragrant of the Tyne's tributaries at the best of times, and today was the worst of times.

When the cop had announced herself in Maz Crawford's apartment, Rats feared he'd go the same way as his old man.

The fear didn't last long, soon overtaken by the excitement of the chase and the adrenalin rush he experienced when he dove into the air conditioning vent on the fifth-floor landing.

He'd contorted himself into the narrow channel and held the grate in place across the entrance. From here, he heard the cop's footsteps echoing down the stairs, noticed the silence when she gave up the chase, and heard her swear when she'd realised her quarry had disappeared.

Rats had rolled onto his back, sucked in air, and began giggling like a ticklish schoolgirl. He'd remained there until darkness fell.

Slowly, he crept out the vent and made his way outside the Byker Wall estate. He'd begged a KFC from a wary patron entering the Clifford Street takeaway. Rats wasn't short of cash; it was more fun getting something for nothing, that's all.

After demolishing the meal, he'd taken a back street route onto Byker Bank and, from there, along James Place Street to his current hiding spot in the stinking sewer.

He'd eaten nothing since. Marvin Scully was cold, hungry, and angry. Angry at Scrapper, at the female cop, the young woman who'd busted his balls, and everyone in-between. Rats was also cornered, and a cornered rat is a dangerous thing.

At the insidious onset of his second night in the cloying mud of the culvert, he made himself a vow. He wasn't changing his ways. They could go fuck themselves, all of them.

Marvin Scully was his father's son and one day, very soon, he'd prove it.

He'd make sure his dad was proud of him.

CHAPTER FIFTEEN

SUNDAY

'How much longer is it going to be? The doc said I was fine.'

The nurse's eyes smiled at Peter Kirk behind her face mask. 'We just need someone to sign the discharge papers. Bear with us – you won't be here any longer than necessary. It won't surprise you to know we need the bed.'

Peter released a sigh. On the bright side, at least he was safe here. He'd spent the night in North Tyneside Hospital – known to all by its previous name of Rake Lane – under observation.

He had eyes like a raccoon and a headache from Hell, but mild concussion was the only lingering effect. Heaven knows what would happen next time he crossed swords with the construction worker, though.

'Any chance of a cup of tea while I'm waiting?'

'There's a vending machine along the corridor. You're free to leave the ward, you know, just not the grounds. You're not in prison.'

'Not yet,' he muttered under his breath as the nurse left the ward.

'Mr Kirk,' a voice beside his bed said, 'We meet again.'

Peter was thrust from one nightmare into another. DC Ryan Jarrod stood over him.

'Let's head to the day room for a chat, shall we?'

Ryan shepherded Peter into the unoccupied day room. They took chairs on opposite sides of a low-level coffee table. A wall-mounted TV played BBC News, subtitles replacing the muted volume. A wire rack beneath the screen held self-help leaflets for every ailment imaginable, and a few which weren't.

'Now,' Ryan said, 'Imagine my surprise back at the station when I see your name flash up on my PC telling me you'd been in an incident. We seem to be running into each other quite frequently.'

'To tell you the truth, on balance I'd say I'm quite happy to see you, even though *'an incident'* isn't how I'd describe it.'

Ryan believed him. The one advantage about interviewing someone wearing a face covering was that it focused all attention on the eyes. Beneath the bruising, Peter Kirk's eyes showed both relief and honesty.

'What happened?'

'I ate some ice-cream. What does it look like? I got jumped, that's what.'

'And why would someone do that?'

'Because he's been following me. Threatening me.'

Ryan rocked back in his chair. 'You didn't answer my question. Why would someone beat you up?'

'Because he saw me at Justin's house. He's been following me ever since.'

'Wait. Slow down. You've been to Mr Warne's house again?'

Peter Kirk lowered his eyes. 'Yes.'

'Despite our warnings, you revisited the crime scene?'

'Yes.' Kirk picked at a fingernail.

'Okay. Assuming I suspend belief for a moment and pretend you have no involvement in Mr Warne's death, why would someone want to follow you?'

'I don't know. I wish I did. I REALLY wish I knew.'

'And this man who's been following you, he attacked you outside your house. How did he know where you lived?'

'When he first threatened me, let's just say I overshared the information.'

Ryan sucked in air. 'Describe the man who attacked you.'

'Big. Muscly. Ugly. He's a construction worker.'

'If you don't know who it was, how do you know what he does for a living?'

'Because he drives a truck covered in shit with Wood Building Contractors plastered all over it. It's a bit of a clue.'

Ryan nodded to himself. 'Stay where you are. I'm going to make a call.'

When the detective had left the room, Peter bent forward and put his head in his hands. His friend was dead. The police suspected he did it. He'd made things worse for himself by going back to Justin's house and, to put the tin lid on things, a gorilla was after his arse. Peter Kirk began to weep just as Ryan re-entered the room.

'Tell me about the truck.'

Kirk sniffed and dragged a hand across his eyes. 'It was white. Or cream. Hard to tell because it was caked in shit, like I told you. I could just make out Wood Building Contractors written on the side.'

'Anything else?'

Kirk shook his head, before something showed in his eyes. 'Wait. Yes. It had a company logo on it. Three pyramids.'

Ryan thumbed something into Siri. While he scrolled through the results on his smartphone, the silence played to his advantage when the Uber driver felt compelled to speak.

'Did she give you my name?'

Ryan looked up from the screen. Considered how to respond. 'Yes.'

Peter's eyes shot to the ceiling. 'She promised me she hadn't. I wish I'd told you myself now. It wouldn't look so bad for me that way, would it?'

'Go on,' Ryan said, pretending he knew what Peter was talking about.

'She said you'd been to see her after I told her about Justin. She said she hadn't mentioned me.'

Slowly, Ryan joined the dots. 'Hayley Mack wouldn't tell us how she knew Warne was dead. Only that a Lesley Smith had told her. Now we know who Lesley Smith really is. Thank you, Mr Kirk.'

Peter swore under his breath.

'And it puzzles me why neither of you mentioned you'd spoken to each other. Unless, of course, you're both implicated in his death.'

'No!'

'So: why the secrecy? Why didn't you tell us you'd been to see Miss Mack? You've got our number. We told you to get in touch if you thought of anything.'

'I didn't tell you because I didn't want her to get into trouble.'

Ryan fixed Peter Kirk with a cold stare. 'Why would she be in trouble with us?'

'I just said *'in trouble'*. Not who with. Let's face it, this,' he gestured around the room, 'Isn't exactly party central, and I'm sitting here looking like I've been in the ring with Tyson Fury.'

Ryan had to concede the point. 'Aye. True.'

'It is the truth. Everything I've said is true.'

'Everything you've said makes sense, except one thing. You see, the trouble is, I called the station. Asked them to run some checks on Wood Building Contractors. Companies House have no record of any such business. At least, not one any further north than Lincolnshire.'

'It's obvious, then, isn't it? Just because it's based in Lincoln doesn't mean its local. Could be nationwide.'

Ryan smiled beneath his face covering. 'Aye, true. Except for one thing. I've checked the company logo on me phone. Not a pyramid in sight.'

Peter Kirk slumped forward again. 'Then I don't know what else I can say. Everything I've said is the truth. I don't know what else I can do to prove it.'

'Did Justin ever tell you about his business deals?'

'No. Never. I have to remind you that we're not that close, officer.'

'From what you know of him, would you say Mr Warne was the type to renege on a contract?'

The Uber driver shrugged.

'You know nothing about a transaction to purchase Moot Hall?'

Kirk shook his head.

'What about…'

Peter Kirk sat bolt upright. 'Moot Hall? That's where the construction worker threatened me.'

'Howay, then – tell us more.'

'After I'd been to Justin's house the second time, I went for a drive. I didn't want to go home in case Bluto was there. I ended up parking up outside the Bridge Hotel, next to Moot Hall. The thug was there. He left a note warning me off.'

'So, he must have known about the deal.'

'I guess so. Does that mean you believe me? You don't think I did it, now?'

Ryan looked at him. 'I'm coming round to that possibility, aye.'

'Thank Christ.'

'Had your horses, bonny lad. You're not off the hook yet. You admitted being back in Warne's house after it'd been sealed. That's against the law.'

'Shit.'

'Why did you go back?'

'I wanted to find something that proved it wasn't me. I had it in my head that you lot were going to pin Justin's murder on me. I thought…I dunno, I thought I might find something.'

'And did you?'

'No. You lot had taken his computers. I reckoned that's where I would find anything.'

Ryan remembered the space beneath Justin Warne's desk. 'You're absolutely sure you haven't taken any of Warne's technology?'

'No, I haven't. Of course not.'

Ryan steepled his fingers beneath his chin. Looked at the man opposite. Finally, he gave the vaguest nod. 'Where else did you look?'

'Nowhere. Before I could look anywhere else, Sally came in and scared us half to death.'

'Sally Sykes? She's been in as well?'

Peter nodded.

'Jesus.'

Ryan began gathering up his things.

'Can I go now?' Kirk asked.

'No.'

'What – you're arresting me?'

'Nah, but you need your discharge papers signed off, don't you?'

'Don't do that to me, man. You nearly gave me a Sean Connery.'

Ryan chuckled. He was warming to Peter Kirk. 'Listen, we've some prints unaccounted for in Mr Warne's property. When they let you out of here, would you mind coming to the station and getting yours taken? It would help if we could rule out those belonging to you.'

Peter beamed. 'Definitely. I've nothing to hide. Will you give me protection, as well?'

Ryan shook his head. 'What do you think you're on? This is real life, not Line of Duty.'

'What if he comes back for me?'

'We'll fix some security cameras up.'

Peter breathed out in relief.

Until Ryan concluded, 'That way, at least we'll get him on camera after he's killed you.'

**

High Level

Newcastle Quayside Market had been held every Sunday, from nine am to four pm, for as long as living memory could recall.

Part of North East culture, it was a vibrant showcase of quality goods and produce, from jewellery to artwork, clothing to kid's toys, perfumes to handmade crafts, all sold by a familiar cast of vendors.

Once known as the Covent Garden of the north, street artists and buskers helped create a warm, friendly, immersive atmosphere, and food trucks, candy floss stalls, and bakery stands always did a roaring trade.

Until the pandemic struck, and everything ground to a sudden, desolate halt. Now, only a cold wind inhabited the riverside streets, dragging with it a cascade of litter which whipped like tumbleweed along the near-deserted quayside drag.

In a doorway in a side-street with the appropriate name of The Swirle, Rats took shelter. He slugged down the last dregs from a can of Strongbow and allowed his imagination to catch the scent of hot dogs and fried onions from a non-existent fast-food van.

He blew warmth onto his hands and struggled to his feet. He was only a few miles from the Byker Wall, but no-one would recognise him. Not here. Not if he hid in plain sight.

Besides, another night, two at most, and he'd be back in The Wall, taking care of business. Specifically, business with the one with the silly name: Maz, wasn't it?

Marvin Scully's hand reached into a pocket. The roll of notes he'd taken from his 'clients' remained in place. All he had to do was find somewhere that was open, somewhere that didn't have CCTV, and somewhere that sold food.

The first place he encountered was a Starbucks next to the Malmaison Hotel.

The girl behind the counter smiled warmly as she asked for his name.

He gave her his dad's name, and the girl wrote 'Lee' on a styrofoam cup despite the fact he was the only customer.

Rats bit into a muffin while the machine at the end of the counter whistled and chuffed like a steam train.

'Sorry. You'll have to wait til you're outside before you eat. Takeaway only,' she said, pointing to a sign above the pastries.

'Fuck off.'

The girl opened her mouth to protest, saw the malevolence in Rats' eyes, and thought better of it.

'When do you finish?' Rats asked.

'I beg your pardon?'

He produced a roll of notes. 'I'm just sayin', like. You look the sort. I'm well flush, me, if you're up for it.'

The girl's mouth curled in distaste and her eyes yawned.

A male barista poked his head above the gleaming contraption. 'For Lee,' he said. 'Take care. It's red hot, mind.'

Rats collected the cup. Removed its lid. Took a sip.

'You should have taken us up on me offer, like,' he said to the young woman.

He threw the mug's scalding contents into the girl's face.

Above her falsetto scream, he said, 'It'll be a canny while before anybody gives you a shag now.'

He ran off, laughing.

CHAPTER SIXTEEN

Ryan wasn't on the work roster for the day, so he was able to quit when he felt like it. Which just happened to be after he'd interviewed Peter Kirk. In other words: lunchtime.

He considered dropping in on his dad and brother for Sunday lunch but decided chicken nuggets and chips – which was all his dad ever made on a weekend - didn't hit the spot. Instead, he went straight home to The Drive and ordered a takeaway roast from Café Lutz.

He was out of luck. They'd sold out less than half an hour earlier.

He buttered three slices of bread and cut some Cheddar from a block. 'Oh, sod it.' He slammed down the knife. Suddenly, chicken nuggets and chips sounded appealing.

The drive to Norman Jarrod's house only took a couple of minutes. Ryan opened the door and was met by the aroma of rich gravy and roast beef. Even Spud couldn't drag himself away from the smell to greet Ryan.

'Bloody hell, have you entered Masterchef or summat?'

'Ah, howay in, son. You're just in time. I thought we'd have a change. Got a couple of meals in for James and me from Café Lutz on Oakfield. We were lucky. Got the last ones.'

Ryan smiled. 'Aye, I should have guessed it would be you buggers.'

'Eh?'

'Never mind. Are you sure there's enough to go round?'

'Why aye, man. You don't mind, do you?' Norman Jarrod said to his youngest son.

'Pull up a seat,' James said, forking the last Yorkie onto his plate before Ryan had an opportunity to snaffle it.

They spent the next forty minutes engaged in mindless small talk. Ryan felt his shoulders relax, the tension in his neck dissipate, and his lower spine sink against the seat's backrest. This was what he needed: the company of family, where he could be himself; the antithesis of his life at the station.

'How's Gran doing? I haven't had a chance to ring the care home this week. Too much on.'

'Much the same, apparently,' James told him. 'They said she's staying in her room more these days. She's had her second vaccination, though. Angela, the manageress, said one of us can start visiting her again once it's in her system.'

Ryan beamed. 'Ah, that's good news, man.'

'Do you want to be her nominated visitor?' Norman Jarrod asked. 'You know I'm no good with things like that. It just upsets us.' He drifted into a melancholy silence.

Ryan began gathering up their empty, gravy-stained plates and cutlery from the table. 'Normally I would but, with work the way it is, it'd be a waste of a visit if I couldn't get in to see her. James – d'you not fancy it?'

'I don't mind but she responds better to you, Ry. You're her favourite.'

Ryan balanced the salt cellar atop plate mountain. 'Don't say that, man. She doesn't have favourites.'

'She gave you her old engagement ring. That's got to count for something.'

'She didn't, really. Her note said it was for whichever of us needed it first.' He carried the plates into the kitchen, James following.

'Aye. And that was you.'

Ryan spat out a bitter laugh. 'Fat lot of good it did me, though. If you ask me, it's still up for grabs.'

James turned on the sink taps and squirted soap under the running water. 'Speaking of which…' The younger Jarrod left the sentence hanging.

High Level

'Don't go there, kidda. Let's not spoil the afternoon by talking about Hannah, yeah?'

James shook his head. 'No, no. I didn't mean you and Hannah. I was wondering…do you think…oh, it doesn't matter.'

Ryan leant across his brother and switched off the tap as bubbles threatened to flood the kitchen. 'Howay, man. Keep your mind on the job,' he dug James in the ribs, 'And spit out what you were going to say.'

James took a deep breath. 'Look, I know you said you couldn't, but if I asked Hannah do you think she'd give me Maz Crawford's number?'

'Absolutely not. She's leading on that side of the case so I couldn't tell you what's happening with it even if I knew, but I'm pretty sure she'll send you packing.'

James shrugged. 'Okay. Just a thought.'

'But you'll never know if you don't ask. Give her a shout. See what she says. Just have your ear-plugs handy, yeah?'

James grinned, before a frown overtook it. 'Will Hannah know you mentioned it? I don't want you getting into bother with her.'

'I don't give a toss, mate. Not anymore.'

It was a lie. Ryan knew it, James knew it, and Ryan knew James knew.

Which is why they were both grateful when James changed the subject.

'Let's leave these to soak. The Toon game's on Sky in a minute.'

Ryan sniffed a laugh. 'Bloody hell. First, you talk about me ex, now the Toon. Heaven knows, I'm miserable now.'

James laughed out loud. 'They've got to win sometime, man. Today might be the day.'

'That's what every gambling addict says every time they waste their last fiver on a dead cert that's more dead than certain. No, they're fucked this season. You and Dad make yersel depressed if you like; I'm off to do something more enjoyable.'

'Oh aye? What's that, like?'

'Sticking needles under me fingernails.'

**

Maz Crawford was delighted to discover the lift closest to her flat was back in service.

She hoisted a heavy roll of fabric she'd purchased from the Silverlink's Hobbycraft store against her thigh and pressed the lift call button. She fixated on the twelve red lights above the door as the lift made its lazy way down from the top floor.

The light stuck on number eight.

Maz cursed. 'Don't say it's knackered again.' She sensed a presence at her back. 'Sorry. Talking to myself. What am I like?' she said, embarrassed.

'It'll come eventually, pet.'

Maz recognised the voice. 'Oh, hello again,' she smiled. It was the woman she'd shared a lift with a few days back. The woman who'd also got out at the tenth floor.

The woman's return smile was framed by terse lines.

Maz tapped her foot as the lift remained on the eighth floor. The silence made her uncomfortable.

'I'm going to cover my sofa until I can get a new one,' she explained. 'What do you think?' She pulled down the lip of the bag to reveal an elasticated fabric the colour of baked beans.

'Doesn't matter what I think.'

The wind caught the lobby door, slamming it shut. The woman jumped.

'Are you okay?'

'Aye. So-so. Aboot your haberdashery – it won't last. Hope it didn't cost you much.'

'What do you mean?'

'Folk roond here know the price of everything and the value of nowt.'

Maz smiled. 'I don't intend inviting all and sundry in to inspect it.'

The woman gave a humourless laugh. 'You mightn't have a choice.'

Maz thought of the kid called Rats. 'Is there something I should know?'

The woman's cackle sounded like dry leaves. 'It's like I said, before: just be careful, reet?'

Marilyn Crawford raised her eyebrows.

'It's not like the owld days,' her companion said in response. 'Byker was reet homely at one time. We mightn't have had two coppers to rub together but what we had was ours. Nobody would dream of robbing us blind or threatening us.'

The woman stared into space. 'But now, the buggers here think the world owes 'em a living. Like I say, you watch out for yersel', hen.'

The elevator light moved again. Seven, six…

'I will. Look, are you sure you're alright? You seem a bit, I don't know, a bit tense.'

Five, four…

'I'll get by. Have to, don't we?'

Three, two…

'We do,' Maz smiled. 'I'm Marilyn, by the way. But call me Maz. Most people do.'

One, Ground. …the door shuddered open.

Maz struggled inside with her load and pressed for the tenth floor.

The woman reached across and hit the button numbered 'two.'

'Sorry. I thought you were on same floor as me.'

The lift shook and moved off.

'Nah, pet. I was just lookin' oot for you last time, that's all. Somebody has to.'

As the door slid open at the second floor, the woman squeezed out.

'I'm Rosina,' she said, 'But call me Mrs Durrant.'

**

Ryan finished the dishes by himself whilst listening to cries of 'For fuck's sake, man, close him down,' and 'It's just a matter of time before they score,' from the living room.

Sure enough, between saying his goodbyes and boarding the Fiat, 'they' did score. Ryan switched channels from talkSport to Heart FM before the commentary sent him spiralling into depression.

Although a bitter wind wrapped itself around the Fiat as Ryan steered the car down Whickham Bank, the sun splashed molten gold tiger-stripes across the road's surface. It was a good day to take his old jalopy for a spin.

He gave Doris Jarrod's care home a deferential nod as he drove by, tutted as Mark Wright made a glib comment over the intro to Miley Cyrus and Dua Lipa's *Prisoner*, before keeping tempo to the song by drumming his fingers against the dash.

His phone chirruped and he cast a glance at its screen.

'*Fucking hell. Two down already,*' James Jarrod's message read. '*Got any needles going spare?*'

Ryan chuckled and brought his eyes up to the road just as a white streak shot across his vision.

He spun the wheel, slammed down hard on the brake pedal, and hit the horn all at the same time.

'Jesus.'

Ryan twisted his neck and watched the sparkling-white vehicle which had cut him up disappear into an industrial estate.

He'd signalled left and turned towards Blaydon Rugby Club when realisation hit with the intensity of a lightning bolt.

High Level

He did a U-turn in the rugby club's car park and retraced his route.

Sure enough, he'd been right.

In front of a large white unit sporting the name *Grande Tyres*, a Berlingo, fresh from the car wash, was parked up. Two men, one tall and rangy, the other older and smaller, inspected the closed and shuttered tyre depot.

It wasn't the men who'd caught his attention. It was their vehicle. A vehicle emblazoned with a logo featuring three pyramids and the words WESTWOOD BUILDING CONTRACTORS.

No wonder the station couldn't find any trace of Wood Building Contractors. They'd been looking for the wrong company.

'It's shut, mate,' Ryan said as he pulled up alongside the Berlingo. 'Doesn't open Sundays.'

The older of the two men rolled his eyes. 'Aye, I can see that now, like.'

'You got a flat?' Ryan asked.

'Tyre looks ok,' said the other man, 'But I think me tracking's out. Wanted to get it checked.' He rubbed at the tattoo snaking out of his shirt collar. 'Can't be helped.'

'You must have a lot of work on, being out on a Sunday and all.'

'I never turn down overtime, me.'

'Is it your company?' Ryan asked the older man.

'You're joking. Wish it was. I'd be living it up in the Caribbean rather than slumming it in Hebburn.'

Ryan snickered. 'Is that where the company's based? Hebburn?'

'Nah. I just live there.'

The tattooed man plonked himself in the driver's seat, listening to the conversation.

'I could do with some work,' Ryan lied. 'Don't suppose there's any jobs going?'

'You'd have to ask HR about that, pal. Way above my pay grade.'

'So, it's a big company, is it? Westwood's?'

'Big enough to pay me wages. That's all that counts.' The older man opened the passenger side door.

'Is it your lot doing the refurb at the Byker Wall?' Ryan asked.

'Nope. Not us. That's not one of our contracts.'

'Really? Just I thought I saw one of your low-loaders there the other day. It looked like it said Wood, not Westwood, but it was definitely the same logo.'

The man pulled his seatbelt across his shoulder and clicked it into place. 'You're mistaken. It's definitely not one of wors. We do the snagging inspections for all the sites. I'd know if we were working on the Wall.'

The tattooed guy threw the Berlingo into reverse.

'See ya,' the older man shouted through the open window as they pulled away.

Ryan watched them leave.

'Yep,' he muttered to himself, 'I think you quite probably will.'

CHAPTER SEVENTEEN

MONDAY

Overnight, Ryan worked out what to do next. He ran his plan past Danskin even though he knew doing so always irked the Acting Super. Stephen Danskin liked his team to work on instinct but, when his plan risked the safety of a civilian, Ryan was always going to cover his arse.

He made his way to the ever-growing estate in North Tyneside and waited for Peter Kirk to answer the knock on his door. When he did, Ryan was pleased to see Uniform had fitted a security chain. Kirk slid the chain from the clasp and stood aside to let the detective through.

'I'm not coming in. I've got a cunning plan, and it involves you.'

Peter looked less than convinced. 'In what way?'

'Well, the good news is I know where the guy who attacked you works. It's not Wood Building Contractors: it's Westwood.'

'Right. And the bad news?'

'You're coming with me to identify him.'

'No, I'm not.'

'You are.'

'Listen, I don't want to confront him.'

Ryan put on a Mother Hen act. 'You won't have to. I promise you'll be safe.'

Ryan saw Kirk glance at the chain on the door, and up to the security camera above it.

Finally, Peter Kirk nodded. 'Ok. You've kept your promises so far. I believe you. Let's go before I change my mind.'

Ryan led the way to his Fiat, parked a few doors up on Cloverfield.

'Which one's yours?' Peter asked.

'The white Uno behind the Mondeo.'

'You've got the wrong guy.'

'Come again?'

Peter stared at the man sitting in the rear of Ryan's car. 'You've got the wrong man. That's not the bloke who assaulted me.'

Ryan laughed out loud. 'I know it's not.'

'Then, who is he?'

'His name's Todd. He's my colleague. Believe me, you'll be alright with Todd.'

Peter looked at the giant frame of Todd Robson squeezed into the tiny car. 'I do believe you. Nobody in their right mind would take him on. Not even the bloke from Wood's.'

'It's Westwood. And you're right. They won't. Which is why my Superintendent insisted I brought him with us.'

**

Back in Forth Street, Hannah and Lyall Parker reviewed the incident report of an assault on a female barista in a Quayside coffee bar.

'Do you reckon it was him?' she asked.

'Description fits. What he was wearing fits. The fact he gave his Da's name fits. Aye, I reckon it was Rats Scully.'

'At least we know he's still in the area, if it's him.'

'We do. It also proves he's a canny wee devil. Nobody's seen hide nor hair of him despite half the station looking for the bugger.'

Hannah sighed. 'I'm more sure than ever Scully's behind Warne's murder. This assault on the waitress shows what he's capable of. We're going to get him, Lyall, and beat Ryan to the punch.'

Lyall spoke clinically. 'It's no' a competition, Hannah. It's not us versus Ryan. It's us versus a murderer – whoever it turns out to be.'

'It's Scully. I know it is.'

High Level

She felt her phone vibrate against her thigh. She mouthed 'Excuse me' to Lyall while announcing herself as 'DS Graves' to the caller.

Lyall turned to the two crime boards while Hannah took the call. He glanced from the three women on Board A to Marvin 'Rats' Scully on Board B, and back again.

Behind him, he heard Hannah say, 'What the hell? Absolutely not! The bloody cheek of it. You should know better than to ask and, as for him, I'll have his guts for garters. I really don't know what to make of him anymore. You listen to me: I never want to have this conversation with you again. Understand? Never. Now, I'm busy. Goodbye.'

Lyall switched attention to Hannah, who stood shaking her head in the direction of her phone.

'Everything ok?' he asked.

'Yeah. Sort of. I think. I really don't know.'

'That's what I like about you, lassie: your decisiveness. Care to share what that was all about?'

She sucked in air. Pondered whether to say anything or not. Finally, she spoke in little more than a whisper.

'Remember what you said about it not being a competition between Ry and me? You're wrong. I think it just became one.'

Hannah continued staring at her phone, wondering why the hell Ryan had primed his brother to contact her about Marilyn Crawford.

**

Ryan's Fiat joined the Coast Road towards Newcastle at the Silverlink interchange. Inside it, Ryan and Todd Robson probed Peter Kirk for more information on Justin Warne.

'I don't know what more I can tell you,' Kirk protested. 'I don't know what he's like these days. Not really.'

'What was he like when you did know him?'

Peter chose his words carefully. 'A bit full of himself, I suppose. I never really knew whether it was false bravado or he really was a cocky so-and-so. He was a bright lad, that's for sure. Always confident he'd make a fortune somehow or other.'

Ryan checked his mirrors and pulled into the outside lane. 'Was he popular?'

'With the ladies, for sure. They warmed to his self-confidence more than the lads at Uni. I think the blokes all felt like I did: that he was a bit OTT with the *'look at me'* front.'

The Wills Building passed in a blur on their right-hand side. 'He met Hayley Mack at the LSE. Tell us about them.'

'She was into him more than he into her. It was because of him that Hayley moved up here. I'm sure you know that already.'

'Do you think she still fancied him? Was she jealous?'

Peter squirmed in his seat. 'You'd have to ask her. I hardly knew the woman. Look, where's this Westwood company based? Are we nearly there yet?'

Todd laughed. 'You sound like a five-year old kid on his way to the Hoppings. It'll be a while yet. Relax.'

Peter Kirk folded his arms and slunk down in his seat.

'Aye,' Todd said, 'Definitely a five-year old.'

They drove passed All Saint's Cemetery as they neared the City Centre. Ryan glanced over his shoulder at Peter. 'How'd he get into the property market?'

'I don't know. Justin did lots of things. Property, blogging, financial advice. That's the only reason I was still in contact with him. He knew the markets better than I know my own face.'

Ryan stopped for the red lights at the bottom of Osborne Road. As they changed to green, he signalled left and swiftly switched lanes onto the Central Motorway.

'He didn't own a car, though, did he? If he was so successful, don't you think it's a bit odd?'

High Level

'Not really, no. When I first met him, we'd just started at the LSE. We were little more than kids, and we were in London. The last thing we needed was a car.'

'You drive, though. For a living. It doesn't explain why Warne didn't.'

'I lasted one term at LSE before I realised it wasn't for me. I came home. Learned to drive then. By the time Justin returned to the area, he was twenty-two. He told me a few years back that he was already setting up contacts for life. Business contacts, like. Justin was focussed on business. I suppose he was already making a good living. Never got round to taking lessons. I'm only guessing, mind.'

A gust of wind caught the Fiat as it stopped and started in the traffic on the Tyne Bridge.

'Where are we going?' Peter asked. 'I thought we were going to catch my attacker.'

'We are.'

'But we're heading out of town.'

'Who said Westwood Building Contractors were based in Newcastle?' Ryan countered.

'*True*,' Peter thought but said nothing.

Traffic eased once they crossed the bridge and hit Old Durham Road, Gateshead-side of the Tyne. Peter relaxed as the questions lessened, too. In fact, it was Peter Kirk who asked the next one as the car left the main drag of the thoroughfare and headed into a residential area.

'Odd place for a building company, this, isn't it?'

Ryan replied with a question. 'How many times did you meet with Mr Warne over the last couple of years?'

Peter thought for a moment. 'I don't know. Probably no more than five. Why?'

'Where did you meet him?'

'Always at his house.'

'In Byker?'

Peter raised an eyebrow. 'Of course. That's where his house is.' Peter corrected himself. 'Was.'

The car drew to a halt. Ryan squinted out the window. 'One of them, yes.'

'Eh?'

'He had others. Several, in fact.' He pointed to a large semi-detached house on Evistone Road. 'This is one of them.'

'I don't understand. I thought you wanted to catch the bloke who's been following me.'

'We do, and we will. No harm in a little detour first, though, is there?'

Todd was already out the car, stretching his arms after their confinement. He stared up at Justin Warne's house. Lying in shadow, it stood dark, abandoned, and not a little forbidding.

'Now, who lives in a house like this?' Todd asked in the pseudo-Bostonian accent of Loyd Grossman.

**

The answer to Todd's question was: nobody. That much was obvious from the moment Ryan opened the front door with the key he'd signed out from the Forth Street basement storage room.

He nudged the door fully open with his elbow.

Justin Warne's house was cold, permeated with the musty odour of damp, while a thin but obvious film of dust coated the hallway's skirting boards. Ryan entered first, looking up at the high ceiling. He noticed a motion-sensor camera spring to life.

Todd followed, while Peter hung back in the doorway. 'Have you a warrant for this?' he asked. He felt uncomfortable breaking into his old friend's house. The house he knew nothing about.

'Uniform and Forensics have already been over the place.'

'That's not what I asked.'

High Level

Ryan turned, hands on hips. 'That's a bit rich, isn't it? I mean, it's not like you've never entered a property without permission, is it? Remember Raby Crescent?'

Peter stared at the floor.

'Now, come in and don't touch a bloody thing. Understand?'

Peter understood enough not to close the door behind him.

Ryan and Todd had donned their standard issue gloves by the time the threesome entered the main living room. The walls and ceiling were finished with artex plasterwork, the hardwood floor covered by a threadbare paisley-design carpet. Two straight-backed wooden dining chairs, an antique bureau, and a round, marble-effect coffee table stood on the carpet. High up in the corner of the room, angled towards the door, Ryan noticed another high-tech camera.

'Uniform were right,' Todd said, 'There's nowt here, is there?'

'Doesn't appear to be, no. Seems strange to me, though.'

'What does?'

'Everything. Like you say, there's nowt here, so why the cameras? And the front door was a composite. Super-strong structural frame, five lever Mortice lock. I mean, compared to the rest of the house, it's way over the top.'

The dining room was equally sparse, the fitted kitchen adequate but old-fashioned apart from another camera aimed at a back door protected by a pull-down metal shutter.

Ryan shook his head. 'Strange,' he repeated.

They made their way upstairs. The first bedroom was little more than a box room. Appropriately, it contained a chest-like Ottoman. Todd tugged at the lid. It opened freely and revealed nothing but stale air.

'Look, there's nothing here,' Peter Kirk said. He shifted his weight from one foot to the other. 'Can't we just find this Westwood firm? Or, better still, take me home?'

Ryan ignored him. 'I don't get it,' he said to Todd. 'There's nothing here. At Byker, he had nowt, either.'

'Apart from the IT stuff.'

'Exactly. All he's got here is a fortune in security cameras. I still think there's got to be something. I'm convinced, somewhere, there's a piece of kit, mebbe just a hard-drive, with the key to all this.'

'There is an alternative, Ryan.'

'Which is?'

'Warne's killing's got fuck all to do with his business interests. That Hannah's right and it's summat else.'

Ryan shook his head. 'Nah. I'm not having it.'

He led them out of the bedroom onto the landing. They headed for the rear bedroom. Ryan's blue gloves pushed at the door. It opened with a creak.

Three jaws dropped.

'What the fuck?' Todd said.

CHAPTER EIGHTEEN

A mid-afternoon, crystal-clear blue sky lured the unwary outdoors. The wind-chill factor of the blustery wind howling along the Ouseburn valley lowered the temperature by several degrees, capturing the foolhardy with its bite. Even in the shelter of the culvert, the cold penetrated Rats to the bone.

He needed food but didn't dare leave his hiding place. Scalding the miserable tart had been a mistake. Even more cops would be hunting for him, now. He smiled to himself. Still, it had been fun, though.

Rats fumbled in his pocket. Not for food, but for something even more warming. He brought out a small plastic money wallet.

'Shit.'

There were only a few grains of Ailsa Black's white lady clinging to the side of the bag, probably less than a quarter. Nowhere near enough for him to need the razorblade to crush it. Instead, he rolled a ten-pound note and inhaled the remnants of the package's contents directly from the bag.

The hit was almost instantaneous. It was also short-lived. He lost the buzz in less than ten minutes, and then the air's chill hit him hard. He shivered. Wrapped his arms around himself and shivered some more.

He gazed out the culvert into bright sunshine. Yet, he was cold, so fucking cold. He curled himself into the foetal position and stared at sewage pooled on the brick floor. White spots of light danced across his vision, but they were the spots of sun-blindness rather than euphoria.

Suddenly, as if a slideshow image had snapped into place, he knew how he'd warm himself.

Ouseburn City Farm, a small inner-city oasis within a desert of industrial land, lay only a few hundred yards away. The pandemic meant it remained closed to the public. There'd be no scruffy-arsed schoolkids twatting about - but the greenhouses of its nursery still stood. On a sunny afternoon, sheltered from the wind, how warm would it be inside? Fan-bloody-tastic.

Rats unzipped himself, added to the sewage, and crawled out into cold sunlight.

**

'Roger that. On my way.'

Michael McNeil smiled to himself. It happened every time he said it. He'd always thought of *'Roger that'* as childish innuendo, but perhaps that was him: childish.

Or, it had been him until boredom, lockdown, and unemployment led to the position he found himself in today.

Michael tugged at the hem of his hi-viz gilet as if it were a lifejacket. The blue Community Support Officer patch stitched to the rear of his coat proudly uncreased itself.

He finished his external tour of the Team Phoenix Martial Arts studio and, satisfied its alarm had sprung to life of its own volition rather than the result of illegal infiltration by a host of ninjas, he stepped into the sunlight of Lime Street in response to his next call.

Michael didn't need catch them red-handed to know they were up to no good. The hoodies pulled over their heads and scarves covering everything bar their eyes, was enough. The spray cans in their hands were simply an added bonus.

'Howay, lads. You got nowt better to do with your time?'

The three youths turned towards Michael and froze. 'Fuck. A rozzer,' one said.

High Level

Michael McNeil knew he needed to ensure the situation didn't escalate. Keep it cordial but let them know who's in charge. That's what he'd been taught.

'If you like this sort of thing, I'm sure there's a painter and decorator who could do with your help. This isn't the place for it, though; you know that, don't you?'

He looked at the paint sprayed on the wall of The Cluny. The youths had begun to daub it with a jungle scene, for some reason too obscure to fathom.

Although he deliberately kept the conversation light, he really meant it when he told them he liked it.

'It's really good, lads. The giraffe's brilliant. You've got it in proportion to the trees and the lion.' He thought it best not to tell them they were wrong including a tiger in the scene.

The smallest of the youths found his voice. 'Are you not going to arrest us, then?'

'Do you want me to?'

'Not fucking likely. Me ma'll kill us.'

'Okay, then; I won't. I should, but I won't. Not if you chuck your cans into those bushes.'

'Is this a wind up? You're letting us gan?'

'I am. But only for one reason. And it's not because of the giraffe.'

'What is it then?'

He pointed towards three letters sprayed on the wall in a 3-D effect. *SMB*, the letters said.

'You're Toonies. It's not the giraffe that's saved you. It's the Sad Mackem Bastards bit.'

The lads laughed. 'Yer aal reet, you. Do you knaa that?'

'Next time, though, I won't be. I'll be far from it. I'm round here all the time and, disguise or no disguise, I'll recognise you. So, keep a low profile, yeah?'

'Aye, we will.'

'You'd better. Now, chuck your cans away and get lost.'

They did. They threw their cans away and got lost via a sprint past Stepney Bank stables.

Michael McNeil gave the all-clear over the radio. He advised the operator to put the wall of The Cluny on the list for Community Service clean-up. 'Got anything else for me?'

'Negative.'

'Champion. That's me shift done. Signing off, and on me way back.'

**

Like hand grenades tossed into a bunker, three cans of spray paint rained down on Rats as he crouched in the bushes. He pawed one of them to one side.

He was yards from the farm; literally, just yards: within smelling distance of the horseshit. Then, he'd seen the bloody copper approaching him. Not even a real copper; one of those pretend ones.

Rats Scully wasn't going to be caught by a bloke living out his fantasy, so he'd rolled into the bushes as if he were in the SAS.

Rats heard the copper say, 'You got nowt better to do with your time?' and knew he wasn't speaking to him. He hunkered in the bushes, out of sight, with the sanctuary of City Farm within spitting distance.

As soon as the cop fucked off, he'd be safe. More importantly, he'd be warm.

Rats listened as the exchange between McNeil and the kids continued. *'Come on. Hurry up and fuck off out of there,'* he thought. He moved a few branches aside. Saw the unmistakeable footwear of a copper within three strides of him.

Rats held his breath.

He heard the yobs run off, laughing at their lucky escape. He listened as the copper signed-off. He waited for the cop to disappear.

And he lost his balance as his calf muscled spasmed into cramp.

Prone on the ground, Rats saw the boots turn in his direction as he rubbed his leg frantically.

'Oh, we've got another one, have we?' he heard the cop say. 'Howay then, son. Follow your mates off down the bank and I'll take the spraypaint, ta very much.'

The bushes in front of Rats parted and the stooped figure of Michael McNeil met him eyeball-to-eyeball.

'Howay, son. Out you come,' Michael said.

But there'd been a moment's hesitation. A change in tone. Rats knew he'd been recognised.

'Aal reet. Just giz a minute to get up, will you?'

Both Rats and McNeill stayed where they were.

'Give us a hand up.' Rats extended his left arm.

McNeil's lack of response confirmed what Rats already knew. The cop's demeanour had changed. He wasn't relaxed anymore. His frame was tense. His voice strained.

Rats struggled to his feet.

McNeill reached for his radio button.

Rats' arm flashed out. Drew a letter X in the air.

'Put your light sabre away, Scully,' Michael McNeil said.

At least, he tried to say it. Instead, the only thing which came from Michael McNeil's throat was a crimson fountain.

The razorblade's incision had been so swift, so neat, that McNeill felt no pain. His hands went to his neck; hands which instantly reddened as blood pumped between his fingers.

He fell to the ground. Rats watched, fascinated, as Michael's eyes bulged, and his legs jerked spastically. McNeil's mouth opened and closed, but no words came. Only a bubbling, gurgling sound and an eerie, haunting, whistle as air escaped the trachea.

Rats bent to wipe clean the razorblade on the grass. His eyes were inches from Michael McNeil's as he spoke.

'That one's for me Dad.'

CHAPTER NINETEEN

If the rest of Justin Warne's home appeared sparse, the chaotic clutter they discovered in the main bedroom more than made up for it. Ryan, Todd, and Peter Kirk stopped dead the moment the door opened, the mess inside a paradox to the rest of the house.

A dining table stood on its side against one wall. Its legs had been detached and were bound together with gaffer tape. Alongside them, a sofa bore the weight of two upturned armchairs. A single bed – no bedding or headboard – also stood upright. On the floor in front of them, a helter-skelter pile of wooden crates and boxes littered the laminate. Every box was empty.

Against the other wall, the surface of two office desks were obscured by a 50" plasma TV, a dozen or more recordable DVDs, a vacuum cleaner and, bizarrely, an electric lawnmower. A faux leather swivel chair completed the ensemble.

Ryan checked the contents against an inventory he'd called up on his smartphone.

'These are all in the report, but there's nothing to say they were all crammed into one room.'

Todd fingered a DVD. 'What's these for?'

'I don't know. For his CCTV, perhaps? He's got enough cameras, that's for sure,' Ryan said, looking at another above the curtainless bedroom window.

'What's Forensics say about them?'

Ryan scanned another document on his phone. 'All the DVDs are blank. There's also no prints on them, apparently.'

High Level

He twisted his mouth. 'In fact, there's absolutely nowt on 'em. No fibres, no DNA, not a sausage.'

Todd wandered to the window. A red light glowed on the camera as he approached it. The camera followed his hand as he waved it in front of the lens.

'The CCTV's the only thing that works in here. Why the hell's he got all this security when there's nothing worth nicking?'

Ryan thought for a moment. 'Not now, there's not. What if there was at some point, though? What if all this stuff's piled up here because someone's already raked through it?'

'Forensics would know if somebody had been at it, man.'

'If it was recent, aye; but what if it's been like this for weeks? Warne spent most of his time in Byker, didn't he? Perhaps somebody rooted through his stuff weeks ago and he never even knew about it.'

Todd frowned. 'What would they want to look for?'

'Details of the deal for Moot Hall.'

'Howay, man, Ryan. Ravi's already said there's no record of the transaction ever showing up.'

'Precisely – and I always said I suspected there was a missing laptop. Some bugger's either got it, or been here looking for it.'

'It'd be on camera, man.'

'Wouldn't matter if somebody took the discs.'

Ryan and Todd stood in silence, taking stock. Outside the window, the burble of lawnmower engine on the cricket club's outfield infiltrated Justin Warne's bedroom. Its buzzing distracted their attention like a bluebottle at a picnic.

'Fascinating.'

Todd and Ryan both said, 'What?'

Peter Kirk tilted his head towards the bedroom walls. They were adorned by framed prints. Although they filled almost the entire room, Ryan and Todd had barely paid them any attention.

'Fascinating,' Peter said again.

'They're fucking pictures, man,' Todd spat. 'And, *Fascinating* isn't the word I'd use to describe them, Mr Spock. They're a pile of shite.'

Peter Kirk gave a benign, almost sympathetic, smile. 'To you, they may be a pile of shite. To Justin, though, they'd be things of beauty.'

Ryan's eyes took in the framed prints. 'They're all of the same thing, aren't they? Different angles, but the same subject.'

Kirk shook his head. 'No, no. This,' he said, pointing at a dowdy grey image, 'Is a close-up of a window frame from Pearl Assurance House.' He looked at another print, a featureless concrete slab. 'And unless I'm mistaken, this is part of Bewick Court.'

'Still just a pile of shite, as far as I'm concerned.'

'That's a shame, Todd. You see, this pile of shite, as you call it, is part of an architectural feat seldom replicated. Bewick Court was a tower block built on top of a raised piazza which straddled John Dobson Street. '

'Look, nowt you've got to say will persuade me it's nowt but bollocks.'

'I'm really pleased I came, now,' Peter said. 'Thanks for showing me this. I feel I'm getting to know Justin all over again.'

Todd began to speak again, but Ryan hushed him. 'Listen, Peter, if there's anything about Warne we can learn from this, I want to hear it.'

'Are we still going to Westwood?'

'Yes. After you've broadened our minds on, to use Todd's words, this pile of shite.'

Peter gazed longingly at the slab of concrete. 'It was part of a dream...'

'Bloody nightmare, if you ask me,' Todd interrupted.

High Level

Kirk ignored him. 'The dream was to build a network of raised walkways. To build a city above a city. The roads and pollution and noise stayed below, the pedestrianised city built proudly above.'

'What happened?'

'The visionary got arrested.'

'Who? Somebody related to Warne?'

Peter laughed. 'No. T Dan Smith, that's who. He's a bit of a hero of mine. I happen to think he was much maligned and totally misunderstood.' Peter's eyes circled the room. 'I think Justin thought much the same.'

'Wait, Smith built the Byker Wall, didn't he?'

'Well, he didn't exactly lay any bricks if that's what you mean, but it was his brainchild. Most of the other shots in this room are part of the Wall, I reckon. Look, there's even a framed blueprint in the corner, over there.'

Ryan scratched his nose.

'Okay. So, I get why Warne wanted to own part of the Wall if that sort of thing floated his boat, but it doesn't gel with his involvement in the purchase of something like Moot Hall. It's like, I dunno, comparing Anne Hathaway to Ann Widdecombe.'

Peter laughed. 'Except you're forgetting something you already know. Justin wasn't buying Moot Hall. He was just a middle-man using it as a means to fill his wallet.'

Kirk was right. Ryan told him so before checking his watch. 'We need to get a move on. Things to do; people to see. Starting with your mate from Westwood's.'

**

Westwood Building Contractor's lay hidden in the strata of Birtley's Portobello Industrial Estate less than five miles from Warne's house overlooking Gateshead Fell cricket club.

As Ryan pulled the Fiat off the A1231 onto Shadon Way, the atmosphere in the car became tense.

'What are we going to do when we get there?' There was a tremor in Kirk's voice.

'Don't worry. You'll be fine. Me and Todd'll make sure of that.'

As if to reinforce the message, Todd flexed his bicep. 'Hard as steel, that.'

'You don't know him. He's no wimp either.'

'I know. I can see by the state of your face. You look like a map of Ireland. Don't worry, he won't get near you this time.'

Ryan jumped in. 'All we'll do, to begin with, is have a tootle round the car park. See if you can spot his truck.'

'It's the bit after the *'to begin with'* I'm worried about.'

Ryan slowed as he looked up at the units. They drove past Tor Coatings before taking an angular left turn.

'If we don't see the truck,' Ryan said, 'You know he's not there. All's good. If we do see it, I note the reg, walk into the office, ask to speak to him.'

'Then what?'

'I nick him, that's what. Job done. And, before you ask, Todd stays in the car with you at all times.'

A JT Dove warehouse lay to their right, beyond it, BOC Gas.

'Here we are,' Ryan said.

Peter Kirk whispered, 'Shit' as the Fiat drove through open metal gates emblazoned with three pyramids.

A twelve-bay car park lay outside an oblong building clad in multi-coloured panelling.

'It's a bloody Rubik's Cube,' Todd joked. Peter didn't laugh as they manoeuvred through another set of gates to the rear of the building.

Here, the car park was significantly larger. A fleet of Berlingos, clones of the one Ryan had spotted at Grande Tyres in Whickham, sat nearest the Rubik's Cube. Beyond it, outside a whitewashed concrete building the size of an aircraft hangar, an assortment of trucks waited to be loaded or unloaded.

High Level

Ryan cruised the plot with the eye of a kerb-crawler.

'Shit. That's it! There!'

They followed the line of Peter's outstretched hand. A truck with a cab so filthy, the first syllable of the company's name was completely obscured. It did, for all the world, read WOOD BUILDING CONTRACTORS. Only the unmistakeable pyramids, gold, red, and blue, gave the game away.

'I want to leave now. I don't want to see the animal again. Let's get of here. Please.'

'Calm doon, man,' Todd said. 'How many times do we have to tell you that he's not getting anywhere near you?'

Ryan photographed the registration plate with his camera phone before he looped the Fiat around the yard and into the front office car park.

'Right. Let's find out who this character is, and what he's up to.'

All three occupants turned towards the building, and all three occupants jumped as a palm slammed against the rear window three times.

They turned as one to see a rugged face scowling in at them, nose pressed against the glass.

Kirk jumped the length of the backseat.

'That's him!'

Ryan was out the car in a second. 'I'd like a word with you, sir.'

'Stay out of this. I'm not interested in you. It's the little runt inside I'm after'. The man raised his voice. 'You,' he shouted at Peter. 'Out the car. Now!'

Ryan moved around the Uno. 'Step away from the vehicle.'

The truck driver snorted. 'Who do you think you are, the frigging police?'

'What's your name?'

'Piss off. I don't need speak to you.'

'I'm afraid you do.'

'Oh yeah?' the man balled his fists.

Ryan raised his hands, a submissive gesture. 'That's not a good idea, sir.'

The hulk stepped forward. Threw a punch which Ryan sidestepped with ease. The man swung again. Hit fresh air as Ryan ducked.

Todd Robson flung open the back door as the man lined up another punch.

'Don't leave me!' Peter shrieked.

Todd left him.

The construction worker saw his opportunity. He flung open the door nearest Peter and grabbed him by the hair.

Kirk squealed again.

Another squeal followed. This time, it came from Kirk's assailant. Todd had one arm around the man's neck in a stranglehold restraint while the other viciously twisted the brute's right arm behind his back.

Robson wrestled the man to the ground, facedown. Todd knelt on his back while Ryan rifled the man's pockets. He pulled out a wallet, flicked through it, and extracted a driver's licence.

'George Riley, you're under arrest for assaulting a police officer.'

**

'What were you doing at the Byker Wall last Thursday?'

Ryan was seated opposite George Riley in Custody Suite three. In the absence of other senior members of Danskin's team, Detective Sergeant Sue Nairn sat in on the interview.

'Seeing a mate.' Riley slouched back in his seat, arms folded across his broad chest.

'Name?'

Riley remained silent.

'What's this friend's name?' Ryan repeated.

'Dunno. Somebody I work with.'

'Do Westwood Building Contractors have the tender for renovation work on the Byker Wall?'

High Level

'No. I didn't say it did. I worked with this guy on another project. Someone – before you ask, I can't remember who – told me he'd seen him at the Wall. I was passing so thought I'd pop in for a chat.'

'A chat?'

'Aye. That's what I said, wasn't it?'

'With a bloke who's name you don't know.'

Riley chewed on his bottom lip.

Ryan took a deliberate pause before switching attack. 'Why were you following Peter Kirk?'

'I wasn't.'

'You threatened him outside the Bridge Hotel, later that same day.'

'I threatened him? Ha! Other way round, more like. He swore at me for parking too close to him.'

Ryan passed a sheet of paper across the table. 'Is this your handwriting?'

Riley gave the note a cursory glance. 'No comment.'

'Okay. We can easily check. For the tape, the note I'm showing Mr Riley is Item 2B. Part of the note reads, *I know where you live. I'll be seeing you, Peter Kirk. Soon.*'

Ryan turned a page of his notebook.

'On Saturday, two days later – I make that *'soon'*, by anyone's reckoning - you assaulted Peter Kirk outside his home.'

'Who says I did? Kirk?' He sneered. 'Not exactly independent, is he?'

Ryan set the papers aside. Interlocked his fingers on the edge of the desk. Rolled his shoulders.

'Earlier today,' Ryan continued, 'You approached Peter Kirk and threatened him.'

'No, I didn't.'

'You said, and I quote, *'It's the little runt I'm after.'* Do you remember saying that?'

Riley tugged at his ear. 'Might have. But that's not a threat, is it? I didn't say what I wanted him for.' His eyes flicked to the floor. 'I'm not that sort of bloke.'

Ryan opened another file. 'That's not true.'

'Are you saying I'm a liar?'

Ryan looked up from the papers and met Riley's stare with one of his own. 'I am.'

Ryan held up an A4 sheet, 'This says you received a caution and a restraining order for stalking an ex-girlfriend.' He sifted out another leaf. 'This one relates to a charge of Criminal Damage.'

'For fuck's sake, that was years ago.'

Ryan nodded. 'Four and a half years ago.'

'Aye. Yonks ago. I'm not the same person, nowadays.'

'What happened?'

'I was stitched up. They said I smashed an ex-gaffer's windscreen after he sacked me.'

'What really happened?'

'It wasn't the windscreen. It was the side window.'

Ryan watched Riley for a full minute. Waited until the big man squirmed in his seat, then he moved in.

'What's your connection with Justin Warne?'

The man across the desk folded his arms behind the plexi-glass divider. 'Who?'

'Justin Warne.'

'I didn't kill him.'

'I thought you didn't know him?'

'That's why I didn't kill him.'

'Why were you outside his Byker Wall address?'

Riley deflated. 'Look, I was only asked to find out what he was doing.'

Ryan and Sue Nairn exchanged glances.

'Who by?' Nairn asked, speaking for the first time.

Riley jumped at the sound of the new voice.

'What?'

High Level

'Who asked you to follow Justin Warne?'

Riley opened his mouth to answer at the same time as the interview room door flung open.

'Don't answer any more questions,' a large, florid-faced woman announced, striding into the room. A sheepish Nigel Trebilcock followed her, mouthing 'Sorry' to Ryan and Sue.

George Riley's eyes shifted towards her.

'I'm Celia Groenweld. I'm your solicitor. The detective's are finished with you. Aren't you?' It was an order, not a question.

Ryan didn't recognise the woman, but Sue Nairn did. She knew Groenweld was a formidable defence lawyer. One of the best.

'I assume you have sufficient to charge my client for the incident in the car park of Westwood Building Contractors?'

Ryan blinked at the front of the woman. 'Yes. Assaulting a police officer.'

'Did you announce yourself as police?'

'Well..'

'It's a simple question, detective. Did you inform my client that you were a police officer?'

'No.'

'Then the charge is attempted assault, not actual assault, and you drop the police officer element. You weren't in uniform, and you didn't declare yourself.'

Groenweld stared at Ryan. 'Get on with the charge, and then you release Mr Riley. You have no grounds for detaining my client in custody. None, whatsoever. This interview is officially over.'

George Riley grinned like the Cheshire cat.

CHAPTER TWENTY

Upstairs in the bullpen, Ryan rocked back and forth in his chair whilst shredding strips of paper as if pulling pork.

'I ballsed up good and proper down there. I could kick myself.'

'Not a bit of it, Ryan. You were most impressive, I thought.' Sue Nairn reached towards him, then withdrew her arm as her natural reticence took charge.

'Okay, if not down there, I did when I arrested Riley. I should have said I was police.'

'Yes. You should.'

Ryan snorted. 'Thanks. That makes me feel a load better.'

'Just being honest, Ryan. Listen, the interview was textbook. Well done. Yes, you made one mistake, but not everybody has Celia Groenweld on their side.'

'I thought she was gonna burst a blood vessel, the colour of her.'

'She always looks like that.'

'Blood pressure?'

Sue shook her head. 'Whisky.'

Ryan laughed. 'Now, that does make me feel better.'

They sat in silence. Ryan had never warmed to DS Nairn. He found her impossible to read, and consequently had never got to know her. It was a bit late for small talk now, but Ryan asked, 'Not long left with us, Sue.'

DS Nairn sat up straight while she looked around her. 'Shhh. I don't want a fuss. No big leaving do or anything, I just want to walk out of here one day and not come back the next. Just like that.'

'Where are you transferring to?'

'I'm going north. Lyall Parker's territory.'

'Really? Granite City Constabulary?'

Sue tittered. 'Not literally Lyall's territory. I meant Scotland. And I'm not transferring. I'm getting out altogether.'

'No way, man. Really? Why?'

'It's just my time, Ryan. I need to go. I'm worn down by it all. The hours. The shifts. The cuts. I've had it up to here,' she angled her hand at brow height.

'So, what are you doing?' His question was almost drowned out by a train squealing like a stuck pig at Platform 9 of the adjacent Central Station.

Sue laughed again, staid and controlled, but a laugh, nonetheless. 'I'm joining that lot.' She tilted her head in the direction of the sound. 'Head of Security and Business Continuity with ScotRail. I'll be based in Glasgow.'

Ryan whistled. 'Bit of a change, like.'

Sue shrugged. 'Who knows? Anyway,' she stood to leave, 'We're in good hands with you and Hannah.'

'I've got to pass the exam first.'

'You've got this, Ryan. Trust me.'

Ryan thought for a moment. 'You off somewhere?'

'Not really, no. Just to file my report of our Riley interview for Lyall and the Acting Super. Why?'

'Do you fancy a coffee? I'd value your opinion on something.'

'Sure.'

'Not here, though. Outside.'

**

They sat on concrete steps outside the Basil Hume Memorial Garden clutching the Styrofoam cups they'd filled from a Sainsbury's Local.

Sue Nairn sat upright, knees clasped tightly together. 'I'm not the right one to give you relationship advice, Ryan. In fact, I'm the last one you should ask. I'm not exactly the most worldly-wise person in Danskin's squad.'

'I disagree. No disrespect, but that's exactly why you're the right one. Hannah and I both work to Lyall, Gavin was my mentor, Ravi and Treblecock I've worked closely with in the past. That leaves Danskin – and I don't want to involve him.'

'He's fine, you know, is Stephen. I think he'd listen.'

'No. I can't.' He didn't expand. Only Lyall Parker knew Hannah Graves was Stephen Danskin's stepdaughter.

'What about Todd?'

Ryan stared at her, open-mouthed and wide-eyed.

Sue let out a genuine, hearty laugh. Coffee exploded from her mouth. 'Yep, that look just about says it all. I guess that leaves you with this old spinster, then.'

'Aye. Desperate times, yeah?'

They both smiled and took a sip from their cups.

'Actually, Sue, it's not Dear Deirdre type advice I'm after. It's more protocol, really. You see, I think neither me nor Hannah really want to hurt each other, or hurt ourselves, for that matter. Because of that, we're a bit frightened to get close again, so we go the other way. We're actively pushing against each other.'

'I should warn you I'm even less of a psychologist than I am Agony Aunt.'

'Bear with me. I'm getting to the point. We all know that it would be inappropriate for Hannah and me to continue a relationship if we're of different rank, yeah?'

'It would.'

'But, if we were equals, we'd be fine.'

'You were together long enough before Hannah got promoted so, as DCs, it might be awkward but it's not against our ethics code.'

A flotilla of buses streamed along Neville Street, offloading their cargo at the stops alongside the Central Station car park. Ryan watched them before speaking again.

'Before, you mentioned you'd be leaving Forth Street in safe hands if Hannah and I passed our Sergeant's exam.

High Level

That's fine, but if only one of us did, me and Hannah wouldn't have a future. So, we either both pass or we both fail.'

'You'll pass. I know you will.'

Ryan stared up at the sky. 'Unless I don't want to.'

Sue Nairn turned to face him. 'You don't mean that, Ryan.'

'I don't know what I mean. Me heed's done in at the minute.'

'Women, eh?'

'Exactly. They mess with your head.'

'Work's the other way, too, you know. That's why I never married. I didn't want any distractions, and where did that get me? Nowhere, Ryan Jarrod; absolutely bloody nowhere – except heading out on a new life on my lonesome.'

She finished the dregs of her drink. The streets filled with men and women spewed out from their closing offices. The few college students not working from home mingled with them.

Sue stood and smoothed the creases from her trousers. 'I need to be getting back. It's been a long day and it's not done yet. Listen, all I can suggest is you think very carefully about what you do. It's not just your career you're playing with, it's your future.'

She looked down into Ryan's eyes. 'You two need to talk.'

Ryan sighed. 'Wait up; I'll head back with you. I've some talking to do.'

**

Ryan and Sue Nairn pushed open the bullpen's swing doors and walked straight into Hannah Graves on her way out.

'The very person...' Ryan said.

'You and me need to talk. Now.'

'You took the words right out of my mouth.'

Sue Nairn winked at Ryan as he and Hannah walked out into the third floor lobby.

'I was just say...'

'What the hell do you think you're playing at?' She pushed him vigorously in the chest, so vigorously he stumbled back a couple of steps.

His hands shot up in a submissive gesture. 'Whoa. What's that for?'

She pushed him again. 'You've lost the bloody plot, you have. What you did goes against everything in the book.'

'Hannah, man, I haven't a clue what you're talking about.'

'Your brother, that's what I'm talking about. Your brother and Maz Crawford.'

'Ah. That.'

'Yes, *'that'*.'

'He called you, I take it.'

Her face was red with fury. 'Yes. What the hell do you think you're doing, sticking your nose into my investigation?'

'I wasn't…'

'You just can't bear the thought that I'm onto something, and you're barking up the wrong line of enquiry.'

Ryan tried to diffuse the situation with humour. 'I don't think that metaphor really works, Hannah.'

'Fuck off with your clever-dick comments. You can't bring yourself to admit that Justin Warne's murder's got sod all to do with his business interests and everything to do with Rats Scully, can you?'

'Wait til I work my way through those double-negatives.'

'Fuck-right-off! Besides, Crawford might not only be a witness in the case, she could be connected to it in some way.'

'Hadawayandshite, man.'

'You. Don't. Know. That. If she is, you could have endangered your own brother.'

Ryan turned away from her. 'This is bollocks. You've no idea what you're talking about.'

High Level

She grabbed him by the wrist. Swung him around. Ryan was taken aback by her strength. Her anger. Her…hatred.

'When this case is solved, one of us transfers out of Danskin's squad. If you don't, I will.'

Ryan opened his mouth to respond when the bullpen doors opened.

Lyall Parker.

'Shit,' Ryan groaned. He thought they were in for a bollocking. Until he saw the sombre look on his face. Morose. Bereft, almost.

'The Super wants a wee word wi' us all,' Parker said, his gentle tones even softer than usual.

The squad were huddled together, social distances ignored. Stephen Danskin stood in the centre of the circle. 'I've got some sad news to announce,' he said, eyes cast downwards. 'One of our Community Support Officers was found dead earlier today. Michael McNeil.'

Danskin raised his head. 'He was only thirty-one, and he was found with his throat slit.'

'Jesus.'

'Fucking hell.'

'Shit, man.'

Danskin allowed them to let off steam before continuing. 'McNeil answered a routine call to sort out some anti-social behaviour near The Cluny. He radioed in to say he'd cleared the incident before he signed off. It was the last anyone heard from him.'

Ryan and Trebilcock exchanged glances. The last time something like this happened, they'd both been at the heart of the incident; PC Frank Burrows taken inside Dunston's Derwent Tower by the Tyneside Tyrant. The fact that neither knew McNeil didn't soften the blow.

'A young lass with her bairn in a pushchair saw his boots sticking out from some bushes. He'd been sliced open like cod by a fishmonger.'

'Bastarding bastards.' Todd's words summed up the squad's feelings.

'I just thought I should let you know. DCI Kinnear's mob are dealing with the initial situation but once we get the forensic reports in, I expect us all to be involved. This is one of our own. This takes priority over everything.'

The assembly nodded their grim agreement.

'But, until then, we carry on with our tasks. I want everything else wrapped up so we can concentrate on finding the bastards who did this. Understand?'

'Sir,' the group responded.

'Good. Now, it's been a long day. I suggest those who have been on duty since first knockings get some rest. Tomorrow will be even longer.'

Danskin returned to his office, the squad stood around murmuring to one another. Despite their downcast heads, Ryan and Hannah caught each other's eyes; their dispute small beer compared to this. They both flushed in embarrassment.

Sue Nairn rescued Ryan.

'Listen, before we all get switched to Michael McNeil's case, I thought you should know something.'

'Yeah?'

'Well, it's just dawned on me. This George Riley bloke, he doesn't strike me as being loaded with cash.'

Ryan had almost forgotten about Riley. Was it really today he'd interviewed him?

'Nor me.'

'It's just his solicitor, Celia Groenweld, is about as expensive as they come.'

'So?'

'So: who's picking up the tab?'

Ryan thought for a moment.

'Westwood Building Contractors,' he answered.

CHAPTER TWENTY-ONE

TUESDAY

Ryan was in his Fiat outside the multi-coloured patchwork exterior of Westwood Building Contractors. He'd had all night to work out an approach. The best he came up with was to wing it.

Inside, the foyer was compact yet tidy and flooded with natural light. A couple of low coffee tables, each with three seats around them, sat next to a water dispenser. On the wall above them, a sign indicated neither chairs nor dispenser were to be used due to Covid restrictions. Ryan's hand subliminally checked his face covering.

A young man with slicked-back black hair looked up from the front desk. 'How can I help you?' His eyes relayed the smile hidden beneath his multi-coloured facemask.

Ryan showed his warrant card and noticed the man's eyebrows lift. 'Detective Constable Ryan Jarrod, City and County police. I'd like to talk to Mr Westwood.'

'Mr Westwood is no longer with us,' the receptionist said.

'He's sold up?'

'He's died.'

'Oh,' was all Ryan managed in response. Inwardly, he chided himself. He should have done his research.

'It was around eighteen months ago. You may wish to speak with Suzanne, that's his wife. She runs the company nowadays.'

'Is she free?'

The man checked Suzanne Westwood's diary on his screen. 'She's scheduled for a Zoom meeting momentarily, but I'll see if she can afford you a few minutes. Bear with me.' The young man disappeared into a back office.

While he waited, Ryan studied the lobby. The walls doubled as a glossy brochure for Westwood, adorned as they were with framed shots of their refurbishment work. Testimonials from auspicious clients hung alongside each picture.

'Detective Jarrod, this is Suzanne Westwood.'

Ryan quickly surveyed Mrs Westwood. He believed she was probably younger than her salt and pepper hair suggested. Unless she'd had some seriously good work done, he guessed she'd be mid-forties at most. Her clothing was dowdier than he'd expected to see, which added to the age conundrum.

'This way,' she said brusquely. 'I haven't long.'

She led the way along a short corridor into an unprepossessing office dominated by Suzanne Westwood's desk. Ryan managed the complicated task of maintaining eye contact whilst taking in the office with his peripheral vision.

Westwood's desk held a monitor screen and a Surface Pro hybrid laptop. A number of post-it notes, in almost as many colours as the building's cladding, lay on the desk's surface. To one side was a framed photograph of Suzanne Westwood with, Ryan presumed, her late husband and their daughter. Next to it was a telephone handset, and a mobile phone plugged in and on charge.

A plastic stress-ball - pink, knobbly, and with arms and goggly eyes – lay in front of the monitor screen. A mug adorned with the corporate three-pyramid logo matched the picture on the wall behind Suzanne Westwood.

'Thanks for meeting me at such short notice, Mrs Westwood.'

'No problem. And, it's Suzanne, please.' She gave him a taut smile. 'I'm happy with you removing your mask in here. None of my staff will interrupt us.' Her hands mimed the unhooking of a mask as Ryan performed the action.

'Now,' she continued, 'I haven't long so I presume this is about Mr Riley's shenanigans in the carpark.'

'Yes, ma'am.'

'First thing you should know is he's been given his P45. He no longer works for us.'

'Did you hire him in the first place?'

Suzanne Westwood chuckled and waved a hand airily. 'I have an HR department doing that sort of thing.'

'Did you do the firing?'

'In this instance, I most definitely did. As soon as I heard of the incident, I instructed my HR director, Stewart Crossland, to sack Mr Riley immediately. Please, feel free to ask Mr Crossland directly.'

'There'll be no need for that.' Ryan leant forward slightly. 'Did you hire a solicitor for him?'

'Who?' She cleared her throat.

'George Riley. Did you book his solicitor?'

Her eyes narrowed. 'Why would I do that?'

'That's what I'd like to find out. You see, his lawyer is Celia Groenweld, and she comes way out of his means.'

Suzanne Westwood straightened in her chair. She interlocked her fingers and looked downwards at them. 'Yes. We arranged for Celia Groenweld to represent him.'

Ryan hadn't expected an honest answer. 'Okay. Let's get this straight. You hired one of the most expensive solicitors in Newcastle to represent a man you'd just fired? Why would you do that?'

Mrs Westwood glanced at the wall above Ryan's head. He assumed there was a clock on the wall behind him.

'I didn't recruit Ms Groenweld for George Riley's sake. I recruited her for my business. You see, Detective Jarrod, in this line of work, what you see is what you get. If word got out that Westwood Building Contractors had been involved in an assault on a police officer, no matter how indirectly, Mr Riley's actions would be seen as my actions. The damage to my business would be incalculable.'

Ryan fixed Suzanne with a glare. 'Were they your actions, Mrs Westwood?'

Anger flashed across her face. 'No, most certainly not. I would never advocate any sort of violence, let alone against a police officer.' She glanced at her watch. 'Now, if we're done, I really need to do some prep for my meeting.'

Ryan ignored her. 'Mr Riley indicated he was asked to look into Justin Warne.'

'Justin who?'

'He brokered a deal to purchase Moot Hall. Turn it into des res apartments.'

'And?' Suzanne Westwood lifted a couple of post-its from her desk. Replaced them in the same position.

Ryan took a wild punt. Make or break time.

'Westwood Building Contractors have the contract for the internal renovation of Moot Hall.'

He knew he'd backed a winner by the look on her face.

'That was supposed to be confidential information.'

'There's no such thing in a murder investigation.'

'Murder?'

'Yes.'

'Justin Warne is dead?'

'Most murder victims tend to be dead, yes.'

Suzanne shrank back in her seat. 'Fuck me.'

Quickly, she regained her composure. 'Sorry. That was most unprofessional. Please, forgive me.'

'So, you see, I'm interested in Mr Riley for more than assault.'

'My God. You think I had something to do with the death of Justin Warne?'

'You've just admitted having a clandestine business relationship with a murdered man, Mrs Westwood. You can see why I'm curious, to say the least.'

'I think I need a solicitor.'

'Celia Groenweld?'

High Level

'I'm not saying anything further, detective.'

Ryan offered Suzanne a reassuring smile. 'For what it's worth, I do believe you're not involved. Not directly, anyway. It would really help us with our enquiries if you explained exactly why you had George Riley check out Mr Warne.'

Suzanne Westwood put both hands to her forehead and rubbed so vigorously the motion left blotchy red marks above her eyebrows.

'I didn't trust the man, that's why.'

'Why not?'

Her eyes flicked to one side, then back again. 'I'd heard he'd been involved in some shady practices. You know he'd been evicted from the office he rented, don't you?'

Ryan said nothing.

'I heard on the grapevine it was something to do with the Moot Hall deal. I didn't want to fall into the same trap.'

'Trap?'

'Yes. The trap Lola Di Marco fell into it. He usurped her on the purchase of Moot Hall. I didn't want the same happening to me.'

'So, this grapevine you heard from: it was Ms Di Marco, I take it?'

'No. It wasn't.'

'But it was somebody in her company, right? North Umbria Estates?'

Suzanne tossed back her head and laughed. 'Wrong tree, Detective.'

'Who was it?' Ryan asked, impatiently.

She rocked back and forth in her chair, more relaxed than at any time during the interview.

'The word came from inside a company by the name of High Level Properties. You need to ask for a Beth Richards.'

**

Ryan stood outside Cale Cross House feeling like he'd just slid down a snake back to square one. In the depths of his mind, he desperately sought a ladder.

He ruminated on the connections between High Level Properties and North Umbria Estates, Beth Richards and Suzanne Westwood, and Justin Warne and the lot of them.

An unsettling ripple washed through Ryan's stomach like a seventh wave. He'd missed something; something so obvious it drove him to distraction. Whatever it was he'd heard or seen, it held the key. He was sure of it. The trouble was, he had no idea where the key lay.

He put the distraction to one side and pushed through the revolving door into the home of High Level Properties.

Lynne Casey, in her pale blue blouse above navy blue slacks, smiled as Ryan approached her redwood desk.

'Nice to see you again, Detective.'

'You've a good memory.'

'We tend not to get many visits from the police, surprisingly enough. How can I help you?

'Beth Richards – is she back from holiday?'

'She is, yes. Miss Richards returned yesterday.'

'I'd like to speak to her.'

The receptionist spoke into a telephone for a few moments, then was put on hold. Lynne covered the mouthpiece with her hand. 'Sorry about this. I won't be long. We're just checking her diary.'

'We?'

'Ursula Maddox, to be exact. She...' her attention returned to the telephone 'Oh, thank you. I'll send him up.'

'She's free?'

Lynne Casey said, 'You know the way. Twelfth floor. Ms Maddox will meet you.'

'I don't want Ursula Maddox. I want the organ grinder.'

Lynne Casey laughed. 'You obviously know Miss Richards by reputation. Twelfth floor,' she repeated.

High Level

Ursula Maddox was waiting for him, but only to shepherd him into an office where Beth Richards sat like a pharaoh queen in a shrine built for herself.

The walls were covered in photographs of Richards with the great and the good. A trophy cabinet displayed an assortment of awards, plaques, and crystal all engraved with the name *'Beth Richards'*.

The woman herself stood and moved around the desk; her hand extended. She wore a short maroon miniskirt and an understated teal blouse. Richards's heels were high and her perfume rich.

She returned to her chair and sat before motioning for Ryan to do likewise.

'I gather we missed each other last time. How may I help you, DC Jarrod?'

'It's about Justin Warne.'

'Dreadful news,' she said with a shake of her head. 'I heard the moment I got back in the office.'

'When was that?'

'Yesterday. I really never know why I take time off. I always have so much to catch up on.'

'How was your holiday?' Ryan asked, building up a rapport, playing it cool.

A shadow crossed Beth's face. 'Not as good as I'd expected.'

'I'm sorry to hear that.'

'Not half as sorry as I am.'

Ryan paused to signify a change in mood. 'How well did you know Justin?'

'So-so. He worked out of this office, was partly employed here, but he did a lot of freelance stuff, too. That's why we charged him for office space.'

'Beyond that?'

Beth shook her head. 'Nothing beyond that. He kept himself to himself.'

'There was a complaint made against him…'

'Lola Di Marco.' Beth's nose wrinkled. 'We don't get on. Competition, and all that.'

'You think she made the complaint to cause trouble for your company?'

Beth flicked her long hair with both hands. 'It happens all the time. I wasn't worried about her. The complaint wasn't why I served notice on him.'

'Why did you?'

Beth Richards sighed. 'Attitude, Detective Jarrod. May I call you Ryan?'

Ryan nodded. 'What do you mean by his attitude?'

Beth pursed her lips. 'Unprofessional. Demanding. Overbearing. Sometimes, almost bullying. I don't need that here.'

'Are you aware of any major transactions Mr Warne was working on?'

Beth inhaled sharply through her nose. Ryan saw her lips tighten before she regained her poise. 'You're talking about Moot Hall, aren't you?'

Ryan inclined his head.

'Yes. He did do work on that for me. I've no doubt Lola Di Marco told you that, too. Well, as it happens, he did renege on his work for her – but he also let me down, too.'

'Go on.'

'He signed a deal with an unknown third party.'

'Not you?'

'It wouldn't be an unknown party if he was acting for High Level.'

'How did you feel about that?'

'How do you think? Pretty pissed off, actually, but not unexpected. As I said, Mr Warne was selfish and unprofessional. It wasn't the first time he'd done it, either.'

'So, that's why you ordered him out.'

Beth Richards gave a light, vaguely sexy, laugh. 'High Level is SOOO much bigger than one deal, Ryan. We can live without it, trust me. And, if you don't, feel free to peruse our accounts.'

'That won't be necessary, but it would be useful to see any files you hold on the transaction.'

Beth flicked a switch and spoke into an intercom. 'Ursula, pull me the files on the Moot Hall transaction Mr Warne was working on.'

Ursula Maddox voice crackled back. 'He took them with him.'

'What?'

'When he cleared his desk. He came into the office and took the files from there.'

Beth's jaw muscles became rigid. 'He's not allowed to remove any files from this office.'

'But...'

'No excuses!' Beth's face reddened.

'He said he only needed them overnight. He'd bring them back the next day.'

'And did he?'

'No.'

'Idiot!' Beth hissed.

Ryan flinched. Beth Richards was indeed an organ grinder, and a ball-buster to boot.

'Apparently, as you heard, the files are missing. I knew I shouldn't take time off, I really shouldn't.' She shook her head.

'Have you any idea why he'd want to take the files?'

'I do, now. He will have had his own copy filed electronically so I suspect he knew the paper records contained something incriminating. If I were a betting lady, that's where my money would go.'

Ryan prepared himself for his coup de grace.

'Why were you in Justin Warne's property?'

'What?'

'Why were you in Justin Warne's apartment?' he repeated.

The colour drained from Beth's cheeks. 'I don't understand. I wasn't.'

'You were. Your fingerprints were found in his apartment.'

Beth's eyes widened for a moment, and then she recovered. 'Oh, I'm sorry. You mean back then. I thought you meant recently.'

'Miss Richards, you've just told me you didn't know him outside of work.'

'I don't. I was in his home as part of the work he conducted on behalf of my company.' She set her jaw again, eyes flaring. 'Are you accusing me of something?'

Ryan looked at Beth Richards for a long moment. 'That's all for now. Thank you for your time. I'll see myself out.'

CHAPTER TWENTY-TWO

Ryan gulped in the exhaust fumes of stationary traffic as he stood in the shadow of Cale Cross House. He didn't look up. He didn't need to. He knew Beth Richards would be at her window looking down on him. Ryan set off and, a few paces into the subway beneath the NHS Business Services Authority, he called Todd Robson.

'Listen, Todd, I've just spoken to Beth Richards about Justin Warne. She's as fishy as cod liver oil. I need you check summat out for me...'
'I can't, mate...'
Ryan's mind was on autopilot. Todd's words didn't register.
'What I need from you is a load of cross-referencing. Beth Richards, Lola Di Marco, and throw in Suzanne Westwood for good measure. After that, I want you to go through any and all connections their businesses have – with each other, and with Justin Warne.'
'Ry, man. Listen to me: I can't.'
'Why the hell not? You're with me on this one, remember.'
'Not anymore, I'm not. Look, Danskin wants us all back pronto. We're only waiting for you and Gav O'Hara.'
'What's up, like?'
'The shit's hit the fan. Big style.'

**

Ryan noticed one of the two crime boards had been pushed to one side. His board.

Stephen Danskin's focus was on the other board, the one populated with the scant details pulled together by Hannah

Graves. The Acting Super took centre-stage alongside it and got straight to business.

'As you know, yesterday was a sad day. We lost Michael McNeil.' He gave a reverential pause. 'Rick Kinnear's team has overseen the initial groundwork, liaising with uniform and sifting through forensic reports. I now have some fresh information to share with you.'

He looked at a sheet of paper in his hands. 'I apologise in advance. This doesn't make pleasant viewing.'

Danskin turned to the board, his frame obscuring the contents. When he moved to one side, his entire squad gasped.

Michael McNeil's crime scene photograph was affixed to the board.

Their eyes homed in on the CSOs throat, where a crimson grin smiled back at them. The slash across the throat seemed more vivid, more alive, than his listless gaping mouth.

Ryan swallowed and shifted his eyes so they surveyed the rest of McNeil's body. Blood had cascaded like a waterfall down the front of his uniform and gathered in a small pool in the hollow between chest and stomach.

'Shit the bed,' Todd Robson whispered.

They'd all seen much the same scene at some point in their careers, but the fact the victim bore uniform hit hard.

'We know Michael responded to a call, gave the all-clear, and signed off. We now know he tried to reconnect to control a few moments later but his wire didn't connect.' He pointed to the gruesome image once more. 'This is why.'

'Do we have any info on the call-out?' O'Hara asked.

'Aye,' DCI Lyall Parker said, 'It was nothing or something. A few scalliwags wi' spray cans. Michael sent them packing, so he did.'

'What do we reckon, then,' Hannah asked, 'One of them came back afterwards to do this?'

'That's the theory we were working on, until half an hour ago.'

'What's changed?' someone asked.

'We got some clarity from forensics,' Danskin replied.

He pinned three more photographs to the board.

'These are the spray cans the graffiti artists used. They were found next to McNeil. This one,' he pointed to one of the photographs, 'Bore no prints. The user either wore gloves, or wiped the can clean. From fibres found on the can, we can safely say it was the former. Cheap, grey, woollen gloves. Poundland specials, probably.'

Danskin indicated a second can. 'We recovered several prints from this one. They're not a match to anyone on record, but we have them on file now and we'll use 'em when we wheel in our suspects.'

'Sir,' Ryan interrupted, 'Does that mean we have suspects?'

Danskin and Parker exchanged a grim smile. 'Yes, we do.'

Stephen Danskin crossed in front of the board to reveal a third picture of a paint cannister. 'We have a shedload of prints from this one, too. They belong to a Brian Thomas. Thomas has a number of minor ASBOs to his name. Nowt serious, but he is known to us.'

'Nah,' Ravi said, 'It's a bit of a leap from a spot of graffiti and making a racket when pissed, to killing one of us. Doesn't seem likely.'

'I agree. Rick's boys have spoken to Thomas and his appropriate adult. He admits to the paint job but claims to know nowt about Michael. Rick reckons the poor kid nearly shit himself when he was told what happened.'

'Doesn't rule him out, though, sir,' Gavin O'Hara observed.

'In itself, that's true; it doesn't. Except, we've recovered the clothes he was wearing. They're covered in paint which forensics prove came from this can,' he pointed to the image on the board, 'But, crucially, there wasn't a speck of blood anywhere on the lad or his clobber. It's not him.'

'You said there were suspects, plural, sir.'

'Aye, I did, Jarrod.'

The Super shifted his weight.

'Although the can was covered in Thomas's prints, forensics recovered a partial print from another person. And that person is someone well-known to us.'

'Who?'

'This fella.' Danskin rapped the board with his knuckles. 'Marvin *'Rats'* Scully.'

**

The moment he'd seen life drain from the cop's eyes, Rats knew it'd be only a matter of time before his buddies descended like flies on shit.

He had to act swiftly but, at the same time, he knew this was his moment. He wanted to revel in it before the bastarding pigs worked out that Rats Scully, son of the legendary Lee Scully, was their man.

Rats turned out his pockets. All they contained was a razor blade, an empty plastic wallet, a debit card lifted from some no-mark's jacket, and a condom. And one-hundred-and ten pounds in cash.

The latter was a start, but he needed more. He planned a new life. Well, the same life but in a new city. Coventry, perhaps. Or Slough. He'd never been to either, but he'd seen something on telly about them and they looked suitably shitty for Rats Scully to make a living the way he always had.

In the distance, the Byker Wall loomed; its outer façade rising like a prison wall above the A193. It was the only prison Rats Scully would ever see, and he knew it like the back of his hand. What's more, it was the last place the police would think of looking for him. They'd have searched it already, and they'd know Rats Scully was long gone.

They were wrong. So wrong.

High Level

All it needed was one final round of his clients. That would raise another three or four hundred pounds. Enough to kickstart his new beginning.

Rats grinned to himself with the realisation it gave him something else.

It gave him enough time to settle an outstanding score.

**

'I want every man jack we have on this,' Stephen Danskin told his squad.

'I've spoken to DCI Kinnear already and he's got a couple of his best lads on their way to Frankland to speak to Scully Senior. I've cleared it with the Prince Bishop Force in Durham: they're more than happy for us to squeeze him 'til the pips squeak, under the circumstances.'

'Do you think that'll get us anywhere, sir? Lee Scully's not the most co-operative soul, from what I gather,' Sue Nairn queried.

'I don't give a shit. We won't know until we try. And, my God, Kinnear's lads will try. Anything we can learn about Rats, where he might lie low, what food he likes, where he might buy it – anything will help.'

'Aye, it's the right call, Sir,' Todd Robson agreed, 'But I also think Sue's right. We'll get fuck all from him. I wish you'd sent me. I'd have got summat out of the bastard.'

'Robson, you'd probably have got yourself fired. And I need you on this with me.' Danskin shook his head. 'Bloody hell. I never thought I'd see the day when I'd say that.'

The line lightened the mood for a second. 'Sangar, as usual you'll monitor CCTV for any sign of Rats. He's a sly bugger but, surely, he'll show up somewhere. I take it you've already got someone tracking social media?'

'Yes, Sir. Martin Lennard's seeing if Scully himself has any hidden accounts, while Ken Collins is monitoring for references to him elsewhere.'

'Good. Lyall, I want you and Graves to check out all known contacts of the little sod, and O'Hara and Robson doing the same with his old man. It's possible the son's with one of them.'

Ryan looked around the room. Only he and Sue Nairn hadn't been allocated a role.

'Sue,' Danskin continued, 'You have a ferret around the Wall. Graves will have the info on his activities there. You okay to hand over what you know to DS Nairn?'

'Of course, sir.'

And then there was one.

'What about me?' Ryan asked.

'While the priority has to be finding Michael McNeil's killer, we still have the Warne case outstanding. 'It's low down on our priorities but we need it to tick over.'

'I can't do it on my own, sir.'

Stephen Danskin inhaled and glared at Ryan. 'Think on it as an opportunity, Jarrod. You have carte blanche to do it your way. Just keep me updated, yeah?'

'But…'

'Enough! Decision made. Okay, we've a lot to do, but before we do, there's one last thing.'

The squad looked on impatiently, eager to be let off the leash and on the trail of Rats Scully.

'If this wasn't urgent enough, we've got the new Super paying an advance visit tomorrow. I don't need to tell you how important it is that we present our best front. We've got Michael McNeil's family to think of first and foremost, but we also have our good name and reputation at stake.'

'Sir, are you able to release the new Super's name to the guys yet?' Lyall asked.

Danskin gave it some thought. 'It's still supposed to be kept under wraps but as the Super will be here tomorrow, I don't suppose there's any harm.'

Todd Robson's sarcasm got the better of him. 'Howay, man; the suspense is killing us.'

'It's Sam Maynard.'

High Level

The blank looks indicated the name meant nothing to the squad.

'Maynard, as in wine gums?' Todd asked.

'The very same. Previously of Basildon parish.'

'Fucking hell. A TOWIE.'

'Yes, Robson. A TOWIE indeed.' Danskin smiled for the first time. 'I'm sure you and Superintendent Maynard will get along just fine.'

He clapped his hands. 'Now, get on with it. I want Scully apprehended before the new Super arrives.'

The squad scurried away to all four corners of the bullpen.

All except Ryan Jarrod.

He couldn't pursue the Justin Warne case by himself. It just wasn't possible. He needed help.

Ryan pulled out his mobile and dialled the number of the only other person able to assist.

**

The bruising around Peter Kirk's eyes was already turning a yellowish-green.

'Healing up canny there, I see,' Ryan said.

'You think? I got some right funny looks in Asda this morning. When your eyes are the only parts of you people can see, this look kind of attracts attention.'

'You going to invite me in, or what?'

Peter stood aside and let Ryan enter.

'Kettle's on if you want a cup of tea. I don't do coffee, I'm afraid.'

'I'll give it a miss, ta.'

While the tea brewed, Ryan took the opportunity to scan Peter Kirk's living room once again. The only difference he picked up on was the fact that Kirk's laptop remained shut down, lid closed.

'Custard cream?' Peter asked.

'You're a bit of an owld fanny, sometimes, aren't you?' Ryan joked.

Peter raised his shoulders. 'Just the way I am, I suppose. Anyway, I take it you're here to tell me Riley's all locked up?'

'Actually, no. That's not why I'm here.'

'But he is locked up, yeah?'

Ryan shook his head.

'What? You let him go?' He set down his teacup. 'Why, for God's sake?'

'He won't be bothering you again. Trust me on that one.'

'How can you be sure? I mean, you've seen what he's like.'

'It's a long story.' Ryan ensured he had Peter's full attention before continuing. 'And it's a story I hope you can help me finish.'

Ryan recounted the facts he knew were in the public domain, being careful to leave out any mention of Rats Scully or Michael McNeil. They weren't his concern.

Ryan summarised his meetings with Suzanne Westwood and Beth Richards and, finally, came to his point. 'Truth is, resources are stretched to the limit at the station, and I really could do with your help.'

'MY help?'

'Yes. Why not?'

'Well, until I ended up looking like I'd been in the ring with Rocky Balboa, you had me nailed on as being Justin's murderer.'

'I wouldn't put it quite like that.'

'You would if you were in my shoes.' He sipped his tea, set the cup down on its saucer, and wiped biscuit crumbs from his lips. 'What is it you want me to do?'

Ryan rested his chin on balled fists. 'You won't be in any danger. I just need to get inside Justin's head. The more I hear about him, the less I know.'

Peter spat a laugh. 'You and me, both. He's like one of those blokes your daughter brings home for tea, acts the perfect gentleman, then as soon as your back's turned, he drags her around by the hair as if he were a caveman.'

Ryan raised his eyebrows in acknowledgement. It was a good analogy. 'Are you not working today?' he asked, with a nod to the laptop.

'No. Heart's not in it, to be honest. Same as the driving. That's gone for a Burton. I can't get motivated since…well, since all this started. Never had the laptop on.'

Ryan picked up the thread seamlessly. 'Speaking of which, Beth Richards seems to think Justin had a copy of the transaction deeds for Moot Hall. You were at his house with us. There were no files there. Our tech guys are adamant there's nothing on his IT, which leaves only one possibility.'

'Somebody's stolen them.'

'Aye. Exactly that. I'm more convinced than ever that there was a piece of kit missing from Justin's property. No, not *A* piece of kit; *THE* piece of kit. The one that leads us straight to Justin's killer.'

'I'm not sure how I can help you.'

'Is there anybody - anybody at all – who you think might have been is a position to break into Justin's house?'

Peter Kirk chewed on a knuckle, deep in thought, before shaking his head. 'No. I'm sorry. There's not. You're the detective here. You're the one with the facts at your fingertips.'

'Fingertips. That's it. We have Justin's, a person unknown, yours…'

'My what?'

'Fingertips. Well, prints, to be more accurate. Beth Richards and…'

Peter Kirk sat upright. 'I know who's got it.'

CHAPTER TWENTY-THREE

Sally Sykes opened the door wearing pink pyjama bottoms and a black lace bra. A three-quarters empty bottle of red dangled between her fingers.

'Well, if it isn't my two favourite boys,' she slurred. 'Come into my parlour, said the spider to the fly.'

In the spider's parlour, Peter remained standing while Ryan took a seat opposite Sally Sykes. It took her two attempts to tuck her leg beneath her. She took a long slug from the bottle and drew the back of a hand across her lips.

'What can I do for you boys today?' She played with the strap of her bra, sliding it off her shoulder, then back on, then off again; lower this time. Her glassy eyes searched theirs for a reaction.

'Where's Justin's laptop?'

'That's for me to know, and you to find out.' She slid the shoulder-strap down again and left it hanging.

'Miss Sykes,' Ryan said, fighting hard to maintain eye contact and prevent his cheeks from colouring. 'Do you have a laptop belonging to Mr Warne?'

'Say, please.' She drained the wine bottle. Set it at her feet. Her bra gaped open as she bent forward, cleavage deliberately and brazenly exposed.

'Oops. Better make it pretty please after that little treat.'

Ryan hadn't time for her silly games. His patience was spent. He got to his feet. 'Miss Sykes. I'm arresting you for being drunk and disorderly.'

'You can't do that,' she slurred.

'Yes, I can. I'm a police detective.'

High Level

'And little ol' me is in my own house.' She burped loudly. 'I can only be drunk and disorderly if I was in a public place. That's what my sloi… my soci… the legal bloke told you lot last time.'

Ryan sat down again. She may be a drunken mess, but she knew her stuff. Fortunately, Peter Kirk saved his embarrassment.

'You see where you put your bottle down?'

'Where? Here?' Sally leant forward and almost toppled out of her chair. She put her fingertips to the floor and her top came away. She flung it against the wall, and her arms open wide. 'Well, hello boys,' she giggled as she gave a little shimmy.

Ryan picked a tea towel from the floor and tossed it at Sally. 'Cover up with that, or I really will arrest you. I mean it.'

Sally tucked the towel under her chin. It was fit for purpose providing she didn't move.

'Now, Sally, listen to me. When I was here before, there was something on the floor where you've just put the bottle. Do you remember?' Peter asked.

Sally shook her head as best she could without dislodging the towel.

'It was a backpack. Bluish-grey. You had to move it out the way to put out your cigarette, I think.'

'Who knows?'

'*I* know, Sally. You did. Now, was Justin's laptop inside the bag?'

Sally's eyelids drooped.

'Don't fall asleep,' Ryan said. 'This is important. You want me to catch the man who killed Justin, don't you?'

'Don't care. Justin was a mean and nasty person.'

'What do you mean by that?'

She shrugged. 'Probably nothing. It was probably me. Not him. Ignore me; I'm pissed as a fart.'

Ryan rubbed his knee in frustration. 'Listen, the bag. What was in it?'

'I don't remember any bag.'

Sally Sykes rolled off her futon. She was snoring like a warthog before she hit the floor.

**

'Peter, are you sure about her?'

They were in the back garden of Justin Warne's Raby Crescent apartment.

'No, Ryan; I'm not. But you told me you wanted my help, and that's what I'm trying to do, okay?'

'Okay. Sorry. She's a messed-up kid, or woman, hard to tell these days, but I don't see her being part of a property scam.'

'Nor me. All I do know is, I'm certain there was a backpack where I said it was, and it was definitely full. Now, the next time I came here – the time I broke in – there was a rucksack lying right there.' He pointed towards a small rockery.

'You're sure?'

'About that, I am. I know because I remember I had to move it to get a rock to break in with. I can't swear it was the same bag, but it was similar. And it was empty.'

Ryan exhaled through his nose. 'I know you said Sally Sykes had a key to Justin's place, but I just can't believe she's got owt to do with it. My gut's generally reliable when it comes to this sort of thing.'

Peter tipped his head towards Warne's house. 'Are we going inside?'

Ryan shook his head. 'Nee point. We've been in umpteen times. There's nothing there for us.'

'Us?'

'Us as in City and County Police, not us as in you and me.'

'Pity. I'm beginning to fancy myself as a cop.'

High Level

Ryan's tongue clicked the roof of his mouth. 'Trust me, it's more shit than giggles,' he said, paraphrasing a popular maxim amongst Stephen Danskin and his team.

'Where do we go from here, then?'

'I take you home, first.'

'Do you have to?'

'Are you for real? Yes, I have to.'

'We're done for the day?'

'You are. Not me. I need another chat with somebody else who showed an interest in Warne's house.'

'I want to come with you.'

'Not a good idea, mate.'

'Why not?'

'Because one other person who we know had an unhealthy attraction to it is a certain George Riley.'

**

'You're too late, pal. We're shutting up shop.' The security guard swung shut the metal gates in front of the multi-coloured cube.

'Has Mrs Westwood left for the day?' Ryan shouted through the wound-down window of the Uno.

'Look,' the man said, turning towards Ryan, 'I told you we're closed. You can come back tomorr...' The final syllable remained unspoken as the man saw the warrant card in Ryan's hand.

He unchained the gate and let Ryan through. 'Half an hour then the locks go back on, okay?'

Ryan saluted as he squeezed through the half-open gate and drove into a car park occupied by a single vehicle; a black BMW adorned with the private plates of Suzanne Westwood.

The reception lobby was eerily silent. No telephones rang, there was no idle gossip filtering from adjacent offices, no clangs or bangs of trucks being loaded, and there was no man with slick-backed hair behind the reception desk.

Dusk filled the lobby with hues of indigo and violet as Ryan slipped behind the desk and into the corridor housing Suzanne Westwood's office.

Ryan entered without knocking.

'Jesus,' Suzanne gasped, banging her knees off the underside of the desk as she jumped in shock.

'Sorry. I didn't mean to startle you.'

'You should have knocked. What are you doing here, anyway? Our gates should be locked. We're closed.'

'I just made it in time. Your security guy is very accommodating. You must thank him for me.'

Suzanne's mouth formed a grim line. 'Detective, I'm busy. I want to get home sometime this evening. What can I do for you?'

'You can answer a few questions.'

'I already did.'

'A few more questions.'

Suzanne let out a wearisome sigh. 'I've nothing more to say.'

'You do realise we could be doing this at Forth Street, don't you? I thought it better to do it here. I was only thinking of your reputation, that's all.'

'I'm saying nothing more without a solicitor present. I don't know what you think I've done but, whatever it is, you're wrong. Now, do you go, or do I call my legal people?'

Ryan held up his hands. 'Okay, okay. I'm going.'

Suzanne Westwood's mouth opened in surprise before she smiled. 'Thank you, Detective. Some other time, perhaps, but make an appointment first, please.'

'Oh,' Ryan snapped his fingers, 'Just to let you know I've prepared a press release about Mr Riley's attempted assault. It'll say how an employee of Westwood Building Contractors was arrested on your premises, and that you were uncooperative in our enquiries.'

Suzanne shot to her feet, her knees rattling against the desk once more. 'You can't do that,' she said through clenched teeth.

'I can, as long as what I say is the truth. And it is, isn't it? Every word of it. What was it you said to me earlier? Something like, *'Mr Riley's actions will be seen as my actions,'* I think it was. Not good for business, Mrs Westwood.'

'You're a bastard, do you know that?'

Ryan shrugged and made his way to the door.

'Wait. What do you want to know?'

'Thanks, Mrs Westwood. You know it makes sense. I genuinely want to believe that you have nothing to do with Justin Warne's death, but you haven't made it easy for yourself.'

'I really don't need this so get to the point, please.'

She sounded tense. Agitated. Nervous. It didn't escape Ryan's attention.

'We look for three things when investigating a crime: MMO – means, motive, opportunity. At the moment, you tick all three boxes.'

'I don't know how you reach that conclusion.' Her eyes darted sideways, as if seeking comfort and support from the family photograph on her desk.

'Okay. Let me explain it to you. We'll start with means. George Riley. He followed and threatened a friend of Mr Warne. Riley assaulted the same man, and he attempted to assault me. He's proved his tendency towards violence. Yes, he had the means to kill Justin Warne, don't you agree?'

'They were his actions, not mine.'

'Ah yes, but you hired a solicitor to defend him. His actions are, in law, now linked to you.'

'No!'

'Now, let's look at opportunity. You've already admitted you had Riley check Mr Warne on your behalf. He's confessed to keeping an eye on Mr Warne and, what's more, we know Riley's been to his property. That gives him opportunity.'

She slumped in her seat, her eyes seeking solace from the photograph.

'Motive, I admit, we struggled with at first. Now, though, I think we have enough. You told me earlier you didn't trust Mr Warne. You said you feared he'd renege on the deal you two had struck for the refurbishment of Moot Hall.'

'Come on, Detective; that was just an idle thought. I don't have any reason to believe he'd actually do such a thing.'

Ryan's eyes seared into Suzanne. 'Where's the laptop, Mrs Westwood?'

Genuine puzzlement crossed her face. 'What? I don't know what you mean.'

'We have good reason to believe a laptop containing details of the Moot Hall transaction has been taken from Mr Warne's property. If the data on that computer implicates you in any way, you're in very, very deep water.'

'Look. Get as many of your buddies here as you like. Search the place. I'm inviting you to search my offices; my home, if you wish. You don't need a warrant. Go on. Do it now.' She slid her telephone towards Ryan. 'Go on. I've nothing to hide.'

Ryan smiled. 'Thank you, but it won't be necessary. The fact you've been so open is enough for me.' He smiled again. 'Like I said, you're tied in tight with George Riley, but I don't think either of you are murderers.'

Suzanne Westwood exhaled like a punctured beachball. Her eyes flitted to the photograph. And Ryan intuitively knew what it was he'd missed on his previous visit.

It was so obvious; so utterly, inescapably, transparent.

Suzanne Westwood had a much more pressing motive for the murder of Justin Warne.

Ryan reached across the desk for the telephone.

'Lyall, I know you're stretched but can you spare some of Rick Kinnear's guys for a search?'

Suzanne's eyes bulged like a cartoon character's.

'No, no warrant needed. We've an open invitation. I want a team at Westwood Building Contractors on the Portobello Estate. Immediately. I also want a party sent to the address of Suzanne Westwood.'

Suzanne wrapped her arms around herself. She thought she heard the voice at the other end of the receiver ask what it was all about. She heard Ryan answer the question.

'We're looking for Warne's missing laptop. Do you remember the girl on Justin Warne's screensaver? The lass on the yacht?'

Ryan stared at the photograph on Suzanne's desk as he spoke.

'It's Suzanne Westwood's daughter.'

**

'Suzanne Westwood, you're under arrest for...'

'You've got this wrong!' Mascara streaked the woman's cheeks. 'Stop right there. It's a mistake.'

Ryan continued reading her rights. When he finished, he said, 'Mrs Westwood, I strongly recommend you seek legal advice before saying anything further.'

'Fuck legal fucking advice. I don't need any!' Suzanne was screaming, tearing at her hair, crumbling in front of Ryan Jarrod's eyes.

'Look, your daughter's photograph was being used as a screensaver by Justin Warne. If the two of them were in a relationship, that gives you a motive for murder. You took the laptop from Mr Warne's home not for business purposes, but for personal ones. You took his personal laptop in order to discover the extent of their relationship, unaware that your daughter's photograph was plastered on other kit he used, as well.'

'There is no fucking laptop!' Suzanne Westwood slumped to the floor in the corner of her office. 'And there's no daughter.' The words came out as a whisper.

Ryan screwed up his eyes. 'Howay, man – there's a photograph of you all right there on your desk.'

'Tanita is my stepdaughter. I've not seen her for eighteen months. She went off the rails when her dad died. She disappeared the day of Derek's funeral, and she's never been in touch since.'

Ryan's heart sank. He didn't know why, but he believed her. Yet, she'd fooled him once before. 'Why should I believe what you're telling me?'

Suzanne reached up to her desk. She plucked her mobile phone off the surface and threw it at Ryan.

'Be my guest. Check it out. Get in touch with the service provider. They'll have records of all calls and messages, received or made? Even those I've deleted, yeah?'

Ryan nodded.

'That'll prove I've had no contact with Tanita.' She looked at Ryan with empty, hollow eyes. 'And it hurts. It bloody hurts, you know.'

She tucked her knees up. Folded her arms across them. Lay her head on her arms. Buried her face. Suzanne Westwood's shoulders shook and heaved.

Ryan picked up the desk phone and pressed redial. 'Lyall, sorry, mate. I might have been a bit hasty. Call off the hounds. Instead, get a few lads out looking for a Tanita Westwood. That's Tango Alpha at the beginning. She's the girl in the photo. We need to find her.'

Between sniffles, Suzanne said, 'That's not her name.'
'What isn't?'
'Westwood. She told me at the very same moment my Derek – her father - was being lowered into his grave.'
'Told you what?'

'That she was taking her birth mother's name. She wants nothing to do with me. Said she didn't want to be associated with me in any way and if I kept the Westwood name, she would disown it entirely.'

Ryan sat on the floor next to her. 'Why?'

Suzanne's watery eyes met Ryan's. 'She blames me for his death. Says I drove him too hard. It isn't true. It was Derek's business. He did what he wanted with it, when he wanted. God, I miss them both so much.'

She leant into Ryan as tears flowed again. Her words came out muffled against his shoulder, but to him they resonated loud and clear.

'She calls herself Tanita Richards, now. Her mother's Beth Richards.'

CHAPTER TWENTY-FOUR

WEDNESDAY

He awoke at four-forty AM. He'd fallen asleep only two hours earlier.

Panic washed over him as he found himself in a cell, staring out into darkness through a metal grate.

'Fuck.' He began to stand only for his head to crash against a concave roof. 'Ow. Shit.' He rubbed his hand across the crown of his head. Checked it for blood. In the darkness, he couldn't tell.

He touched his head again. A bump was already forming, but the bang had served a purpose. He was wide awake, and he knew where he was. It wasn't a prison cell.

He exhaled loudly. Breath condensed above him like a halo.

'Thank fuck,' Rats Scully said to himself.

Once night fell, he'd used the irrigation sprinkler in the Ouseburn City Farm nursery to hose the copper's stinking blood off his hands and face. He could do nothing with the stains on his clothing. That would have to wait.

Using the razor blade, he sliced through the perspex sheets surrounding the nursery and snuck out into a black, moonless night.

He usurped main thoroughfares in favour of dimly-lit industrial land and made his way back to the one place he knew best – the Byker Wall.

In eery silence, he climbed a staircase until he reached a point of sanctuary. It was a place he'd used before; the fifth-floor air conditioning shaft where he'd hidden from the bitch

High Level

of a copper. Once there, he'd dislodged the grille, clambered in, and wedged the metal wire screen back in place.

He yawned. Stretched as best he could in the cramped space. His cheap Timex eked out a faint glow when he touched a button.

Four-forty-eight, it read.

Soon, he'd discover if the maxim 'old habits die hard' held true. If it did, he'd be fed, watered, and ready for action within three hours.

Rats lay flat on his stomach, eyes peering out from the vent, and waited.

**

The bullpen was always at its fullest first thing, before the officers went on their separate lines of enquiry. Today, there were no separate lines. Everyone was focused on apprehending Rats Scully. Everyone bar Ryan Jarrod.

'Sir, can I have a word?'

Danskin glanced at his watch. 'I'm expecting Sam Maynard any minute. Make it quick.'

'I need some assistance with the Warne case.'

'Not that again.'

'I'm onto something. It's just a matter of time before…'

'You fouled up, Jarrod. Look, you're a good detective. And I like you. But our priority has to be finding Scully. I had to calm Rick Kinnear down yesterday. He'd scrambled his squad to go off on your wild goose chase, only for you to say you'd made a mistake five minutes later.'

'It wasn't like that, sir.'

Danskin scratched his forehead. 'It was exactly like that. If you're onto something, great. You'll crack it, in your good time. Scully killed a serving officer. Everyone else stays on that case.'

'But…'

Danskin's phone chirruped. 'Bugger. Maynard's here already.' He got everyone's attention by clapping his hands. 'Listen up, everybody. Superintendent Maynard's in the house. I'll be escorting the Super upstairs. I want to see you hard at it, heads down arses up, when we come back.'

The squad instantly made to their desks and booted up their monitor screens.

Danskin lowered his voice as he spoke to Ryan again. 'Look, I've smoothed things over with Kinnear. He's sorting out support for you. Uniform only, mind, and just a couple. It's the best I can do.'

'Thank you, sir,' Ryan said with no gratitude in his voice.

'When Maynard arrives, keep a low profile. I don't want you standing out for the wrong reasons. The Super's attention is bound to be on Michael McNeil's case. I can't have Maynard think I haven't got everyone and their dogs working the case.'

'So, I'm the naughty boy in dunce's corner, am I?'

Danskin sucked air between his teeth. 'No. I want you to crack the Warne case. I want you to get all the kudos for it. I want you to pass your sergeant's exam next week. To be honest, I want you back with Hannah, okay? Satisfied?'

Ryan remained open-mouthed as Stephen Danskin made his way to the lift lobby and the waiting Superintendent Sam Maynard.

'Are you okay?'

Ryan realised Hannah had sidled up alongside him.

'Aye. I'm aal reet.'

'You don't sound it.'

'It's all tits up.'

'What is?'

'Life, the Universe, and everything; that's what.'

'None of this is my doing, you know.'

'Isn't it?'

She sighed. 'Look, let's get these cases solved and next week's exam out the way then we can get this sorted. I mean, properly sorted.'

High Level

Ryan was about to reply when the bullpen door creaked open.

'He's here,' Todd Robson stage whispered.

The room fell silent. No-one looked towards the door. They all followed orders. Head down, arse up.

Until Stephen Danskin and Sam Maynard passed Todd's desk and he saw their legs walk on by. 'Bloody hell. He's a she.'

Samantha Maynard stopped dead.

No-one dared breathe as, slowly, she turned towards Robson, face like a stern headmistress.

Suddenly, Maynard's countenance changed, and a mischievous grin creased her face. *'And she says, hey babe: take a walk on the wild side.'* She gave Todd a wink before she and Danskin set off towards the Super's office amidst raucous laughter.

'Y'knaa,' Todd said, 'I think she might be aal reet, TOWIE and all.'

**

'Pssst.'

The youth stopped at the sound.

'Ower here, man.'

He looked around, perplexed.

'How man, you daft twat. I'm doon here.'

The youth shrunk back against the concrete stairwell. 'You!' he whispered.

'Aye, me. Who'd you think it was?'

Rats hauled himself out of the air con shaft. Almost lost his balance as the cramped veins and arteries of his legs feasted on the renewed blood flow.

'What do you want?'

'I want some scran. And a Red Bull or summat.'

'Piss off. Why'd I want to do that for you?'

'Because of this.' He grabbed Scrapper by the wrists. Turned them upwards so the scars became visible. 'It's healing canny. Not sure what'd happen if the cut opened up again, mind.'

Scrapper looked around him. 'You're aal ower the news. They're saying you killed a copper.'

Rats beamed. 'Aye. I did. What've they been saying about it? About me? Tell us, man.'

'Howay, man. I can't be seen with you, and YOU can't be seen, full stop.'

'Then get yersel' doon to Greggs. I'll have a steak bake and a sausage stottie. Divvent forget the drink. I'll disappear back into there. I won't be *'seen'*, as you call it.'

'Money?'

Rats fumbled in his pocket. Produced a tenner. 'Tight arsed get. Now, be back here in twenty minutes, or I'll come looking for you.'

Twenty minutes passed. Twenty-five. Half an hour.

Rats wriggled towards the rear of the shaft, where a downward chute led to the lower floors. He suspended himself, arms and legs held against the narrow tube in a star shape. If that bastard came back with the cops, he'd let himself go and drop to another level. Then, he'd find the little runt and do for him.

After forty minutes, Rats was sure that's what Scrapper had done. He became jittery, couldn't think clearly.

'Rats. I'm here. Sorry I'm late.'

Wary, Rats Scully remained silent.

'Are you still there? I've got your stuff. And your change.'

Rats eased himself into the horizontal plane and edged along the vent until he could see Scrapper's legs. And only Scrapper's legs.

'You've been ages. Where the fuck you been, Mackemland or somewhere?'

Scrapper laughed. 'Nah. Couldn't get into Greggs. Didn't have me mask. Got you a Maccy D's though. I knaa a lass who works there. She let us in. Will sausage and egg do you? I got one of those shitty potatoey things an' aal.'

'What about the drink?'

'Coffee.'

Rats smirked, remembering the last coffee he'd had. 'That'll do.'

He crawled up to the grate. Twisted his head so he could see to Scrapper's right, and again to the left. No coppers.

Rats pushed against the grate, unscrewing it with his hands in the same motion. 'Howay in. You'll give the game away out there.'

Scrapper squeezed his wiry frame through the gap. 'It stinks in here, man. You had a piss or summat?'

'Aye, I've had a fucking piss. Where do you expect me to have one, up me own arse?'

Scrapper laughed. 'Look, about what happened before. Me wrists, and that. I know it was the drugs. I mean, I don't blame you or owt.'

Rats remained silent.

'But the copper, man. What've you done, mate? You're fucked.'

'I've got plans. I'll be okay.'

'What plans?'

'How I'm gonna get away. Where I'm going. It isn't here, that's for sure.'

'You need to go. Now. They'll find you.'

Rats shook his head. 'Not yet. I need more cash.'

'How're you going to get that, man?'

Rats stared straight ahead.

'Rats? Are you listening?'

Scully turned towards Scrapper. 'Why all the questions?'

'Cos I'm your mate. Despite these,' he held up his wrist to show the scars, 'We're still mates, aren't we?'

'Depends.'

'Depends on what?'

'On why you took so long to get me scran.'

'I told you. I didn't…'

'No. I don't believe you. You've been to the filth. You've grassed us up to save your scrawny twattish neck.'

'I haven't. I wouldn't.'

Rats turned his head towards Scrapper until their foreheads touched. 'Fucking grass,' he hissed.

The razor slashed across Scrapper's throat, then back again, and down his face. An eye popped like jelly. The blade went to Scrapper's groin and slashed back and forth.

Rats Scully once more dripped red with the blood of a victim as he lowered himself down the air con chute with a last look at his butchered friend.

**

'You didn't tell us you had a daughter.'

Ryan sat in Beth Richards's office, watching her intently.

'I didn't think it relevant. In fact, it isn't relevant.'

Ryan remained silent as Ursula Maddox entered with a tray containing a cafetiere, a jug of cream, and two cups. Beth Richards played mother.

Ryan sipped from his cup until Ursula closed the door behind her. 'Thank you, Miss Richards. For the coffee.'

'You're more than welcome. I wish you'd tell me why you're here, though. I told you everything I know yesterday.'

'Not everything.' He took another sip. The coffee was too hot for his taste, but he wanted to gauge Beth's reaction to every question.

'I'm sorry your holiday was disappointing. Where did you say you were, again?'

'I didn't say.'

Another sip while he let silence shout out loud.

'I went to the Lake District, if you must know.'

'Windermere?'

Beth Richards' right eyebrow shot up. 'Yes, but how did you know?'

'Where did you stay?'

'Is this relevant?'

'I think it is, yes. That's why I'm asking.'

Beth shook her head. 'A little B&B. Not sure of the name. I can find out for you.'

'Ah. Right. A B&B.'

'Yes.'

'Not a yacht?'

'What? What are you talking about, Detective Jarrod?'

'How old's your daughter? Tanita, I believe, isn't it?'

'Yes. That's her name. She'll be eighteen next month.'

Ryan looked around the four walls to disguise his shock at learning the girl's age. Everywhere he looked, the image of Beth Richards smiled down on him.

'Did you know your daughter was in a relationship with Justin Warne?'

'I beg your pardon. How dare you!'

'Where is your daughter, Miss Richards?'

'That's none of your business.'

'We think she's material to the investigation of Justin Warne's death.'

Beth tossed her head. 'Hah. Preposterous.'

Ryan fought hard to conceal the realisation which had just hit him like a hammer blow. This time, the sip of coffee was to calm his own excitement. He didn't want anything to show in his voice.

'I'd like permission to speak to your daughter.'

'No. I won't permit it. It's out of the question.'

'Strictly speaking, I don't need your permission, but I'm doing you a courtesy here.'

'A courtesy? You call dragging my daughter's good name into this a courtesy?'

'I'm sorry your holiday didn't work out how you'd hoped. I guess it's probably because Tanita didn't like what you had to say.'

Ryan looked into the woman's eyes and knew with absolute certainty he was right.

'Thank you, Miss Richards. That'll be all for now.'

'I meant what I said, you know. I don't want you pestering my girl.'

'Thank you,' Ryan said again.

This time, he didn't even wait until he was outside the offices of High Level Properties before putting the call through.

'Ravi, it's Ryan. I need your help. I know you're up to your neck with Scully, but I think I'm down to the last wicket stand on the Warne case. I'd like you to go back over some of the trolls who commented on Warne's blog posts.'

'I'd love to help out, mate, but it'll have to be quick and easy, and we've been over them all already. The senders are untraceable.'

'Is there any way you can do a reverse Google? Like you did with that picture of the lass on Warne's yacht?'

Ryan could almost hear the unoiled cogs turning in Ravi Sangar's brain. 'Not sure. What exactly are you thinking?'

'Well, if I give you a name, can you work it backwards and see whether it fits a handle?'

There was a moments silence. 'I can't promise anything, but I'll give it a go.'

'Right. This is the one I want you to check.'

'Fire away.'

'Okay; it's the comment that says, *Warne: you are high-level filth.*'

'Yep. I remember it.'

'I think I know who sent it, but I need proof.'

'Right. Just a sec, I'm calling it up now.' Ryan heard Ravi Sangar whistle while scrolling through the files. 'It's the one from someone using *Beer* as their handle, am I right?'

'Spot on. I think *Beer* might represent something else.'

'Such as?'

'I think it's a representation of the sender's initials. Rather than *Beer*, I'm hoping it's B.R.'

Ryan paused.

'I want you to dig out everything we have, and then stuff we don't have, on Beth Richards.'

CHAPTER TWENTY-FIVE

Ravi Sangar's head gave a wobble. 'Not yet, I haven't; no. It's not easy when my focus is supposed to be on Scully.'

'Okay,' Ryan said. 'I hoped it would be straightforward, that's all.'

'No such luck. Before I can even start a trace on the sender, I have to access…'

Ryan held up a hand. 'Enough already. I won't understand the explanation anyway. Thanks for trying, though.'

'And I'll keep trying, but I can only do it on the Q.T. I've already been caught once.'

'Shit. Who by?'

'Danskin and Maynard.'

'Shit.'

'Aye, that's what I said.'

'Sorry, mate.'

'No bother. Danskin realised what I was up to, but Maynard was oblivious. She just wanted to be seen, I think. Visible management, and all that.'

'Pleased I wasn't there.'

Ravi laughed. 'She just had a whistle-stop tour, but she seems canny. Completely different approach to Connor, mind. I think Danskin's relieved Connor's been replaced, to be honest.'

'Yeah. He can get back to being a *'proper copper'* again.'

'And we can get back to calling him Foreskin.'

They laughed.

'Danskin was cool once Maynard had gone. He gave me the okay to give you a hand - but only when I wasn't needed on the Scully case. He told me a couple of Uniforms were allocated to you, so I asked them if they'd do the background checks on Beth Richards while I worked on the IT trace.'

'Cheers, mate. You're a star. I'll see where they're up to.'

Ravi spoke again as Ryan stood to leave the bullpen.

'Good luck.'

'Cheers.'

'No. I mean, next week. The exam, and all.'

'I didn't think you knew.'

'Howay, man. Nowt's secret here. We all know.'

'Danskin told me he'd only told a couple.'

'Did he, now? Did he really?' Ravi smiled. 'We're all on your side, you know. You might still be the newbie, but we're behind you.'

For the third time, Ryan found himself saying, 'Cheers.'

'Aye. We're with you all the way, and with Hannah. Mind, we're bloody sick of your soap opera love life, though,' Ravi chuckled. 'Get yourselves sorted, the pair of you. I'm in no position to give you an order, but it's an order.'

Ryan sighed. 'Your little speech was going so well. Why'd you have to go and spoil it?'

This time, he did leave the bullpen.

**

In the calm of the breakout area, Ryan sat alone at a table, its surface decorated with a pen, notebook, crumpled Twix wrapper, a cooling Mocha, and the chocolate-smeared reports printed out by PCs Lucy Dexter and Jamaal Locke.

He already knew most of the information they'd unearthed on Beth Richards. Her marital status, education and employment history, and her Companies House listings were in the public domain. Her minor criminal record had already been discussed amongst Danskin's team, and Lucy Dexter hadn't turned up anything new on that score.

Ryan drank from the cup and read up on her early employment background. Credit to Dexter, she'd located a photograph of a young Beth with Derek Westwood's arm draped around her waist. On the back, Lucy Dexter had scribbled the location, *'Grand Opera, Briggate, Leeds,'* and the event; *'The UK Estate Agency 'Rising Star' Awards.'*

The photograph was dated. It tallied with Tanita Richard's age.

Ryan sat back and gazed up to the atria roof. He grabbed his pen and scribbled, *'Was Tanita conceived as a result of a one-night stand?'*

He continued browsing the reports. There were no other public photographs of them together, no press releases, no nothing. What's more, for the thirteen months following the Awards ceremony, Beth Richards went completely off-grid.

Lucy Dexter had reached the same conclusion as Ryan. In her report, PC Dexter hypothesised, *'Query: Did the Westwood's bring Tanita up as their own?'*

It had to be the answer but, if so, why would Tanita reach out to Beth Richards? They must have maintained contact in the intervening years.

Ryan picked up his phone. 'Is Lucy Dexter around? It's DC Ryan Jarrod. I'd like her to do something for me.'

'She's not. Can I help? It's Jamaal Locke here.'

'Jamaal; listen - I wanted to ask Lucy a favour, but you can do it. I'm as sure as I can be that Beth Richards kept in touch with her daughter throughout her life. I want you to check when Beth took periods of leave from work. Start with periods of three days or more. Crossmatch them against school holidays or, even better, times where Tanita Westwood was known to be away from the Westwood's home. Not sure how far you'll get with the latter, but owt you find will be great.'

'I'll do what I can, sure. By the way, what did you make of my report?'

Ryan hesitated. The young cop sounded so enthusiastic he didn't want to admit he hadn't looked at it yet.

'I started with Lucy's, if I'm honest. I've just started on yours, but it looks fine from what I've seen,' he lied.

High Level

'Great! Thank you. That's great. Finding the holiday cottage took some doing, mind, seeing as it's registered in another name. I hope it was worth the effort.'

'I'm sure it will…' Ryan stopped. 'Wait, I'm not up to that bit yet. Where do I find it?'

'Page five, I think. Somewhere around there, anyway.'

'Okay, Jamaal – I need to press on. Good work.'

Ryan ended the call and opened PC Locke's report at page five.

**

The telephone number Ryan had been given was discontinued. A quick internet search provided him with the number of the estate office, from where a prissy secretary refused to divulge any information.

Ryan gave the secretary the number for Forth Street, persuaded her to check its validity, and asked her to call him back. Pronto.

'Pronto' turned out to be twenty minutes but, finally, he had the information he needed. His first call went unanswered, as did the second. He waited half an hour and tried again.

'Yeah?' The voice held a cautious tone.

'Is Tanita there?'

'I think you've got the wrong number.'

'Tanita, my name's Ryan Jarrod. I'm a detective with City and County Police.'

'Wrong number.'

The line went dead.

'Bollocks.'

Ryan tried again, six times in total, before she answered again.

'Look, leave me alone, will you? There's no Tanita here.' The girl sounded more irritated than concerned.

'Don't hang up! If you're not Tanita, who are you?'

The girl spat out a disdainful laugh. 'I'm not telling you that! You could be some perv, for all I know.'

'Is that what you thought of Justin Warne?'

The girl fell silent for a moment too long before saying, 'I don't know what you're talking about.'

'Last chance, Tanita. All I want is to ask you a couple of questions. That's all. Just a few simple questions.'

'I'm not this Tanita person you're looking for.'

'Okay. Fine. We'll do this the hard way. I'll talk to your mother. Or, should I say, I'll talk to her AGAIN. Both of them.'

He heard an intake of breath.

'Yes, that's right,' he continued, 'Both your mothers. We know a lot about you already. Answering a couple more questions can't do any harm, can it?'

'Listen, fuckwit,' the girl hissed, 'I don't know what you're on about.'

'When I do meet you, please remind me to charge you with obstruction.'

Ryan hung up.

**

'Do you, or do you not, understand basic English?'

They were in Ryan's Fiat, heading north-west, and Beth Richards was as vitriolic as ever.

'I expressly told you NOT to speak with my daughter.'

'You see, that's where the problem lies. Legally speaking, Tanita has two mothers, and Suzanne Westwood didn't have a problem with it.'

Ryan had checked in with High Level Properties only to discover Beth Richards was working from home. He'd arrived unannounced at her four- bedroom detached bungalow in the hamlet of Higham Dykes, five miles from Newcastle Airport.

Beth wasn't amused but, when Ryan made it clear he'd be interviewing Tanita regardless of her wishes, she insisted on coming along as the appropriate adult.

It was exactly what Ryan had hoped for.

High Level

'I really don't know what you expect to get from this harassment. My daughter will have nothing to say to you because she has nothing to hide.'

The Fiat slowed as it drew through Kirkharle village. 'That's fine. If she knows nothing, it rules her out of the investigation. Good news all round.'

Beth Richards harrumphed behind a diamante facemask which glittered and sparkled in the sunlight.

Ryan glanced to his left. 'Is that why you went to the Lakes?'

'Is what why? You're really starting to piss me off, do you know that?'

'To give Tanita the keys to your cottage?'

'Lodge, detective. It's a lodge, not a cottage.'

'Is that why?'

Beth Richards stared out the passenger-side window. 'Yes.'

She waited for Ryan's follow-up question. It didn't come.

Beth loosened a button on her blouse, slid her face covering beneath her chin, and fanned her face with her hand as the silence suffocated her.

Twenty minutes later, as Ryan pulled sharp left onto a B-road at Otterburn, he spoke again. 'Why didn't you tell us about the lodge?'

Beth raised her shoulders, a gesture Ryan interpreted as evasive.

'Why didn't you tell me that's where Tanita was?'

'Because I didn't want you to talk to her.'

Ryan steered his car across a bridge over the River Rede. 'Why did you send her to the lodge?'

Beth flipped down the visor as they drove into a lowering sun. 'I didn't *send* her,' she drew quotation marks in the air with her fingers. 'I suggested she go there, that's all.'

'Why?'

'So she'd be safe, that's why.'

The car weaved across the cats-eyes as Ryan looked towards Beth. 'Safe from who?'

'Safe from anyone. Everyone. Come on, detective. Tanita's seventeen years old. She was on a yacht, for Christ's sake. Not the most secure of environments, is it?'

Ryan agreed with her, but added, 'Especially the yacht of a dead man.'

Beth Richards turned her head and stared at the scenery.

A milepost informed them their destination lay nine miles ahead.

In less than quarter of an hour, they'd be at Kielder Water.

**

They pulled onto loose shale outside a two-storey Scandanavian-style lodge on the water's edge. Two kayaks tethered to a wooden stake pulled against their restraints as the wash from a passing motorboat rippled the lake's surface.

Ryan removed his face mask and used it to swat away a swarm of omnipresent midges. Beth Richards, next to him, looked up at the lodge.

'She won't answer the door to you,' she said.

'Be my guest,' Ryan gestured towards a bronze door knocker in the image of a brown trout.

Beth hesitated, took in air, and rapped on the door. 'Tanita, it's me, your mum.' When only silence followed, she added, 'Beth.'

'Who's that?' The voice came from an open upstairs window.

Ryan used his hand to shield his eyes from the setting sun as he looked up at the girl on Justin Warne's screensaver picture.

'My name's Ryan,' Jarrod said.

'Toyboy?' Tanita sneered.

'Open the door, love,' Beth asked.

Tanita disappeared from view. A minute later the door swung open.

'I'm Detective Constable Ryan Jarrod of City and County Police.'

Tanita Westwood, or Richards, looked him up and down. She was fresh-faced and, dressed in cropped jeans and marshmallow pink T-shirt, looked considerably younger than she had appeared in the provocative pose on board Justin Warne's yacht.

'So?' she bristled.

'I'd like to ask you some questions about Justin Warne, if I may.'

'No, you may-fucking-not.'

'Tanita!'

'Mum, what are you thinking? Fucking hell - you're as bad as the other one.'

Ryan stepped forward. He didn't say anything, just looked closely at her.

Tanita smirked. 'Are you trying to act all macho? It won't work.'

'When did you last see Justin?'

'I'm saying fuck all.'

'Tanita! Just answer the man's questions and get it over with.'

'Man? That's not a man. Not a real one.'

Ryan took a step even closer. 'That's twice you've referred to me in that way. Is that what attracted you to Justin? That he was older?'

Tanita narrowed her eyes. 'You think I've got daddy-issues?'

'I don't know. Have you?'

The girl looked downwards. 'I miss him.'

Time for a change in approach. Ryan softened his tone. 'My mam died when I was about your age. I know what it's like.'

'Really?'

'Yes, really.'

Tears pooled in Tanita's eyes. 'I miss him,' she said again.

Ryan motioned for Beth Richards to give them some space. 'You'll miss him for the rest of your life, but there's ways to get over it. You don't need an older man in your life to compensate, you know.'

Tanita sniffed noisily. 'That's not the way it was. I'd already started seeing Justin when Dad was still here.'

'What was it about Justin?' he asked.

'We had fun. He took me to nice places.' She lifted her head and stared over Kielder Water, its surface stained blood red by the last of the sun's rays. 'He liked water. He liked me in a bikini.' A sad smile appeared on her face.

'Did he know how old you were?'

She stiffened. 'I'm old enough. He did nothing illegal. I did tell him I was twenty, though, because I thought he might dump me if he knew how old I really was. I let it slip, once, after we'd been together for a while.'

'He didn't dump you, though.'

She chuckled. 'No. I needn't have worried. I think it turned him on.'

Ryan heard Beth give a sigh of anguish from behind them.

'Did your mum ask you to break up with him?'

Tanita glanced towards Beth.

'No,' Ryan corrected, 'I meant your other mum; Suzanne Westwood.'

A tear rolled down her cheek. She wiped it away with the heel of her hand. Tanita nodded so briefly Ryan would have missed it if he'd blinked.

'I wouldn't do it. Part of the fun of being with Justin was that it pissed her off so much.'

'Did it piss her off so much she'd want him out the way?'

'What do you mean?'

'Do you know a George Riley?'

'Don't think so.'

'Do you know anyone who might have wanted to hurt Justin?'

Tanita picked at her fingers. 'Not by name, no.'

Ryan wrinkled his brow. 'Does that mean there was somebody?'

'Justin wasn't sure. He had a big property deal on the go.'

'Hah!' Beth laughed, scornfully. 'Don't I know it.'

Tanita ignored her. 'He said he'd take me to Vegas if it came off.' She gave a wan smile. 'He was a bit paranoid about it. He thought somebody might be following him.'

Ryan glanced towards Beth, who didn't react. 'Did you ever see anybody following him?'

The girl shook her head.

'Please, think carefully: are you sure you don't know a George Riley?'

'I am, yeah. Never heard of him. Why? Who is he?'

Behind them, Beth Richards looked at her watch. 'Are we finished here? It'll be late by the time we get back and I've a busy schedule tomorrow.'

'Did Justin ever say why he thought he was being followed?'

'Nah. He didn't really talk about it. He knew I wasn't interested in work and stuff. We girls just wanna have fun, you know.'

'Was he taking any precautions?'

She gave him a look and Ryan blushed.

'No, I didn't mean it like that. I meant by way of security.'

Tanita thought for a moment. 'Not really. I remember he took some records away to his house, once. Like, files and stuff. Papers. He said he wanted them to be safe.'

'Was this his house in Byker?'

The girl looked confused.

'Gateshead, then?'

'Of course not.'

Ryan stiffened.

'If neither of them, where was it?'

He waited, expectantly.

'Tanita – where did he hide the files?'

CHAPTER TWENTY-SIX

THURSDAY

While the rest of Tyneside woke up to battleship grey skies and a bitter easterly wind, the weather outside meant nothing to Rats Scully ensconced within the darkness of the Byker Wall infrastructure.

He'd spent the night exploring his surroundings. The experience was exhilarating and terrifying in equal measure, and now it was time for sleep. He curled up like a cat in a basket, secure in the knowledge he'd never be found in the labyrinthine ductwork.

The first hour after nightfall had been thrilling. Rats lowered himself to the fourth floor, where he discovered a network of channels and tunnels running the length of the floor.

Every now and then, he came across a vent which looked down into one of the apartments below. Most were silent as death and he hardly dared creep away in case his movements alerted the occupants to his presence.

A further shaft veered off to his right. Narrower than the first, he had to lie on his belly. He wriggled along it like a worm. The tunnel seemed to drag on for miles but common-sense told him he was traversing the width of the Byker Wall.

Rats struggled for breath as he manoeuvred in the cramped space, but he was rewarded with a glimpse down into a bedroom where a young couple were lost in noisy, dirty, sex.

Scully lingered. Watching. Grinning. Somehow, he managed to stifle the manic laugh which built inside him. Instead, he reached inside his trousers and worked himself until he came.

High Level

For a moment, he wondered if he could spend the rest of his life hidden away, spying on his neighbours, thieving from them when they left their flats. He almost regretted killing the cop. If it hadn't been for him, that's the life he could have lived. He *almost* regretted it, but not quite.

When the man below rolled off his lover, sweaty and spent, and stared up towards the air con vent, Rats moved on before he was spotted.

He'd lost his bearings after having stopped to witness the spectacle below. With the spatial disorientation of a pilot lacking a visible horizon, Rats no longer had the ability to determine angle or direction; whether he was heading up, down, or parallel.

Instinct took him into the first opening he encountered. Inside, there was barely enough space to wipe the beads of sweat from his brow. He sucked in stale, musty air extracted from the apartments below. Or was it above? He couldn't tell.

He sensed the air was warm and getting warmer and the space tighter and tighter, until the ceiling seemed to move down, the walls crept in, and the floor. . . well, the floor pressed up, pushing him toward that lowering ceiling.

Rats panicked, fight or flight reflex kicked in but there was nothing to fight, and nowhere to flee. He couldn't see what was in front of him, didn't know what was behind him, but onwards he pressed.

Shallow breaths made him lightheaded. He began hallucinating. He was in a coffin; a tight, airless box deep underground. He coughed, almost choked on bile, and felt himself convulse in terror as his thoughts, his imagination, his fear, spiralled out of control.

Rats realised this was where, when, and how he'd die; lost forever in the Byker Wall catacombs.

Ironically, it was death that saved him. Not his death, but the death of the cold, stiffening body his fingers reached out and touched.

Scrapper's body.

By chance, he'd made his way back to his starting point. He knew where he was. Hysterical laughter echoed around the shaft. Rats didn't care that someone might hear. All that mattered, at that moment, was he was back with his friend, safe and sound.

Rats curled up in a ball and clung on to Scrapper, his friend for life, and drifted off to a sleep filled with glorious nightmares.

**

Peter Kirk insisted on driving this time. 'I need to get on the bike again,' he'd told Ryan.

They were on their way to another of Justin Warne's homes; the one in Stocksfield which, Ryan discovered, had been rented by a League One professional footballer for almost two grand per month until his transfer to a Championship team during the January transfer window.

Ryan had been astonished the house remained empty almost as much as he was to learn anyone from a higher league would want a Sunderland player.

'Why would Warne want to throw away two grand income a month?'

'Perhaps he didn't need it,' Peter said. 'There was the Moot Hall scam, on top of his other business interests. Don't forget property wasn't Justin's only income source.'

Ryan directed Peter into the market town of Hexham, where the rivers North and South Tyne converge to form the Tyne.

'What are we doing here?' Kirk asked.

'Picking up the keys. Warne hired a management company to maintain his house.'

'Sorry, Ryan. I meant why bring me with you?'

'Because you're the only person I trust who knew Justin. I want to use your nose when we get in there. See if you sense anything out-of-place, owt that doesn't sit right with the Justin Warne you know.'

'I'm not sure I know him well enough to help on that score.'

'Too late now. Over there, that's the office.'

Kirk pulled the car onto double-yellow lines outside the office situated on the curiously named Priestpopple, close to Hexham Bus Station. Peter kept watch for traffic wardens while Ryan donned a facemask and headed into the office.

'I'm DC Ryan Jarrod. I called you earlier,' he said to the thickset man behind the only occupied desk.

'Got the warrant?'

'Yep.' Ryan passed the document over to the man, who's lips moved as he read it over.

'Seems in order,' he said.

'You've seen a lot of search warrants, have you?' The fact Ryan's smile went undetected behind his mask meant the clerk misunderstood the jovial comment.

'We're a respectable letting agency, I'll have you know.'

'I'm sure you are. May I have the keys to the property, please?'

The man had them at the ready. 'We've had a ton of interest in the place. Can't understand why he's paying us to leave it standing empty Throwing money down the drain, he is.'

'He won't be paying you much longer.'

'No? Is he selling up? He didn't let us know it was on the market.'

Ryan signed for the keys. 'I'll be back with them before you close.'

It was a ten-mile drive to Stocksfield, but it wasn't until Peter turned in left at the village's Baptist Church that he reminded Ryan he needn't direct him every inch of the way.

'I'm an Uber driver, remember. I can follow directions without you doubling up as a second Satnav.' The quip was good natured, and Ryan took it in the right spirit.

From Cadehill Road, Peter took a right and crawled along Crabtree Road until they found Justin Warne's third home.

'Nice,' Peter said as they pulled to halt on the driveway.

Ryan gave a low whistle. 'Aye. This is a proper detached house, like. Much as I like it, I hope this is the last house of his I see. I'll be presenting Escape to the Country next if I have to gan to more.'

He put the key in the lock.

'Let's pray we find what we need in here.'

**

What they found inside was a proper home, properly furnished, and properly equipped. It bore no resemblance to the Byker or Gateshead Fell houses.

'What, exactly, are we looking for?' Peter asked.

'I'm looking for files, folders, documents – anything that Justin may have moved here in the weeks leading up to his death. As for you, you're looking for anything that looks out of place.'

Methodically, they worked from room to room. Ryan opened every drawer in every piece of antique furniture. Peter cast his eyes over the contents of each. Jarrod encountered nothing which resembled a secreted document while Kirk saw nothing which jarred with his knowledge of Justin Warne.

They completed the downstairs search before climbing a staircase which wouldn't have been out of place on a cruise ship.

Ryan pushed open a bedroom door and did a double take. 'Bloody hell.'

On the back wall, a floor-to-ceiling black and white portrait of a slim man in a full-length coat was etched onto the wall itself. Either side of the man, paintings of post-modern, brutalist architecture hung brazen and proud.

'They're like the ones in his other house,' Ryan said.

'Probably because they are.'

High Level

'Who's the gadgy?'

Peter shook his head. 'I thought better of you. That's T. Dan Smith, that is.'

Ryan plucked at an eyebrow. 'What is it about Warne and Smith?'

'The more I hear of Justin Warne, the less I know about him, Ryan. The only thing he and I have in common is that we both think a lot of T. Dan. We're probably the only ones who do.'

Ryan's knees disappeared into a thick pile carpet as he felt beneath the bed. 'You tell me about him while I look for the files.'

Peter's eyes sparkled. 'To most people, Smith is anathema. They see him as the man responsible for ruining much of Newcastle's character. Some of it's true, much is urban myth.'

Ryan crawled underneath the bed. 'Can Smith teach us anything about Warne?' His voice sounded distant.

'Not sure, to be honest. In his own way, Smith was a visionary. You could almost call him an entrepreneur, a bit like Justin. He purified the Tyne with the aid of new sewage pipelines. Transformed it from a coal-blackened murk into what is now one of the best salmon rivers in the country. Unthinkable before Smith's involvement.'

Ryan re-emerged from beneath the bed, wiping his hands. 'Anything else?'

'Oh yes. He drew up initial plans for a European-style transport system. You see, the Metro was his brainchild, really.'

'Bugger me. I never knew. And he designed the Wall, as well?'

'No, but he commissioned Robert Erskine to do it for him. Smith was fiercely determined to rid Newcastle of its slums; the rows-upon-rows of crowded terraces which swept down to the Tyne in places like Elswick and Scotswood.'

Ryan pulled open a wardrobe. 'And Byker, yeah?'

'Yes. He spearheaded council projects which demolished these unpopular buildings and replaced them with modern public housing. The Byker Wall was his greatest achievement, in my humble opinion. And, I guess, Justin's as well.'

The doors of the empty wardrobe closed. 'Really? The place seemed a bit of a dump to me. What went wrong?'

'Timescales, Ryan; that's all. Byker may have been a slum but the community were together. Strong. Resilient. A proper support network, you know?'

'So?' Ryan asked, arms on hips looking at the image of T. Dan Smith.

'You can't demolish houses while folk are still in 'em, and you can't build until the land's been cleared. Before the terraces could be demolished, folk had to be rehoused elsewhere. By the time the Wall was completed, they were settled in their new locations. Fewer than forty percent of the original community returned to the area.'

Ryan began to understand. 'Which meant the rest of the people were newcomers?'

'Precisely. They didn't '*get*' the area. The spirit which had once been the heartbeat of the community had left the body.' Peter stared at a photograph of the Byker Wall. 'Instead, it became just another inner-city housing development, with all the problems and none of the solutions.'

Behind the door, a shelf housed half a dozen books wedged between brass figurines. 'There's another copy of Smith's biography here. How many of the buggers did he need?' Ryan asked rhetorically.

Peter laughed. 'There's one thing Justin and Smith had in common, though.'

'What's that?'

'Smith was jailed for six years for gifting the contract for the development of Peterlee New Town to a corrupt property developer by the name of John Poulson. Does that sort of behaviour remind you of anyone?'

Ryan looked around the room. His gaze settled on a picture out of place amongst the army of concrete obelisks. He was looking at a framed picture of Moot Hall pinned to the chimney breast.

'Certainly does,' Ryan said.

He reached up inside the chimney. Felt his fingers graze across something. He yanked on it. A bluish-grey rucksack fell into the open fireplace.

Ryan unzipped it.

'Eureka.'

In his hands were three files. They were labelled *'Moot Hall: Transaction, Contracts, Plans.'*

'Back of the net.'

Beneath the files lay Justin Warne's missing laptop.

**

He may have grabbed less than two hours fitful sleep, but Rats awoke, enlivened and clear of thought, in the arms of his desecrated friend.

Rats knew he'd never be traced in the network of tunnels. Even if the cops brought in tracker dogs, it'd be impossible for them to pick up his scent from within the Byker Wall's bowels.

They might, though, identify the smell of a dead body. Especially one only feet from the corridor.

Rats dragged Scrapper by the ankles and hauled him away from the grate. It was hard, strenuous, energy-sapping work, but he lugged Scrapper's dead weight through the internal maze for fifteen minutes until he came across his salvation: a central maintenance shaft which ran from the twelfth floor down to the basement.

The shaft had a metal staircase, encircled by a safety cage. On the wall opposite, he saw a red number five painted on the wall. Fifth floor. Now, he had the means to navigate the Wall to his heart's content, each floor clearly identifiable.

'Bye Scrapper,' he said. The cadaver thundered downwards. Rats heard heavy thumps as the boy's body ricocheted off the wall on its descent.

Without a downward glance, Rats wiped his hands on the staircase and began to climb. On his way up, he noted in which direction the air con vents ran from the main shaft at each floor; left or right or both ways.

He hadn't planned it. Not deliberately. But, when he came face-to-face with the ten marker, he knew it was fate. Time to have some fun. Lots of it.

Rats levered his way into a tube-like tunnel and inched his away along it until he could look down into a flat he recognised.

For the second time in a few hours, he took a grip on himself as he watched Maz Crawford strip for her shower.

CHAPTER TWENTY-SEVEN

Rats lay on his back, eyes shut, fantasising about what he'd do to the blonde girl with the canny tits, and how many times. After he'd finished with her, he'd make sure she had a painful end. She owed him.

Despite his anticipation, he found himself yawning. It had been a long couple of days, and he hadn't eaten since yesterday's McDonald's breakfast. Shame about Scrapper. He was always good for some scran.

His stomach gurgled like a geyser at the thought of food. He rolled over and looked back through the vent. The bathroom was empty, and he'd heard no noise from inside the apartment.

Rats thought he'd heard a door close at one point, but he needed to be sure it had been the girl going out, not coming back in. He gave it another ten minutes before gently removing the vent cover.

He could lower himself down okay, but how would he get back up again? The vent was directly above the toilet bowl. Although it was difficult to gauge height, he guessed he'd be able to reach the entrance if he stood on it.

He breathed in and went for it.

Rats hung by his arms for a moment before letting go. The floor was closer than he'd anticipated but he managed to cushion his landing so he touched down in Maz Crawford's flat without a sound.

He put his ear to the bathroom door.

Silence.

He pulled the handle and inched the door open.

The flat was deserted.

He took a good look round. There was another air con hatch in the living area, just above the sofa by the window, but it was far too small to climb through. His only escape route was back through the bathroom, where the hatch remained uncovered.

Rats opened the fridge door. He grabbed a pack of bacon and shoved the contents under the grill. He licked his lips as the bacon sizzled and spat. An open carton of orange juice stood inside the fridge door. He gulped from it and smacked his lips.

The smell of the bacon was too much for him. It wasn't crispy, but it would do. He ripped a sheet of kitchen paper from a roll and wrapped the food in it.

Rats re-entered the bathroom, stood on the toilet bowl, and muscled up through the gap. He took a last look down into the flat below. He'd used no plates, no cutlery, left no trace. Satisfied, he secured the vent and sat back to enjoy his breakfast.

'This is the life, man,' he said to himself through a mouthful of bacon.

**

Hannah Graves, Sue Nairn, and Nigel Trebilcock huddled around a laptop wading through reported sightings of Rats Scully. Gavin O'Hara and Todd Robson stood in animated conversation around Hannah's crime board. Ravi Sangar was in his tech room combing over social media, while movement within Stephen Danskin's office indicated he and Lyall Parker were reviewing progress on the hunt for Michael McNeil's killer.

Justin Warne was forgotten by all but the runt of the litter. Ryan Jarrod perched on the end of a desk far from the others, studying his own crime board.

He'd reversed it, put the crime scene photograph of a crumpled Justin Warne top centre and, from left to right beneath it, affixed the images of Lola Di Marco, Beth Richards, Suzanne Westwood, Tanita and, finally, George

High Level

Riley. Alongside each photograph, Ryan had scribbled some notes, decipherable only by him.

He focused on each face, one-by-one. Lost in thought, he didn't notice someone steal up behind him.

'I don't think we've met.'

Ryan turned and found himself looking into the most vivid blue eyes he'd ever seen. The face to which they belonged was anonymous, but he couldn't shift his gaze from those eyes.

'I'm Superintendent Maynard,' the woman said.

Ryan took her offered hand. 'No, we haven't been introduced. I was out on call when you came around, I gather. I'm DC Ryan Jarrod, ma'am. Pleased to meet you.'

She sat on the desk next to him. 'Tell me, what role do you have in the McNeil enquiry?'

'I don't, ma'am. I'm working another case.'

'Really? Tell me more.'

Ryan summarised the case as best he could. He relayed Warne's history, summed up the Moot Hall deal, and discussed the potential significance of the missing laptop.

Maynard showed a genuine interest and Ryan was impressed by the way she quickly assimilated the information.

She tipped her head towards the board. 'Who are these reprobates?'

Ryan snickered. 'I'm pretty sure one of these is the killer.'

'Enlighten me.'

He took a deep breath. Ordered his thoughts. 'Lola Di Marco. Owner of North Umbria Estates. She believed she had the Moot Hall deal signed, sealed and delivered. Warne corporately gazumped her.'

Ryan pointed at the second image. 'Beth Richards. Owner of High Level Properties. She, too, believed Warne was working on her behalf. He wasn't. I believe she also sent Warne a threatening note via a blog site he hosts. That's being checked as we speak. I hope.'

Maynard pulled her head back like a strutting pigeon. 'You *hope*? Don't you know?'

'Sorry, ma'am. It is, but way down the priority list. The Super... sorry, the Acting Super's focus is on catching McNeil's killer.'

'Ah, yes. Marvin Scully.'

'Aye, ma'am.'

She fixed him with eyes as blue as the waters of a Nordic fjord. 'Continue, please.'

'This is Suzanne Westwood. She had a contract for the internal refit of Moot Hall. So far as I know, Warne didn't renege on that part of the deal. Hopefully, the laptop I recovered will prove it.'

'And then, we can rule her out?'

Ryan inhaled through his nose. 'Not sure, ma'am.' He pointed to Tanita's headshot. 'This is Suzanne Westwood's stepdaughter, Tanita. Justin Warne was in a relationship with her.'

'Really? She's a bit young for him, isn't she?'

'Yes, ma'am. What's more, her birth mother is Beth Richards.'

Maynard whistled. 'Oh, what a tangled web we weave, when first we practice to deceive.'

'Walter Scott.'

She raised her eyebrows. 'Well done. I'm impressed.' She returned her focus to the board. 'Who's the odd-man out?'

'George Riley. An employee of Suzanne Westwood.'

'And he fits in, how?'

Ryan gave the question some thought. 'Westwood assigned him to check up on Warne. She says she feared he'd drop her in the shit...sorry, ma'am – the same as he had Di Marco and Richards.'

'Interesting.'

'Yeah. He also attacked a friend of Justin Warne's. And, he made an attempted assault on me.'

'Even more interesting. Who's working the case with you, DC Jarrod?'

'No-one, ma'am. Everyone else is after Scully.'

'What? You're telling me you've done all this work by yourself?'

Ryan felt the damned blush rise again. He looked at his shoes. 'Pretty much. DCI Kinnear has leant me a couple of uniform officers to do a bit of my donkey work but, basically, it's just me.'

'Wow. That is impressive.' Maynard gave him a quick smile. 'What do you need from me?'

'With respect, Acting Super Danskin's still calling the shots.'

'Good. Loyal, too. I like it. Let's assume I was in charge. What would you want from me, other than manpower?'

Ryan stared at the board. 'I'd like to know what's on the laptop, and I wouldn't mind some advice on where to go next.'

'I suggest you have another word with Riley. He seems Mr Probable, to me. Lie to him. Tell him it's unofficial. Off the record. Let him believe anything he tell us won't be used against him. We'll see if it he'll open up that way.'

'If he doesn't?'

'You bring him in. You make it official.'

Ryan thought of Celia Groenweld and prayed it wouldn't come to that.

'As for the laptop, leave that with me. My train to Basildon is due in an hour, but I'll have a word with Stephen. I'm sure he'll bump it up the list if I flutter my baby blues at him.'

Ryan was confident Danskin would order Ravi and the cybercrime team on the case within the hour.

How could he possibly resist those eyes?

**

George Riley used his elbow to prop himself against the door jamb. His eyes drifted up and down Ryan.

'What do you want?'

'I'd just like a quiet word, if that's okay with you.'

'Okay with me? Really? After last time? It'll be okay when my solicitor says it's okay; okay?'

'Fine, I can bring you to the station if you want. Keep you hanging around for hours until Celia Groenweld finds an empty spot in her diary for you. Or we can get it over with here. It's not about your attack on me or Peter Kirk, and it's not about Justin Warne. Not directly, anyway.'

He gave Riley what he hoped was a sincere smile. 'It's also completely off the record. No notebooks, no tapes, no nowt.'

'Will you drop the other charge? I'll never get another job with that hanging over me.'

'I can't do that, Mr Riley. But I can mention you've been fully co-operative in an ongoing enquiry of a different matter. In my experience, both the CPS and magistrates take kindly to such commendations.'

Riley pushed himself off the doorframe. Folded his arms. Finally, he gave a terse nod. 'Works for me.'

Ryan followed Riley into a small but tidy living room. A framed portrait of Muhammed Ali decorated an otherwise plain, white-washed wall. Ryan, though, fixated on a plastic table supporting a glass case. Inside the tank, a snake, its deep red bands ringed with smaller black and yellow interruptions, snoozed in a tight coil.

'That's Hannibal,' Riley said. 'He's a milk snake. The little buggers are cannibals. He sleeps most of the day, but if I dropped a frozen mouse in there now, he'd soon wake up. Wanna see?'

'No thanks. You're alright.'

Riley sat down on a lumpy sofa. Ryan pulled a chair from beneath a small dining table and sat astride it.

'Last time we spoke, you said you'd been ordered to follow Justin Warne.'

'Had on; you said this wasn't about him.'

Ryan held up his hands. 'No pens. No notebooks. I'm not trying to catch you out.'

Riley crossed his arms in front of him. 'Jury's out.' He laughed at his own irony.

The two stared at each other before Riley admitted, 'I did want to rough the bastard up a bit, but I didn't kill him.'

'Who did you want to rough him up for?'

'For myself.'

Ryan shook his head. 'That doesn't sound true.'

George Riley shrugged. 'I didn't kill him.'

'Good. Because if you didn't, that's a win-win conversation. And, if you only wanted to beat him up but didn't follow through, that's good, an' aal.'

Riley squinted.

'I'm not pissing you about here, George. I'm only trying to see the bigger picture. Anything you say won't be admissible in court. Now, if you really did want to sting him like a bee,' Ryan jerked a thumb towards Muhammed Ali, 'Why?'

George Riley ran his tongue along his front teeth as he thought. 'You're only interested in Justin Warne, right?'

'That's right, George.'

'And you're not trying to pin owt on us?'

Ryan traced a cross over his heart.

Riley chewed on a lip. 'I wanted him to get rid of them.'

'The Moot Hall files?'

Riley shook his head.

'What did you want him to get rid of, George?'

The man on the sofa squirmed in his seat. Sighed deeply. 'I had a lot of time for Mr Westwood. He gave me a job even though he knew I had a record. Not many would do that, you know what I mean?'

Ryan remained silent.

'Imagine how you'd feel if a creepy bastard was seeing your teenage daughter.'

'Derek Westwood knew?'

'Of course he did. Why do you think the poor bastard had a heart attack? Enough to push anyone over the edge, that.'

Ryan sat back, unsure of his next move. Riley owed Derek Westwood. Warne's actions killed Westwood. Ergo, Riley had motive for Justin Warne's murder.

'George, I ask you once again. Did you kill Justin Warne?'

Riley sat forward. 'No, I fucking didn't. Do you think I'd have just told you all that if I had? I mightn't have any poncey qualifications but I'm not stupid.'

'Did Suzanne Westwood hire you to sort Warne out?'

'No, no.' He shook his head. Laughed. 'You're missing the point.'

'What is the point?'

George Riley sat back. He turned his head and looked towards Hannibal, asleep in the vivarium.

'Listen, man. Imagine a snake was screwing your teenage daughter, and he also wanted to screw you for every penny he could. Wanted you to do work on the cheap. A lot of work for less than cheap. For free, to be exact.'

'Shit.'

'Exactly. The bastard's had the Moot Hall deal in his sights for years. He approached Derek. Told him to do the refit free gratis when it went through, *'or else'*.'

'He told you this?'

'Na.'

'Suzanne did.'

'Aye. That's why she wanted me to sort Warne out. Not to kill him, but to make sure he got rid of them.'

Ryan was still missing something. 'Let's backtrack a bit. You said Warne used Tanita so the Moot Hall refit wouldn't cost a penny. How was he going to use Tanita?'

'Howay, man. It's obvious, isn't it?'

Ryan worked things through in his head. It still didn't add up. 'What was Warne supposed to get rid of?'

'The photos, man. The photos he took of Tanita.'

High Level

George Riley saw the lightbulb moment illuminate Ryan Jarrod's face.

'Aye, detective. *Those* sort of photos.'

CHAPTER TWENTY-EIGHT

FRIDAY

Sam Maynard proved good to her word. Ravi Sangar had called Ryan late the previous night, just as he'd settled down in front of Netflix.

'I've got Justin Warne's laptop open in front of me, Ry.'

'Jeez, do you live in Forth Street? You're never away.'

'And who's fault's that? I've enough on me plate with Scully, without you exerting your baby-faced leverage over Maynard.'

'Sorry, Ravi. I have to say, though: Todd's right. She's aal reet.'

'Crawler. Anyway, what am I looking for?'

'Where do I start? Okay; firstly, print-out all files relating to the Moot Hall transaction. That was my initial interest in the missing computer, so we'll start with them. Check against the paper records. See if there's any differences.'

'Whoa. Hang on. I'll get the papers to you, but I'm not your errand boy. You can do the comparison yourself.'

Ryan ran his fingers through his hair. 'Aye. Fair comment. Also, I want all of Warne's e-mails sent to or from Beth Richards, Suzanne Westwood, Lola Di Marco, and anyone associated with their companies.'

He heard Ravi let out a breath. 'You any idea how many e-mails he's got? There's thousands of the buggers. Doesn't look like he ever deletes any.'

'That's good.' Ryan paused for a moment. 'Though I also need you to recover any he has deleted. You can do that, can't you?'

'Shove a broom up me arse as well and I'll sweep the floor, if you like.'

Ryan chuckled.

'Anything else I can help you with, sir?' Ravi chided.

'I don't suppose there's any dodgy porn on there, is there?'

Ravi laughed. 'Probably. He's a bloke. Don't we all?'

'Maybe, aye; but not porn we've made ourselves.'

'Huh?'

'I'm reliably informed he took intimate photographs of Tanita Richards, or Westwood; whatever you want to call her.'

'She's the lass in the boat on Windermere, right?'

'The very same.'

**

The lass from the Windermere boat spread her length along her mother's sofa in the luxury of the Higham Dykes bungalow.

Tanita's hair hung loose, rays of sunlight tinting it with shades of gold and orange. She wore a tight top which clearly showed there was nothing beneath. A pair of silk running shorts rode up her tanned thighs. It was easy to see her allure to Justin Warne. Less clear was what attracted her to him.

'I thought I'd seen the last of you,' she said.

'Just a couple more questions,' Ryan assured.

'I've got nothing to hide,' she said, tugging her shorts even higher.

Ryan glanced towards Beth Richards. 'If you want to leave at any time, you can, Miss Richards.'

'I'm going nowhere.'

Ryan looked out the lead-framed windows at mature trees which bowed like servile waiters in the strengthening nor' easterly. This wasn't going to be pleasant.

'Did Justin Warne take photos of you?'

A mischievous grin played on the teenager's lips. 'Yeah. All the time. He said I was pretty.'

Ryan studied her with his eyes as he probed deeper. 'I meant nude photos.' He heard Beth Richards gasp behind him.

Tanita's grin grew wider. 'I knew what you meant.'

'You were okay with that? He didn't force you?'

The girl sat up. She tossed her hair and looked directly at Ryan. 'No. 'Course not. Why would I mind?'

Ryan glanced at Beth. Her lips were thin. A nerve quivered on her jawline. She nodded her assent for him to continue.

'Those pictures are forever, Tanita. They could be on a website somewhere, right now. They could come back to haunt you.'

Tanita shook her head. 'Justin wouldn't do that to me. Besides, I look good, don't I?' She struck a pose like the one on Warne's screensaver. 'I'll probably never look this good again. Why wouldn't I want him to photograph me?'

Ryan heard Beth Richards whimper. When he looked towards her, she had her eyes tightly shut.

'Did Justin send you the pictures?'

Tanita shrugged. 'No. But he did show me them. They were good. I loved posing for him.' She lowered her eyes, then raised them to meet Ryan's. 'I wish he had sent them to me. Then, I could have showed you them. You'd love them, I'm sure.'

Her little grin sickened Ryan. 'How many did he take?'

'Dozens. Hundreds. I dunno, really.'

'When did you start posing for him?'

Tanita laughed. 'As soon as he asked.'

'Let's not be clever, shall we? When did he first ask you?'

This time, Tanita's eyes sought out Beth's. 'Our first date. We had sex…'

'You were sixteen!' Beth sobbed. 'Sixteen, baby, and he was in his thirties. He had sex with you on your first night.'

'Doh – yeah. 'Course he did. It's legal. It's what I wanted, not just Justin. We made love together. Both of us. Not just him.'

Tanita turned her eyes to Ryan, the smirk back on her face. 'Soon as we finished, he picked up his 'phone and started taking pictures. He said he wanted to capture the afterglow.'

'Oh God,' Beth said.

'You do know he showed the photographs to your father, don't you?'

'What?' mother and daughter said, together.

'I'm sorry, Miss Richards. Do you want to leave?'

'Not fucking likely. What did that bastard Warne do?'

Tanita stared out the window, tears in her eyes, confusion stamped across her face, the smirk gone along with her innocence.

'Tanita, listen to me.'

She turned towards him, glassy-eyed.

'Justin Warne showed your father those photographs. Photographs of you, in the nude, in the *'afterglow.'* And he probably showed him more.'

Tears glistened on Tanita's cheeks. 'Videos,' she whispered.

'I didn't catch that,' Ryan said.

'Videos. Of me doing stuff. You know - stuff.'

Ryan didn't need to hear more. 'Listen. This is important for you, and your future. Also, Beth's future, and Suzanne Westwood's, too.'

'Her!' Tanita snorted.

'Yes, her. Make amends with her. Your father didn't have a heart attack because of work pressures. He had a heart attack because he was being blackmailed into signing contracts under threat of your nude photographs going public.'

**

Rats lay above the bathroom of Maz Crawford's flat, camera phone at the ready.

He'd been on the seventh floor when he realised he'd developed superpowers. He'd heard Ailsa Black on the telephone telling her boss she was sorry for being late and she was on her way in.

Below him lay Ailsa's bathroom; the room in which she stashed her drugs.

He removed the grate from the air con unit, dropped to the toilet bowl, and from there to the floor. He stripped off, dove into the shower, and watched Scrapper's blood run from him, its dried brownness regaining a crimson hue and, finally, a diluted pink as it swirled down the outlet.

Once dried, he lifted the cystern and snorted Ailsa Black's cargo.

In the living area, Ailsa had left her phone charger plugged in. Rats attached his own phone to it and devoured three packets of Walkers and a handful of Jaffa Cakes while the percentage charge went up sufficient for his needs.

By the time he'd finished, his superpowers were in full flow. He could hear every word said in the building, every baby's cry, every TV programme being watched.

Having superpowers wasn't easy. He had to cover his ears with his hands to shut out the constant racket in his head but, every now and again, it proved ever so useful. Like the moment he heard Terry Strang lock the door on his way out of the flat next to Ailsa's.

Rats disappeared into the infrastructure and crawled the short distance to Strang's apartment. The vent above the bathroom was wedged tight, but not tight enough to defeat Rats' superpowers.

Once inside Strang's flat, he raided the wardrobe for a t-shirt which was too tight and jeans too loose, but they were less conspicuous than the blood-soaked mess he had been wearing.

High Level

He deliberately chose downbeat clothes to ensure Terry Strang wouldn't miss them. Nor would they attract attention on his route to Coventry, unlike the stained gear he bundled up and carried with him to his next destination: the tenth floor and the girl in the shower.

Rats closed his eyes and waited for showtime.

When he opened them again, the room below was protected by a swirl of steam. The girl was wrapped in a towel and she was on her way out of the bathroom.

'Shit.'

Rats scuttled along the vent, took a sharp left into an even narrower tunnel, at the end of which a letterbox-shaped grille allowed the room below to breathe.

Rats fumbled for his camera. Swiped it alive and pointed it downwards. Just as Maz Crawford wiggled into her jeans.

'Ah, man. Balls.' He kicked the wall in frustration.

Maz stopped at the sound. She looked around. Saw nothing. She walked to the window and turned her head from left to right. Finally, back in the centre of the room, she tilted her head and looked upwards.

Rats superpowers deserted him. All he could do was shy away from the grille and listen to a hubbub of mechanical noise and hissing air filtering through the air con system.

He crawled back to the bathroom. Perhaps the girl would strip for bed. Even better, she may need a pee. Rats steadied his camera and stared down.

Sure enough, the girl appeared. 'Yes,' he mouthed.

He brought the viewfinder to his eye, readied himself for the girl to squat.

She didn't squat. Instead, she stood on the toilet pan and reached for the grille.

'Fuck, fuck, fuck,' the voice in Rats' head said.

He was out into the maintenance shaft heading down the ladder by the time Maz Crawford ran a finger over the air vent cover.

She looked down into the toilet bowl, then at her fingertip, and frowned.

**

Ryan knocked on Stephen Danskin's office door and waited.

'Howay in, man. No need for ceremony with me.'

'Sir.'

'How's the Warne enquiry going? I probably shouldn't tell you this, but Sam Maynard thinks you're a bright spark, tackling it on your own. Don't let it go to your head, though. You haven't solved owt yet.'

'I'm getting close. I'm nearly there. I can sense it. Actually, that's why I'm here. I know you're up to your eyes with the McNeil case, but I could do with a hand. Just for a couple of days.'

Danskin pulled at an ear lobe. 'You've got it.'

'Thank you, sir. Who's most expendable: Todd or Treblecock? Either will do.'

Danskin shook his head. 'Neither. What I meant was, you've already got your help. I boosted your request for Warne's IT check up the queue. Sangar's looking at it now.'

Ryan scoffed. 'You boosted it, or Superintendent Maynard did?'

Danskin glared at him. 'Now listen…'

A breathless Lyall Parker burst in without knocking. 'We've got a breakthrough, sir.'

Danskin was on his feet. 'We've got Scully?'

'Nothing as substantial as that. We've had a report of a missing person from the Byker Wall. It's a known associate of Scully who goes by the name of Scrapper. We are confident he's the accomplice Scully uses for his racketeering, so we think there's every likelihood they're both linked to Michael McNeil's murder. Wherever one is, we'll find the other. I'm a canny Scotsman, but I'd still stake a wee fortune on it.'

Stephen Danskin clapped his hands. 'Which also means it doubles their chances of fouling up, and ours of apprehending them.'

He headed for the door into the bullpen.

'Sir; about Todd or Treblecock…'

'Forget it, Jarrod. And forget about Sangar, too, for now. Once we get our hands on the bastard Scully, you can have every resource I've got.'

With a look over his shoulder, Danskin ended the conversation. 'You're on your own.'

Ryan watched the rest of the squad assemble around their crime board, animatedly gesturing towards it. Hannah Graves doled out photographs of Scully's accomplice to the team.

She had a word and a smile for everyone as she did so.

'Aye, I'm on my own, all right,' Ryan said to Danskin's empty office.

CHAPTER TWENTY-NINE

SATURDAY

In the darkness of the early hours, Ryan climbed out of his old-fashioned bedroom and made his way downstairs to the uber-modern living room designed for him by Hannah.

There, he hoped to grab the sleep denied him by his bed. It had proved a fruitless exercise. He lay across the cream sofa, sat up on it, reclined in it; still sleep evaded him. Eventually, he gave up.

He scrolled through the content of Sky Movies, Amazon Prime, and Netflix. Nothing appealed. He made himself a flask of coffee and, at three-fifty am, closed his eyes, pressed a few random buttons on the remote, and settled down to watch whatever fate had selected for him.

Fate's selection was a Robin Williams movie Ryan had never seen before. He almost switched it off once he realised the character played by Williams had a humdrum life uncannily like his own. The character lived alone, had no friends or love life, and existed only for his work.

Ryan decided to stick with it but sought the company of a crate of Stella in place of the coffee. Once he got over his morbid, self-centred sentimentality, he realised the movie was okay. He became engrossed in it and, before he'd even finished his second can, the film drew to its climax.

As dawn broke behind the closed curtains of Ryan Jarrod's house in Whickham, Robin Williams' on-screen character was in California, armed with a knife and a camera, taking pictures of two lovers he'd forced to pose naked in sexual positions.

High Level

As the credits to One-Hour Photo rolled, Ryan knew where the Justin Warne case was taking him next.

**

She appeared to have been swallowed whole by the oversized orange chair which engulfed her. A cup of spiced tea sat on a table, and a copy of Susan Hill's 'The Woman in Black' lay next to it.

'Good book?' Ryan asked.

'Let's just say it's better read in the morning than in bed if you want to get any sleep.'

'What's it about?'

'You didn't come to see me this early to discuss my reading habits, I'm sure.'

'No, you're right.'

'So, what do you want? It's the weekend and I fancy going for a drive once it warms up.'

'Anywhere nice?'

She rolled her eyes. 'Look, get to the point: what the fuck is this about?'

Ryan steeled himself and prepared to fight the blush he knew would come.

'Did Justin Warne ever take photos of you?'

Hayley Mack stared at him.

'Not ordinary photos…'

'I know what you mean,' she snapped. 'Why do you ask?'

Ryan raised his eyes and looked out of the Wills Building window. A golfer fluffed his bunker shot and flung his club into the sand. *'Someone else having trouble with etiquette,'* he thought.

'It's come to our attention that Justin Warne took compromising photographs of a former girlfriend. Inappropriate ones. I know you and Warne were an item, once, and I wondered if…' He hoped he didn't need finish the question.

'I know what you're talking about, detective.'

Ryan blew out his relief. 'Warne was being followed as a result of the photographs he took. The man following him also beat up Peter Kirk.'

Hayley's face blanched and she, too, turned to watch the golfers.

'Did he take pictures of you, Hayley?'

She remained silent for a minute before saying, 'It was, like, ten or twelve years ago. When we were together. He said he'd deleted them.'

'Had he?'

She stayed silent longer this time. 'He wanted us to get back together again. Recently, this is. I told him to get lost, or words to that effect.'

'And?'

'Out-of-the-blue, he texted me. It said, 'Remember this?', and he'd attached a photograph of us. It was raunchier than I'd remembered.'

'Did he contact you again?'

Her head gave a series of jerky nods. 'Oh yes, he did. He sent me another picture, much the same as the other. This time, the text said, 'We need to do this again. Or I might just accidentally on purpose send this to mummy and daddy.'

'Jesus.'

She met Ryan's eyes. 'Before you ask, I deleted them.'

'I'm sure our tec crew can recover them.'

Hayley looked embarrassed.

'Only if we need to, you understand.'

'Thank you. Anyway, that's when I went to Byker and wrote '*Die, you shit*' on his door. That's why I did it, detective. Revenge porn – you read about it but never think it'll ever affect you. Trust me, no-one ever knows, for sure.'

'I'm sorry,' Ryan said.

She gave a wry chuckle. 'Not your fault.'

Ryan thought of the movie he'd just seen. 'Did he force you into having your photograph taken?'

'Oh, no. Nothing like that. I was okay about it, back then. I trusted him. But I didn't really know him, did I?'

Ryan looked Hayley in the eye. 'Did he ever threaten you?'

'Apart from the text telling me he'd send my folks the photos, no. I half expected him to turn up demanding money, but he didn't.'

'I don't think he needed money, Hayley. I think he needed to feel powerful. I also think there's something else, but I don't know what yet.'

It was Ryan's turn to remain silent. Hayley watched him, waiting for him to speak again. Finally, he stood.

'Thanks for your time. I'm sorry that was so difficult.'

'Don't worry, detective. I think it was more difficult for you than me.'

She was right; it had been. He stepped into the corridor.

Before Hayley Mack closed her door, she said, 'I'm not sorry he's dead. Not one little bit.'

**

Rats Scully craved sleep. The cramped and cold confines of the Byker Wall's intestines made sleep virtually impossible. His entire body wracked with pain. He doubted he'd ever manage to stand up straight again, forever going through life deformed and bent double.

The only difference between him and Quasimodo was that he, Marvin Scully, had superpowers. He turned out a pocket and gazed longingly at the tiny blue crystals in the bag.

He had no idea where Ailsa Black got her money from but, wherever it was, he was grateful for it. Christine - crystal meth – was his new girlfriend, and he loved her more than anything else in the world. More than his dad; more, even, than the girl in the tenth floor flat.

Below him, Maz Crawford performed her early morning workout, dressed in a short slinky dressing robe. He watched her toned body flex as she went through a series of squats before she struck a pose and shot out a stiff-arm punch, a Choku Zuki, followed by Haito Uchi.

Rats had no idea what her movements were called. The way her unfettered breasts jiggled beneath her robe was all that mattered to him. He breathed noisily, the noise drowned only by the machinations of a wheezing ventilation fan in a vent somewhere nearby.

Maz brought her knee up and, in a second motion, swept her foot to head height.

'*She's flexible, an' aal*' Rats thought.

She followed the Ashi Barai with a mind-boggling Tornado Kick and, finally, a manoeuvre he recognised all too well: a Kin Geri groin kick.

He winced at the memory, but it reminded him it wasn't all play. He had work to do, too.

Scully's fingers tenderly caressed his well-used razor blade.

**

'I can't tell you something I don't know, Hayley,' Peter Kirk repeated.

'You must know. The detective said you'd been beaten up by somebody stalking Justin.'

Peter took the phone from his ear while he sipped tea from a china cup. 'Yes, but that was something to do with a business deal. I don't know anything about any photographs.'

'This is serious, Peter. You have to be honest with me.'

'I am. I have no idea what you're talking about.'

He heard her take a long intake of breath.

'Justin took some dodgy photographs of me. Years ago. That detective bloke thinks they might be why he was killed.'

'Really? He took photographs of you?'

'Never mind that. Was he killed because he was taking dirty pictures of girls?'

'Girls plural, you said. There was more than one?'

High Level

'Does it fucking matter?' she hissed. 'Look, you came to me for help because you thought the police were framing you. I lied to them for you. The least you can do is be upfront with me.'

'Hayley; I shall say this only once: the police were looking for a missing laptop because they think Justin had stitched up some important people over a property deal. It's got nothing to do with photographs.'

'Then why has Jarrod been to see me about them?'

'Perhaps he wanted to see you nude.'

'Fuck off.'

Peter tried to keep the exasperation out of his voice. 'It was a joke, Hayley.'

'It's not something to joke about.'

'They've got the laptop now, anyway. They'll have all the evidence, all the proof, they need.'

'You'd better be telling me the truth. The last thing I need is for me and him to be spread all over some dodgy website.'

'I know. It'd break the internet if you were.'

'You're almost as bad as Justin.'

Hayley picked up a can of beer. Swallowed half of it down in one.

'If I were you, I'd be careful,' she said. 'You don't want to end up the same as him, do you?'

CHAPTER THIRTY

Rats scuttled along the tunnel as fast as he could. The girl had finished her workout and he hoped she was heading to the bathroom.

She didn't disappoint him.

He reached the grille overlooking the shower just in time to see Maz slip out of her robe. She stepped under the steaming hot spray, her body soon glistening and slick beneath the jets.

Rats watched her soap up and massage herself beneath the foam. *'Who needs crystal when I can have all this, all to myself?'* the voice in his head told him.

It also told him this could be the last time he ever saw her. Alive, that is.

He had to take it all in, every last moment. Imprint it in his memory for when he was in Coventry. She needed to be treasured.

'Shit!' He'd forgotten he had his phone with him. Of course! He could film her. She'd be with him forever.

He fumbled in his pocket. His fingers rubbed against his erection. For a moment, he wanted to make it his priority until he remembered he could do that anytime, again and again, once he'd taken the video.

Beneath the meth and a roll of banknotes, he felt the smooth screen of his phone. He pulled it out and steadied his hand. 'Yeah, babeee!'

Maz Crawford reached up. She ran her fingers through soapy hair. Her movements pulled the flesh and muscles of her breasts taught.

Rats' sweaty fingertip brushed the camera icon. He prepared to record.

And, in the moment, forgot to change the setting from 'Photo' to 'Video.'

The flash lit up the confines of his hide like a supernova. He blinked, but all his eyes could see was a residual, blinding whiteness.

Rats blinked again, and again. By the time he regained focus, he was aware the shower had stopped running. Without his superpowers, he hadn't noticed.

What's more, a naked Maz Crawford stood directly beneath him, her eyes trained upwards.

**

Police work wasn't a nine-to-five, five days a week job so, when Ryan entered the bullpen, it was eerily quiet, even for a Saturday. With a major investigation ongoing, he expected more activity.

Ryan and one of DCI Kinnear's lads exchanged nods, another spoke into a telephone, and a third stared at a PC monitor hooked up to the Mis Per database.

None of Lyall Parker's squad was around and, although Ryan could see two shadows moving in Danskin's office, he could tell neither belonged to Stephen.

He stood before his crime board, lost in thoughts which rapidly disappeared up their own backside. His eyes flitted from one image to the next, then back again. Each time, he reached the same conclusion.

Ryan so wanted it to be one of Beth Richards or Tanita.

Both had motive. Warne had reneged on the Moot Hall deal with Beth, not to mention sleeping with her teenage daughter. She'd pleaded innocent to knowing about Tanita and Warne. It wasn't important: the property scam provided sufficient motive to charge her.

As for Tanita, she was being used by an older man. 'Hell hath no fury like a woman scorned,' came to mind, yet

Tanita was neither furious about her relationship with Warne, nor had she any knowledge of being scorned.

More compelling, though, was the fact both had been in Windermere at the time of Warne's killing.

Ryan picked up a red marker pen and scrawled 'X' through the names of Beth Richards and her daughter, Tanita.

Ryan tapped the tip of his middle finger against the centre of his forehead as he looked between the photographs of George Riley and Suzanne Westwood. They came together as a package.

Riley had means and opportunity, Westwood motive. And plenty of it. For some reason, Ryan felt in his gut that Riley had told him the truth. He put it down to instinct, nothing more, but enough for him to scroll a '?' above his photograph.

As for Westwood, not only did she have the welfare of her stepdaughter at stake, she also had the anger that Warne was the cause of her husband's death. And, that he had her over a barrel with the Moot Hall refurb.

He chose a green pen to draw a green tick, boldly and confidently, through the name of Suzanne Westwood.

Ryan closed his eyes, tipped his head skywards, and gave a satisfied smile. Only one thing remained before he brought her in. Danskin would ask him one question. It would be the question he always asked: *'Have you seen what you expected to see?'*

Ryan needed to be sure his answer was 'No.'

He walked to the window and looked down at the empty bars and restaurants lining both banks of the Tyne. God, how he could do with a beer right now.

A beer.

He logged onto a PC, scrolled through the menu, identified the item he wanted, and pressed print. The image emerged from the printer at a snail's pace.

High Level

The door to Danskin's office opened. The two female occupants, Sergeants Sue Nairn and Hannah Graves, emerged.

Sue beamed the smile of an officer nearing the end of her tenure; Hannah, looking pale, drawn and twice her age, gave him a tentative, thin-lipped smile. Both women moved to discuss the contents of the Lee Scully / Michael McNeil crime board.

Ryan muttered, 'Good morning' as he walked by them and pinned a new image to his board.

Hayley Mack.

Ryan needed proof he'd considered all options before making his case to Danskin, and Mack had also been photographed, blackmailed, and coerced. What's more, she'd illustrated Justin Warne's house with the word '*Die*' in dog crap.

Ryan placed a yellow question mark against Hayley Mack's name. If he could prove she'd also commented, '*You're high-level filth*' on a blog post, she might achieve green tick status.

He glanced to his right.

'Ladies, I don't suppose Ravi's around, is he?'

**

Ravi Sangar shut down the monitor screen as soon as he sensed the tec room door open.

'Aye, aye. Looking a bit shifty there, mate. Trawling through Naughty Nurses again, were you?' Ryan gave him wink.

'Bloody hell, man. I thought you were Danskin. No, if you must know, I'm looking at the info you asked me for. Saturday's the only chance I get.'

'Oh, cheers, man. I owe you one.'

'Too bloody right, you do.'

'What've you managed to come up with?'

Ravi was surrounded by a plethora of screens and keyboards and cables as if he were a prog rock keyboard player from the seventies. He spun his chair so he faced Ryan.

'Not a lot. Nothing that would convince either Danskin or Parker to divert resources your way.'

'Ah, hadaway, man. There's got to be something in the plans that shows up dodgy.'

'There's absolutely nowt, pal.'

'Not even with the refurb contract he had with Westwood Building Contractors?'

'Not even that.'

Ryan swept a hand through his hair. 'There's got to be, man. He was blackmailing Suzanne Westwood. He got them to agree to do the work for nowt.'

Ravi shook his head. 'Not according to the paperwork. Westwood was charging him the national debt of Bolivia for the work.'

'In that case, there must be something on the paper files. Some discrepancy there. Get them to me asap, will you?'

'I don't need to. That Lucy lass from Kinnear's team's been through them already. She's a good 'un, she is. Even she said the computer records are an exact match of the paper files.'

Ryan made a noise like a camel. 'Okay. What about the e-mails?'

'So far, they're all business-like and professional. He doesn't seem to have deleted many, although I haven't had a chance to check deleted files. Warne's been quite open about it. There's communication from Beth Richards about terminating the lease for his office in High Level Properties, Richards was open about Lola Di Marco's complaint against him and, although there's a notable cooling in the wording of e-mails from Di Marco, there's no hint of threats or wrongdoing in any of the content.'

'Fuck.' Ryan massaged his temples with the index finger of each hand. 'What about this *Beer* character?'

'It's not Beth Richards.'

Ryan exhaled. 'I'd come to that conclusion myself. At least I was right about summat.'

Ravi gave a mirthless chuckle. 'I do have some good news, though. Well, sort of.'

'Which is?'

'I know who Beer is.'

Ryan sat up, gripping the arms of his chair. 'Who?' He prayed he was about to hear the name, Hayley Mack.

'Bruce Bicker.'

'What? Who?'

'Bruce Bicker.'

'I knaa, man, but who the fuck is Bruce Bicker?'

Ravi shrugged. 'I don't know, apart from the fact he's a software technician.'

Ryan groaned. 'S'ppose I should talk to him, still.'

'Don't think Danskin will allow it. Too expensive.'

'Ravi, man, have you turned into The Riddler overnight? What's that supposed to mean?'

'It means, the IP address the '*High Level filth*' message was sent from is based in good ol' US of A. Bruce Bicker lives in Idaho.'

Ryan let out a groan and slumped in his seat. 'Jesus Christ. What does some redneck have to do with the toon, let alone High Level and Justin Warne?'

Ravi's only answer was, 'Sorry, mate. I did what I could.'

Ryan sat sullen and silent. Finally, he struggled out of his chair. 'Sod this for a game of soldiers. I've had enough. I'm away h'yem.'

'Before you go, I might as well put the old tin lid on it. There was no porn on his computer at all. No cookies, bookmarks, not a thing.'

Ryan harrumphed and moved to the door. He lay his hand on the door handle. Stopped.

'Wait a minute. We've been working on the theory that Warne's laptop was the key to all this. What if we've been wrong?'

'I'm not following.'

'What if we've spent all this time looking for something that isn't linked to his death?'

'Nah. You've still lost me.'

'Warne didn't have a mobile phone on him when he was found, remember. What if his phone's the key to all this, not the laptop?'

CHAPTER THIRTY-ONE

It was a weekend, a Saturday afternoon. Ryan had no idea what shape she'd be in, though he guessed no worse than usual. He imagined every day would be pretty much the same to her.

Still, he should have brought somebody with him. Just in case.

'What are you doing here?'

'Can I come in?'

'You can come anytime,' Sally Sykes said, with a wicked emphasis on the penultimate word.

Yep. He should have brought somebody with him.

'Can I ask you a question? About your…friendship, with Justin Warne?'

She sighed. 'Him again.'

Ryan wanted in-and-out of there as quickly as he could. He cut to the chase. 'Did he take photographs of you?'

She lifted her head and stared somewhere over his head.

Ryan could see the sadness on her face. 'Did you want him to?'

She looked down at her nails and picked on their cuticles.

Ryan reached out a hand. He thought of the possible consequences, or accusations, but went ahead anyway. He touched her gently on the knee.

'It is important. And, for what it's worth, I'm truly sorry.'

Her eyes teared. 'You're a nice person.'

'Please, can you answer the question.'

'The first time, I didn't know anything about it. I'd passed out. Pissed out, more like. Pissed out of my head. When I came round, he was standing over me, taking pictures.'

'Did he say anything?'

She gave a brisk nod. 'He said I was beautiful. He said that every time he wanted sex.' She rubbed her hands together.

'He'd come around whenever he wanted to, you know. Whenever he wanted me. And he'd always take pictures.'

'Did he use a camera?'

She shook her head. 'No. Just his phone. He said something about taking it *'point of view.'*

They sat in a silence interrupted by a barking dog and its owner's curses.

'After a while, I got used to the camera. The sex was good. It compensated for lots of things. Even for the camera.'

'I'm sorry to ask this, but was sex always consensual?'

Her brow furrowed. 'How do you define that?'

'Well, in a court of law, it means both partners agree to sex every single time.'

Sally Sykes gulped down air. 'What does the law say sex is?'

Ryan squirmed. The lid of Pandora's Box lay open, and out flew Ryan's embarrassment.

'The law says, without consent, any sexual activity - oral sex, genital touching, and vaginal or anal penetration - is sexual assault. Rape, if you like.'

'It was consensual,' Sally said. 'At least, by that definition, it was.'

'What does that mean?'

Sally Sykes looked skywards. 'All of that was consensual. What I didn't consent to was the beatings, the whippings, the third parties. None of that rough stuff I agreed to. None of the violence. That's when I felt dirty, Ryan; when he did those things to me, and when he filmed me doing it.'

Ryan didn't know what to say. He had an urge to hug her, to take her pain away, but protocol, yet alone Covid restrictions, prohibited it.

'He didn't just use me, he abused me. I was a mess before he came into my life and, for a while, it was sweet knowing someone thought I was beautiful. Wanted me. But if I thought I was a disaster before Justin Warne, look at me now. And it's all down to him. Dr Jekyll was fun to be with. It was Mr Hyde who did this to me.'

'Sally, did you kill him?'

'Did I kill him?' She took his hand from her knee and held it tightly. 'No, I didn't.'

She brought his hand to her lips and kissed it, before adding her name to those who'd told him, 'I wish I had, though.'

**

'Where's Ravi?'

Sue and Hannah looked up from their screens. 'He's gone home,' Sue said. Not long after you spoke to him.'

'Shit.'

'Anything I can do for you?'

'I was right. It's not the laptop. It's the phone. It's all on his phone.'

Sue raised both hands. 'Whoa, whoa. What's on who's phone?'

Ryan took a breath. If he said anything, he'd drop Ravi right in it. 'The Warne case. I've found where the evidence is. It'll lead me to his killer.'

Hannah spoke calmly. 'Listen, Ry. What if you're wrong about this?'

His lip curled as he looked at her. 'What would you know? This is my case, not yours. You and your pals have enough on your plate, so Danskin says. Leave the tea-boy here to pick up the shitty stuff.'

Sue Nairn put her hand on Hannah's wrist and took charge of the situation. 'We're all one team. We might be following different lines of enquiry, but we're all on the same side.'

Ryan laughed bitterly. 'That's what Steve Bruce says to his substitutes, is it? *'Look, I know the others are nee good but they're still better than you so man up and warm the bench.'* Is that what you're telling me?'

'You need a rest, Ryan. I'm not being patronising here, but you're conducting a major crime investigation all on your lonesome. That's some task. It takes its toll. And, right now, you're at breaking point.'

Ryan sat down. Nairn was right, he knew she was. He just didn't want to admit it.

'Go home. Stay away tomorrow. Come back on Monday. I'm senior officer today. It's my call, and I've called it.'

Ryan let out a yell. 'Sod it.' He slammed the palm of his hand on his desk, again and again. Slammed it until his old burn scars screamed in protest.

'Feel better?' Sue asked, softly.

'Do I fuck. You know what's worse, though? You're right.'

'Good. You know it makes it sense.'

Hannah looked at him with something resembling pity. He'd forgotten she was there.

'You're not looking too clever yersel,' he said. 'You look older than me gran.'

Hannah's complexion was sallow, her curls unwashed and greasy. She'd chewed her fingernails to the quick and the sparkle in her eyes had given way to the cloudiness of a cataract patient.

'The difference is, Ry, I admit it. Sue and me have just been talking. That's why we've been here all day. It's her last couple of days but she's kindly offered to take the lead on the Michael McNeil investigation until Tuesday. I'll be back then.'

She looked at Ryan. 'We're only human, Ry. Sometimes, we have to admit it to ourselves. What was it you told me old Frank Burrows used to say? The job gets to all of us in the end. He was right. We just have to admit it, now and again.'

Before he could respond, Hannah's phone rang.

High Level

'Hannah Graves,' she answered. Inadvertently, she'd left her phone on speaker mode. They all heard the voice on the other end.

'It's Marilyn. Maz Crawford, remember?'

Hannah sighed. 'Hello Miss Crawford. Is this urgent? I was just going off duty.'

'I'm sorry, but I think it is. Please don't think I'm crazy, but I think I'm being stalked.'

Hannah thought she was crazy.

'What makes you think that?' she rolled her eyes towards Sue Nairn.

The voice came back, hesitant. 'Well, I came home the other day and had the feeling someone had been inside the flat.'

'You had a feeling,' Hannah repeated, unable to keep the scepticism out of her voice.

Sue Nairn held both hands in front of her, palms downwards. *Calm down,* the gesture said.

Hannah nodded an acknowledgement. 'Can you describe this feeling?'

'I know it sounds stupid, but it smelt like someone had been cooking.'

Hannah rubbed a finger beneath her nose. 'It'll have been from next door. The air con units are all linked up, aren't they?'

'That's the other thing. I've heard noises.'

'I live in an apartment block, too. There's noise all the time.'

'It's different, though. I can't explain it. Like, knocking sounds. As if something's moving around up there.'

'Mice. Rats. It could be anything, Maz. Why don't you try Environmental Health?'

'And there's bits of rust lying on my toilet seat. It looks the same as what's on the air con grille.'

Hannah flexed her fingers. 'Look, I don't mean to be rude, but the place is falling apart, and the bloke who used to maintain it is dead. No wonder there's bits of rust.'

The voice at the other end trembled. 'I wouldn't bother you if I wasn't sure. Believe me; I wouldn't. I'm scared, Hannah. Really scared.'

Hannah clenched her fists. 'I'll get some PCs round to check things over.'

'No. I want you.'

'Miss Crawford, it's been a long week. A police officer was murdered. I'm exhausted, I was due off duty yesterday, and I'm ready for my bed.'

'But...'

'No buts. This doesn't warrant a detective...'

Maz Crawford was about to tell her about the flash above the bathroom when Sue Nairn grabbed the telephone.

'Miss Crawford, I'm Detective Sergeant Sue Nairn. I'm working with Hannah, and what she's saying is true. Poor Hannah needs some rest.'

'Please...'

'Let me finish. I'll come check around for you. I can sit with you for a while, if you want. How does that sound?'

'Are you sure?'

'Yes. I don't mind. In a few days I'll have all the time in the world to recover.'

'Thank you. Thank you so much.' They almost heard Maz cheer.

Sue ended the call.

'There,' she said. 'That wasn't too difficult, was it?'

**

Rats wormed his way along ever-narrower channels until he found himself in a dead end as far away from Maz Crawford as possible.

He was six floors down from her and on the opposite side of the Wall, the side facing the Tyne and overlooking the remainder of the Byker estate. Not that he could see any of it, but his mind pictured the scene, crystal clear.

Crystal. That's what he needed after the clusterfuck that had just happened. He wanted his superpowers back. Soon, he would have them.

Rats drew the pack from his pocket. He wished he could shake and bake, but even in his moment of desperation he realised it would be suicide in the claustrophobic tunnel. Instead, he snorted. Squeezed his nostrils together to prevent sneezing out his precious Christine and waited.

He waited only seconds before his powers returned amidst a wave of euphoria and pounding heartbeat. Nothing could stop Rats Scully. Not now. Tonight, would be THE night.

He'd read about snuff movies. He'd never seen one. Wasn't even sure if they really existed but, tonight, he'd make one of his own.

The Oscars awaited Marvin Scully. He'd be director, producer, screenwriter and lead.

Fame and stardom called for him. Him, and his leading lady, the one-and-only Miss Marilyn Crawford.

CHAPTER THIRTY-TWO

SUNDAY

Five past midnight, and Maz Crawford still babbled endlessly.

DS Nairn knew it was nervous energy, so she let the tsunami of words wash over her, interspersing them with the occasional question relevant to the girl's complaint. Not enough to upset her, just sufficient to ensure she wasn't completely wasting her time.

Maz ran through her family history, told Sue about Willow, the German shepherd dog she missed so much, how she never intended living in the Byker Wall for long, anyway, and how she wished she'd left earlier.

Sue noticed Maz didn't say regretted coming there in the first instance, but it went without saying, she supposed.

'If you work with Hannah, you'll know Ryan, as well, do you? Ryan Jarrod?' Sue heard Maz say.

'Yes. He's a good lad.'

'I went to school with his brother. What school did you go to? Sorry, it'd be a while ago. It's not important. Weather's crap again today. Have you seen the forecast? I hope tomorrow's better. I used to fancy his brother, you know.'

Sue glanced at her watch, used by now to Maz's incessant chit-chat.

'James. Jam Jar, we called him.'

'Sorry?'

'Ryan's brother. Jam Jar.'

Sue flicked her head. She was sure, somewhere in Marilyn Crawford-land, it all made sense to her. She let the conversation drift by.

'What was that?' Marilyn sat stock still.

'I didn't hear anything.'

'You didn't?'

Sue stifled a yawn. 'No.'

'You must have.'

Sue looked at the young girl opposite. Considered her words. 'Is that what you've always heard?'

'Yes. No. I mean, I've heard lots of things.'

'I didn't hear anything, Marilyn.'

Maz was on her feet, looking up towards the letter-box vent above their head. 'He's here.'

Sue released a sigh. 'Have you actually seen anybody?'

Marilyn shook her head.

'Why don't you try to get to sleep? Things will seem better in the morning.'

'I don't think I can. You're not going, are you? Please. Don't.'

Sue plucked at an eyebrow. This wasn't the self-confident, affable Marilyn Crawford described to her by Hannah. This Marilyn Crawford was edgy, twitchy. Hyper.

Drugs, Sue wondered. The Wall was well-known in Forth Street for its drug use. Or was Marilyn Crawford genuinely terrified?

'Stay. Just for tonight. Please. It's the only way I'll get any sleep.'

Sue made a sucking noise. 'Okay.'

Maz let out a breath she seemed to have held forever. 'Thank you.'

Sue smiled. 'Go to bed, Marilyn. Get some sleep. I'll be here when you wake up in the morning.' She glanced at her watch. 'Which is now. Grab a few hours. I'll be right here.'

She patted the old green sofa in its new stretch cover.

**

Several floors below, Rats unscrewed the bathroom air-vent. It was the third one he'd tackled that night, but this proved frustratingly stubborn. Rusted with age, the final bolt refused to budge in his skinned fingers.

What now?

He counted the banknotes in his pocket. He'd started the night with a hundred quid. Now, he'd raised that threefold. One more apartment to pilfer, and he reckoned he'd have enough.

After what he had planned for tonight, he'd have to get away, and fast. Coventry beckoned. And, for that, he'd need cash.

Yes, one more raid should do it. If only the bastarding cover would shift.

Folk in Byker may be poor, but Rats knew the exceptions. They were the ones he and Scrapper targeted regularly. True, the majority of their 'customers' had to make trips to the bank or Post Office especially for them, but at least they had sufficient means at their disposal.

And the flat below offered more than most.

Rats put his foot against the cover and pushed, hard.

The grate came away and clattered off the porcelain below. To him, the noise was louder than a volcanic explosion, but that was because he had superpowers.

Still, he waited a few minutes before dropping to the floor. He snuck out the bathroom, crept into the living area as if he were the childcatcher, and ferreted around in a Ming vase until he found it.

In the dark, he couldn't see the denomination, but by touch he reckoned there were at least twenty notes in his hand. That meant he had two hundred, possibly four hundred, quid to add to his spoils.

He kissed the notes. 'Get the fuck in,' he whispered.

Light flooded the room.

Rats spun around.

Rosina Durrant was on him, hammering his head with a broomshank.

'Get out!' she screamed. 'Get out of my house! Help!! Somebody…'

Rats flung the vase in her direction.

Bullseye.

It caught the old woman flush in the forehead.

She dropped the broom. Her hands shot to her head. Blood seeped between her fingers.

'Shut the fuck up.' Rats floored her with a backhander.

On the way down, Rosina Durrant's head caught the edge of a table. The back of the woman's skull cracked like eggshell.

**

Sue Nairn snored softly from her bed on the cramped sofa.

In a nanosecond, she went from sleep to alert mode. Sitting upright, she strained her ears. She'd heard something.

Hadn't she?

She listened. And waited.

The omnipresent rhythmical thrum of the ventilation system, like white noise on an aircraft, masked out all other sound.

Except, there was no other sound to mask. All was quiet.

Sue remembered to breathe as she lay back down.

There it was again. This time, she was certain. She stood. Looked upwards at the ceiling.

Silently, she padded to the door. Put her ear to it. Inched it open.

Nothing.

She tiptoed to the bedroom. Listened intently. All she could hear was the sound of Maz Crawford breathing the sleep of contentment.

And the sound of something being moved aside, somewhere else in the flat.

Sue Nairn's jaw knotted. She gritted her teeth until she thought her fillings would dislodge.

She flung open the bathroom door and pulled the light cord.

Bedlam.

'Fuck!'

'Jesus.'

'Fucking hell, who are you?' Rats didn't wait for an answer to his question. His face disappeared from view as he scuttled back into the claustrophobic tunnels he knew so well.

Sue jumped onto the toilet rim, reached upwards, and struggled to haul her lanky frame through the gap.

She stayed still for a moment. Let her eyes adjust to the demonic black of the Byker Wall's innards. Let them adjust for a moment too long. Already, the sound of Scully scrabbling in the distance began to fade.

Lying on her belly, one hand levering her forward, the other searching for obstacles in her way, Sue Nairn set off in slow pursuit.

She burrowed through spider webs and filth, spitting out the detritus which filled her mouth and nostrils.

Just when she thought she'd lost Scully, she'd hear a movement, or a breath, or a curse as he bumped into something. It wasn't much, but it was enough to keep on his trail.

'Bugger.' She should have called for backup. 'Damn, damn, damn.' Sue pulled out her phone. No signal. Of course, there'd be no signal. Not here.

'Shit.'

She ploughed forward, head first into overhanging ductwork. She took the blow hard. It stunned her. Knocked her face down in the tunnel.

She stayed there, fingers touching her temple. She couldn't see them, but her fingers came back wet and sticky.

Sue raised herself to her elbows and knees. Felt woozy. Blood streaks trickled down the left side of her face, but the sound of Rats breathing somewhere in the inky blackness drove her on.

She'd reached a vertical shaft. For a moment, she didn't know what to do but, if Scully had made it, so could she. Sue pressed onwards. Onwards, and upwards.

She made herself into a star shape and braced her limbs against the wall. Hand on hand, foot after foot, she began to climb.

She breathed heavily. Inched her way upwards. This was her at her most vulnerable. If Scully had found a foothold, all it needed was the gentlest of pushes and she'd be falling, falling, falling.

She didn't fall.

Instead, she came to a horizontal passageway, off to the right. For a moment, she had no idea how she'd manage to extricate herself from vertical plane to horizontal.

In the end, she launched herself into it.

The surface here was different. Beneath her knees, it was no longer smooth. It was etched with ridges, and it was damp.

The drip-drip-drip of a leaking pipe counted down time, diluted the blood masking her face, and covered the channel in hellish slime.

With every inch Sue moved, with each ounce of energy she expended, desperation replaced it.

Spent and exhausted, she lay back against the slick wall, head down, and swore.

She'd lost her quarry.

Slowly, despondently, she set off to check on Maz Crawford, and to find a signal to call the whole nightmare in.

Sue squirreled her way around a Z-bend.

'Shit.'

She hadn't come this way. She was lost.

Somewhere up ahead, above her, she sensed something. A sound. A light, perhaps. Something she couldn't put her finger on.

Sue shivered violently but pressed on; on to another Z-bend, and beyond.

Then, fresh air hit. High above, wind howled through the ventilation outlet like the Seven Trumpets of Revelation.

Sue gulped down oxygen, panting as if she were an elderly dog, blood and sweat stinging her eyes.

She gathered herself, prepared to move off deeper into the apocalyptical maze, when she heard it.

Faint at first, barely discernible above the raging wind, she struggled to make it out.

'Help. Please. Help me.'

It was the voice of Rats Scully.

**

Maz woke in desperate need of a pee.

She jumped out of bed, then remembered DS Nairn was asleep in the next room. 'Damn,' she whispered, fearing she'd disturbed her.

When there was no reply, Maz inched open the bedroom door, and sneaked into the corridor clasping her thighs tight together to prevent leakage.

She dashed to the toilet bowl and let the floodgates open, sighing with relief.

Maz shivered. And again. It was cold. Colder than cold.

She tucked her hands inside the sleeves of the over-sized T-shirt she slept in, and looked up into a gaping black maw where a cover should be.

Maz didn't wash. Didn't flush. Didn't even wipe.

'Sue? DS Nairn?'

She yanked open the door to the living room.

'Shit, no.'

Maz pulled out her phone and called Hannah Graves.

**

'I'm over here. Hurry up, missus. I can't hold on much longer.'

'Keep talking. I'll follow the noise.'

The tunnel began to widen, but the roof remained low. It didn't help.

'Ower here, man. Keep gannin.'

She stopped to pick up the direction. 'Say again.'

'Fucking hurry up, man.'

Sue scuttled forward.

'I think I can here you,' Scully's voice said. 'You must be nearly here. Hurry, will ya?'

Sue Nairn saw a faint glow; a light at the end of the tunnel. One last bend…

And there she saw him.

Scully hung by one hand from a ladder on the opposite wall of the vertical tunnel.

A dim light illuminated a faded number eleven painted on the maintenance shaft wall. The light flickered as Scully's frame passed in front of it, back and forth like a metronome.

'I can't get me other hand up, man. Me arms knacking us. I'm ganna let go.'

'Don't!'

'Well, fucking do something, then. Help us.'

Sue's mind raced. What could she do? Nothing. Absolutely, nothing.

'Please, missus.'

She lay on her stomach. Inched towards the precipice. Stretched out her arm.

'Swing towards me.'

Scully swung like a gibbon.

And missed.

'Again,' Sue panted.

Their fingertips brushed.

'And again. Come on. You can do it! This time. Go!!!'

Rats swung towards her. His fingers wrapped around her wrist.

'There. I've got you. I've got you. You'll be okay.'

Rats flexed his arm and pulled with all his might. Muscles and tendons ripped apart, but it worked.

The stupid cow had trusted him.

She hung below him, eyes wide, staring up the maintenance shaft.

One-by-one, Rats peeled open his fingers.

Until Sue Nairn tumbled and twisted through eleven floors of nothingness.

'Say hello to Scrapper for me when you get doon there, won't you?'

Rats gave a demonic laugh. 'Superpowers!' he roared. He laughed again as he brought his left arm onto the staircase.

'Coventry, here I come.'

He took his right arm off the stepladder, prepared to move it to the next rail. Readied his foot.

And the left arm he'd ruined hauling Sue Nairn over the ledge gave way.

In less than four seconds, Rats Scully would be able to say hello to Scrapper himself.

CHAPTER THIRTY-THREE

'Aal reet, man. I'm coming. Had yer horses, will you?'

Ryan hurried down the stairs, knotting his dressing gown as he went.

The knocking became more urgent.

He flung open the door, saying 'Where's the fi..'

His assailant landed on top of him. The weight pushed him to the floor.

Ryan grabbed his attacker's hair, yanked it, and rolled his body so he lay on top. He held the intruder's wrists and landed his knees on the man's arms, pinning him down.

Except, it wasn't a man.

'Hannah. What the hell?'

She was a mess. A complete and total mess. Her eyes sat in hollow sockets, the sclera red and raw. Drool and spit and snot hung from her nose and lips, and tear-stains streaked her cheeks.

She babbled incoherently. Wailing sobs slipped between lips which trembled like jelly. She lay beneath him, her soul laid bare.

Ryan looked down into those eyes he knew so well, yet he didn't recognise them at all. He saw only pain and suffering.

'Hannah. What's up? Is it Stephen? Has something happened to him?'

No words came.

'Hannah?'

She shook her head, still pinned beneath him.

Slowly, gently, Ryan raised one knee from her. Then the other. He took hold of her arms and hauled her into a sitting position. Her arms immediately encircled his neck, clinging to him like ivy to oak.

Ryan held her for as long as she needed. He didn't speak. Didn't pretend to understand. He just waited.

The wait lasted five minutes whilst Hannah bubbled into his neck, soaking his gown.

Finally, she released her grip and, between whooping breaths, mumbled, 'It's Sue.'

'What about her?'

When Hannah clung to him again, he understood.

'Christ, no.'

He felt her head bob against his cheek.

'How?'

Hannah managed one word.

'Scully.'

**

She sat on the edge of his sofa, head down, tea-cup cooling in her lap. Ryan was alongside her, staring at the surreal site of his neighbours laughing in the garden, teasing their pet cat with a ball of wool.

Getting on with life.

'How are the others?' It sounded pathetic, but he had to break the silence.

She shook her head. 'Todd's in bits, bless him.'

'Todd is? Wow.'

He thought she managed a smile. 'Big softie that he is.'

'Stephen?'

'Not good.'

'You don't think he'll...'

'Drink again? I hope not.'

'Bollocks.'

'I'll get him some Corsodyl, just in case.' Her dimple made its first appearance for weeks. This time, he was sure she smiled.

'The rest?'

'Don't know. Stephen wants us back at the station for twelve.'

Ryan checked the clock opposite. 'We need to get going, then,'

Hannah sniffed. Wiped away dried up tears. 'You didn't mind me coming here, did you?'

'What? Of course not.'

'I just needed to be with someone. And, you needed to know.'

He took a gulp of air. 'Is that really why?'

She hesitated. 'I don't know, Ry. Now's not the time to talk about it, either.' She met his eyes. 'You don't mind if we wait a while to talk, do you?'

'No. Now isn't the right time; you're right.'

He helped her up.

'Come on. We need to get going.'

She cried again. Collapsed onto the sofa. Curled into the foetal position.

Through her sobs, he heard her say. 'It should have been me. Not Sue. I should have been the one with Marilyn.'

Icicles ran down Ryan's spine.

It hadn't dawned on him, not until now.

She was right, again.

He'd almost lost her.

**

The mood in the bullpen was sombre. Much, much worse than when Michael McNeil's news broke. He was one of theirs, but Sue; Sue Nairn was one of them.

It made a vast difference.

With McNeil, there'd been anger. With Sue, just a deep, overpowering loss. A chasm of sadness into which they all fell.

No-one spoke; no-one except Stephen Danskin who went round them all, one by one, a quiet word for each member of his team.

Lyall Parker produced an Islay malt. He poured a healthy dram into a series of plastic cups, enough for everyone. When he reached Danskin, Ryan noticed Hannah stiffen, then relax when her stepfather shook his head. Ryan relaxed, too.

A second bottle appeared. Danskin made a touching speech which brought Todd Robson to tears, and forced Gavin O'Hara to leave the bullpen 'til he'd composed himself.

With the opening of the third bottle - only Bells this time, but it served a purpose – the mood had lightened somewhat, as all wakes do.

Ryan passed on the whisky third time around and took a moment to himself at the back of the bullpen. Hannah saw him log into a PC and walked up to him.

'You okay?' she asked.

'Aye. Sound as a pound.'

She screwed an eye. 'Sure?'

He bobbed his head in confirmation. 'What about you?'

She nodded, too. 'I'm getting by.'

Hannah took the seat next to him. 'I think I'll see Occ Health, though.'

He looked at her.

'I'm healthy. Don't worry. It's just…oh, I don't know. Guilt, I suppose.'

'For what?'

She vibrated air through her lips. 'Being alive.'

Ryan looked at her.

'It should have been me. I can't think like that. I want to nip anything in the bud. Occ Health have a counselling service. Might be worth giving it a go.'

He said nothing, memories of his own past experiences with counselling and where that nearly went so wrong for him. For both of them.

Hannah read his thoughts. 'Different kettle of fish, Ry. Don't even go there.'

They settled into an uncomfortable silence.

Occasionally, Nigel Trebilcock's donkey bray of a laugh reached them as someone – probably Todd – made a humorous remark. The mood was lightening as the alcohol hit the spot.

'What're you doing?' Hannah asked.

'I've got a case to solve, remember. Might as well make use of my time.'

'Why? With a line drawn under the Scully case, you'll have every resource at Stephen's disposal tomorrow.'

He ignored her and typed three words into the browser.

'Come on, Ry. Do it for Sue. She told you to take a break.'

The results of Ryan's search arrived on his monitor screen.

'Bloody hell, man!'

The squad looked at Ryan as one.

'Jarrod! This isn't the time,' Danskin roared.

'Ryan. Sssh,' Hannah urged.

He ignored her. 'Ravi. Ravi – get your arse ower here. Quick.'

Hannah stared at the screen. Her mouth curled. Her brow furrowed.

'Jesus,' she whispered. Then, loudly, 'Ravi, shift your arse!!'

**

'Call yourself an IT expert? All it took was three little words, and I found it.'

Ravi's eyes popped as he stared at the monitor. 'What did you do?'

'Simple. Something in all this doesn't add up. I can't get that comment on Warne's blog post out of my head. It has to mean something, so I typed '*High Level Filth*' into that little box there – it's called a search bar, by the way,' he glanced sideways at Ravi, mockingly, and Sangar dug his knuckles under Ryan's ribs, 'And voila: this is what yer get.'

They were staring at a vibrantly coloured screen, HD quality images partly hidden behind a black box asking for credit card details.

The images may have been masked, but there was no denying what they were, or who it was.

Beneath a website banner proclaiming itself to be *High Level Filth*, Tanita Westwood-Richards lay spreadeagled on the deck of a yacht, bronzed, alluring, and naked; her modesty barely hidden behind a box which flashed with a promise to the watcher that they were only 'One-click away.'

One click, and several pounds, dollars, euros, Iranian Rial or any other tin-pot currency away, to be more exact.

Ravi assumed control of the keyboard as Danskin and Todd Robson moved in.

The screen turned black. Lines of coded hieroglyphics filled the screen. Ravi typed in various symbols and nonsense words and, in a few minutes, the screen came alive.

This time, there was no box to shield Tanita's innocence.

'Jesus Christ, man. What the hell do you think you're doing?' Danskin looked like he was about to explode.

'Policing, sir. This is a lass Justin Warne was sleeping with. Sleeping with and photographing.'

Ravi clicked on a link and a pop-up box appeared. Ravi enlarged it.

Tanita moaned and writhed in front of the camera. A faceless male rode her.

'Fuck me,' Ravi said.

'I bet you wish she would,' Todd commented.

'He wasn't only photographing. He filmed the girl, too.'

'What else we got on there?' Danskin asked.

Ryan already knew. 'I think you'll find this lass is there, somewhere.' They followed the line of his finger and saw it pointed to a photograph on the crime board.

Not Tanita. They already knew her, intimately. Instead, he pointed at another image.

'That's Hayley Mack. Warne was photographing her, too.'

It took Ravi seconds. Sure enough, Hayley was there.

High Level

'The dirty bastard,' Todd said.

Ravi delved deeper. Other images appeared, other videos. Sally Sykes, unmoving and catatonic, was having unspeakable deeds done unto her by two men. One, surely, was Warne; the other, person unknown.

It didn't matter who it was. All that concerned them was that Warne was an entrepreneur, financial blogger, property dealer, pornographer, and, as Todd eloquently put it, a dirty bastard.

A dead dirty bastard.

Hannah looked at the faces gathered around. Whisky fumes swamped her nostrils. Made her gag as much as the on-screen images.

'Have you boys seen enough? I'm bloody sure I have. Let's think of Sue. Have a bit of respect and stop ogling this filth.'

They muttered agreement. Began to move off.

But not Ryan. 'Nah,' he said. 'This isn't filth. It's High Level Filth.'

'What the fuck?' Todd responded, 'Are you auditioning for M&S adverts now?'

'I need to get to the bottom of this. It might lead us to his killer. It's still a live case, remember.'

Hannah shook her head and moved to the back of the group. She looked out the window as the images became evermore graphic. Degrading. Filthy.

The quality took a serious hit. Once he'd lured customers into the website with the promise of Tanita, Warne hit them with any old rubbish.

Todd recognised the setting of a couple of scenes. 'That's the house in Gatesheed. Now I know what all the cameras were for. Looks like you were wrong, Ryan. Warne didn't just use his phone.'

Ravi led them on a quick fast-forward tour of the website.

The settings became less salubrious. Gone were expensive yachts and plush carpeted floors. These were filmed in the flats of the Byker Wall.

Ravi skimmed over the scenes.

'Tell me when you find something meaningful to your investigation, Jarrod,' Stephen Danskin said as he and Lyall Parker moved away to discuss how to inform Sam Maynard of Sue's murder.

'Stop!' Hannah's voice.

Danskin and Parker obeyed. Turned to her.

'Sorry, sir. I didn't mean you. Play that bit back, Ravi.'

Sangar rolled the screen back.

'There!'

'Well, bugger me,' Danskin said, staring at the screen. 'Hook, line, and sinker.'

Ravi paused the playback. Clear as day, two naked women, not attractive women in any sense of the word, romped on a bed with a male.

'Rats Scully, as I live and breathe.'

**

'It's a wrap, folks. Well done, Graves. Super work, in fact. Warne used Scully in his videos. That's the link between them. I guess Scully asked him for cash, threatened him. Warne thought he could treat Scully the same way he treated the lasses. It's the way Warne ran all his businesses. Difference is, we know what Scully's capable of; by Christ, we do. Michael McNeil, poor Sue, even his best mate. Aye, Scully killed him, right enough. It was a vengeance killing, pure and simple.'

The team dipped their heads in agreement, and in memory of their fallen colleagues.

'Pushing Warne down a lift shaft would be nowt for Scully. Closed case.'

Danskin stared out at the Sage on the opposite bank of the Tyne. 'I just wish we'd found this footage first.' His voice broke. 'DS Nairn might still be with us.' He coughed to clear his throat.

High Level

'Jarrod, I'm sorry. If I'd given you the manpower you deserved, we'd have cracked this earlier.'

'No, sir. You don't need apologise. You did what you thought was right. You went after a police killer.'

Stephen Danskin nodded his thanks.

'You got him, sir,' Ryan said. 'You got him.'

The team moved away. Prepared to head for home.

Danskin reached for his phone. He had to speak to Sue's family.

Lyall Parker collected up the plastic cups and rinsed the whisky dregs from them.

Ravi draped an arm around Todd.

Hannah slipped into her coat.

Ryan prepared to shut down the PC, and the High Level Filth of Justin Warne.

As he went to log off, his finger brushed the keyboard. Another of Warne's disgusting files jumped on screen.

'Oh no. Please, God, no.'

Hannah turned. 'Ryan?'

Ryan stared forward, trance-like.

'Ry: what is it? What's wrong?'

He motioned for her to join him.

She looked over his shoulder. Sat down with a thud. Crossed herself.

'Sweet Mary,' she gasped.

CHAPTER THIRTY-FOUR

'Oh. Come in.'

Ryan and Hannah followed through whilst two uniformed officers waited outside.

'I suppose you know why we're here,' Ryan said, his voice flat.

'Probably.'

A rain shower rapped against the window despite bright sun streaking the sky with chrome and silver flecks. They turned their heads, staring out over Tyneside.

Ryan took a step closer. 'Want to talk about it?'

'Not really, no.'

'It'd help if you did.'

'Help who - you? Can't see what difference it'll make to me.'

Ryan dipped his head, an invitation Hannah picked up on. 'How did you meet?' she asked.

'My cousin introduced us. She knew him through work.'

'Your cousin – does she work for High Level Properties?'

A shake of the head.

'Westwood Building Contractors?'

Another shake.

'Tell us,' Ryan stepped in. 'It might help. Help YOU, I mean.'

'She works for a company called Priory and Longsands. It's an...'

'Investment company. Yes, we know.'

A nod, this time.

Ryan and Hannah waited for the resumption of the story. When none came, Hannah provided a prompt.

'We know Justin Warne did some work for them. I've been to their offices.'

'Velma, that's my cousin, knew he had a property portfolio. She also knew I was looking for somewhere, so she arranged for us to meet. It was a Tuesday.' She gestured towards the window. 'Weather was a bit like this. Maybe colder.'

Ryan looked into eyes filled with self-pity. 'What happened?'

'Nothing. He was lovely. Charm itself. He told me he was sure he could help, and he gave me his card. No pressure, he told me, just call him when I was ready.'

She swallowed hard.

'I wasn't ready for a couple of weeks. When I rang, I was surprised he remembered me. A bit flattered, if I'm honest, him having so many important clients, and all.'

Ryan and Hannah saw her retreat into herself. Waited for the moment to pass. In time, it did.

'He said he'd hunted out a few properties and had been hoping I'd call to view them. He said he'd make sure I got a good deal.'

'I bet he did,' Ryan mumbled through gritted teeth. Hannah slapped the side of his thigh with her hand. He shut up.

'Anyway, he said he had the catalogues and brochures and options ready for me. Did I want to see them? Of course, I did.'

'Where did you meet?'

She shuddered. 'I suggested Starbucks, in the MetroCentre, or Eldon Square. Justin said he didn't think they were open yet, lockdown and all, so why didn't I come to his? He'd pay for a taxi.'

Hannah flexed her fingers. Relieved the tension building in her forearms. 'Go on,' she encouraged.

'Well, the cab turned up, and took me to his house.'

'He took you to Byker?'

'No. Gateshead Fell. It was a nice house, from the outside. Once he let me in, though, I realised it felt odd.'

'Empty. Not lived in,' Ryan prompted.

'Yes. Yes, exactly that.'

'But there weren't any catalogues for you to see, was there?'

'Yes, Hannah, there was. Loads of 'em. I didn't know where to start, so Justin asked me to think about what I really needed, not what I wanted. We drew up a list of requirements and weeded out those that didn't fit the criteria.'

Hannah saw the girl's eyes glisten with moisture. 'Take your time.'

The girl gulped. Nodded. 'I ended up with half a dozen properties to look over. And that's exactly what he said: *'Take your time.'* He left me alone, good to his word. No pressure, at all.'

The girl's eyelids slid shut. She shivered again.

'He came back into the room with two glasses of wine. *'You're not driving,'* he said. *'The cab will take you home again. Enjoy.'* He clinked his glass with mine, and he smiled at me. I smiled back, just to say thanks, of course.'

The girl fell silent. Ryan and Hannah shared a disconsolate look. They knew what was coming next, but she had to tell them.

'Next thing I remember was this bright light. Brighter than anything I'd seen before. I couldn't understand what it was. Then, I realised I was looking up into the light. I thought I must have fainted or something. I started to get up.'

She continued talking as the tears breached the well of her eyelids and spilled over onto her cheeks.

'But I couldn't. I couldn't get up. I couldn't get up because I couldn't move. And because he was on top of me.'

Her mouth curved in revulsion, her eyes screwed tight.

'He was on top of me, naked. And…and so was I. He was inside me and…'

She convulsed into rending sobs. Ryan and Hannah shared her pain, hated the sadism of forcing her to speak about it. Finally, she calmed sufficiently to continue.

'Anyway, the light shone so brightly into my eyes, but I couldn't even close my eyelids. I was paralysed. Literally, paralysed. And beneath the light was the camera. Pointing at me. Pointing at us. Capturing what he was doing to me. I've no idea how long I'd been like that, or what he'd else he might have done to me in the time I was out.'

Ryan knew. So did Hannah. They'd witnessed it. It was best the girl didn't know.

Her tears flowed again. 'When he'd used me, he bundled me into the back of a cab – a different one this time – and told the driver I was pissed. He gave him my address and told him to drop me at the end of the garden if I hadn't 'sobered up' by then.'

She paused her story. The pain, the heartache, was over. She'd told someone what Justin Warne had done to her, and she felt weightless as a result.

Ryan spoke next. 'You need to tell us what happened after that.'

She smiled. 'I decided to get even, that's what happened next.'

'And that's why you killed him.'

She shook her head. 'It's not that simple. I didn't mean to. I didn't think he knew I was here, but it seems he was around when I arrived. He saw me before I saw him. Sod's bloody law, huh?'

Ryan said nothing, though he felt Hannah tense next to him.

'Anyway, he was watching for me. Caught me unawares. I was out getting my bearings, just having a general look around the place, when I felt a tap on my shoulder. When I turned around, he was there; that same, pervy smile on his face. '*Hello, precious,*' he said, as if he genuinely thought he'd just bumped into an old flame or something.'

The girl returned to her trance-like state until Hannah, gently, coaxed her into continuing.

'This time, I knew what he was like. That meant I had the advantage over him. He knew nothing about me. He didn't what I could do.'

She rotated her neck until it cracked.

'Warne made a big, big, mistake. He thought he could frighten me. Threaten me. He goaded me, saying he'd done the same to dozens of girls, and he'd do it to me again, and again, and again, and there was nothing I could do to stop him. Absolutely nothing.'

The girl drummed her fingers against her thigh as she spoke.

'Warne taunted me. He held up his phone and asked me if I wanted to see the pictures of him with the others. I snatched the phone out of his hand.'

She adopted a vacant look, as if replaying the moment in her mind. She gave an ironic chuckle. 'You should have seen his face.'

'What happened next?'

'The lift door opened. Same as everything here, it did its own thing. Nobody pressed the button. It just decided to open by itself. Warne stretched his arm out towards me to take his phone back, and I raised my foot and pushed him into the lift.'

A small smile played on her lips; a smile which developed into a large grin as she said, 'I remember he cracked his head against the back wall and just disappeared, as if I was David Blaine or summat. You see, there was no lift for him to fall into. Like everything else in this place, it's shot to shit. I'd pushed him into an empty space, and a long, long way down.'

'Where's the phone? Did you keep it?' Hannah asked.

High Level

The girl motioned to a drawer. Hannah slid it open, nodded to Ryan, and gently slipped the phone into an evidence bag.

Ryan stood. Opened the front door. The uniformed officers stepped inside. As one of them read her rights, the other gently secured her wrists behind her back.

'Ryan,' she said, 'Will you do something for me?'

He raised his eyes to her, neither agreeing nor refusing.

'Tell your James I'm sorry. I wasn't lying. I really do think he's cute. Who knows what might have happened if thing's had turned out differently?'

She took a last look around her tenth-floor Byker Wall flat as the constables led Maz Crawford out.

Ryan collapsed onto the sofa. Hannah sat next to him and took his hand.

'Hey, come on, big guy. You've got to get over this,' she said. She gave him an encouraging smile. 'You've only got a couple of days.'

He looked at her, curiously.

'The exam, silly. OUR exam. The one we're both going to pass. We're going to pass, then we can talk, yeah?' She gave his hand a squeeze.

'I don't want it, Hannah.'

'What? You don't mean that.'

'I do.'

'Ry, come on. 'Course you want to take it. You're the best.'

He looked at her, emptiness in his eyes. 'Well, I don't feel like I am. I've been shit these last few weeks, and I've treated you like shit.'

'We're both as bad as each other.'

He shook his head.

'Honestly, Ryan, I mean it.'

'I still don't want it.'

'But you will, right?'

He didn't reply. That was enough for Hannah.

'Attaboy. But don't do it for me. You've got to do it for yourself.'

Ryan got to his feet. Smoothed down his trousers. Ran a hand through his hair.

'I'm not doing it for you, or for myself.'

He looked out the window, at the streets of Newcastle's east end where the tight-knit community moved on with their lives, counting their blessings for what they had, not dreaming of what they had not.

'I'll do it for Sue Nairn.'

******

Acknowledgements:

Chris Ward
Helen Cherry
Sam Leighton
Peter Knowles

And, to you:

Thank you for taking the time to read High Level. Your interest and support means the world to me.

If you enjoyed this, the fourth Ryan Jarrod novel, please tell your family, friends, and colleagues. Word of mouth is an author's best friend so the more people who know, the greater my appreciation.

I welcome reviews of your experience, either on Amazon or Goodreads. Alternatively, you can 'Rate' the book after you finish reading on most Kindle devices, if you'd prefer.

If you'd like to be among the first to hear news about the next book in the series, or to discover release dates in advance, you can follow me by:

Clicking the 'Follow' button on my Amazon book's page
https://www.amazon.co.uk/Colin-Youngman/e/B01H9CNHQK%3Fref=dbs_a_mng_rwt_scns_share
OR
Liking/ following me on:
 Facebook: @colin.youngman.author
Twitter - @seewhy59

Thanks again for your interest in my work.

Colin

About the author:

Colin had his first written work published at the age of 9 when a contribution to children's comic *Sparky* brought him the rich rewards of a 10/- Postal Order and a transistor radio.

  He was smitten by the writing bug and has gone on to have his work feature in publications for young adults, sports magazines, national newspapers, and travel guides before he moved to his first love: fiction.

  Colin previously worked as a senior executive in the public sector. He lives in Northumberland, north-east England, and is an avid supporter of Newcastle United (don't laugh), a keen follower of Durham County Cricket Club, and has a family interest in the City of Newcastle Gymnastics Academy.

You can read his other work (e-book and paperback) exclusive to Amazon:

The Lighthouse Keeper *(Ryan Jarrod Book Three)*
The Girl On The Quay *(Ryan Jarrod Book Two)*
The Angel Falls *(Ryan Jarrod Book One)*

The Doom Brae Witch
Alley Rat
DEAD Heat

Twists *(An anthology)*

****

COMING NEXT FROM

COLIN YOUNGMAN:

OPERATION SAGE

A Ryan Jarrod Novel

Printed in Great Britain
by Amazon